How

Dolly Parton

Saved My Life

How
Dolly Parton
Saved My Life

Charlotte Connors

BROADWAY BOOKS   NEW YORK

PUBLISHED BY BROADWAY BOOKS

This book is a work of fiction. Names, characters, businesses, organizations, places, events, and incidents either are the product of the author's imagination or are used fictitiously. Any resemblance to actual persons, living or dead, events, or locales is entirely coincidental.

Copyright © 2008 by Charlotte Connors

All Rights Reserved

Published in the United States by Broadway Books,
an imprint of The Doubleday Publishing Group,
a division of Random House, Inc., New York.
www.broadwaybooks.com

BROADWAY BOOKS and its logo, a letter B bisected on the diagonal, are trademarks of Random House, Inc.

Book design by Carol Malcolm Russo

Library of Congress Cataloging-in-Publication Data

Connors, Charlotte.
How Dolly Parton saved my life / by Charlotte Connors.—1st ed.
p.   cm.
1. Women—Southern States—Fiction. 2. Motherhood—Fiction.
3. Work and family—Fiction. 4. Caterers and catering—Fiction.
5. Women-owned business enterprises—Fiction. 6. New business
enterprises—Fiction. 7. Atlanta (Ga.)—Fiction. I. Title.
PS3603.O5492H69 2008
813'.6—dc22
2007049908

ISBN 978-0-7679-2656-0

PRINTED IN THE UNITED STATES OF AMERICA

1 3 5 7 9 10 8 6 4 2

First Edition

For Trish,
and for Dolly

How
Dolly Parton
Saved My Life

Jo

THE CAR BEGINS TO SHAKE. I PUSH MY FOOT DOWN on the accelerator, but nothing happens. The engine quiets, and I begin to coast.

"Not now, not now," I chant under my breath. It had to happen on today of all days.

I steer the car to the side of the road as it shudders to a halt, then turn the engine off. I look up. "You have an impeccable sense of timing, you know." I press my hands to my face and smell my lemon-scented moisturizer. Deep breaths. Stay calm. Stay calm. Just think, and you'll get out of this in no time. You won't be late. I pull my hands down.

I could call AAA, but they aren't exactly known for speed. I squint through the windshield, trying to read the signs down the deserted side street. There. At the end of the block. That looks like a Shell. Problem solved.

I push the door open, then step out and smooth my wool skirt down. I unbutton my suit jacket and toss it onto the front seat. I bet if I just wait here long enough someone will stop and help me. It's the South. People are friendly here. I glance at my watch.

Okay, forget it. No time for that. I look down the street. It's all downhill, but no sidewalks. I begin to make my way to the Shell station, as quickly as possible. I knew I shouldn't have worn heels today. Thankfully, the street is empty, so no one can see my humiliation: sweating like a pig, hobbling down the road in a suit, running late on the most important day of my life.

The stems of my stilettos sink into the hot Southern muck, but I press on. At last, my heels touch the gas station's concrete driveway. I walk over to the dingy little shop and blot the beads of sweat on my forehead.

Inside, there are a few ancient bags of Fritos and air fresheners for sale, and a mechanic with a handlebar mustache balances on a stool, his wide paunch resting on his thighs. The name patch sewn on his stained shirt says "Sonny."

"Darlin'?" He looks up from a crossword book. What's he been eating, inflated basketballs?

Emily Post says that if someone addresses you inappropriately, you should address him very formally in return and he'll follow your lead. Darlin'. The nerve.

"Sir," I say, smiling politely. "There seems to be a problem with my car. It's just up the road there. Is there any chance—"

"Ed!"

I jump at the volume of Sonny's voice.

"Ed!" he screams again, and a slack-jawed twenty-something appears in the little shop.

"Go on up the road a piece and see what's wrong with this nice lady's car. It's a . . ." Sonny looks at me, and I realize I need to chime in.

"It's a champagne, *erhm*, gold-colored Lexus."

Ed nods and strolls out the front door at a leisurely pace.

"Thank you," I call after him, then slip outside to call Gerard. He's going to have to come and get me if I'm going to make it to my meeting on time.

It's the first meeting of my new company, my new start in life. I'm the owner. What kind of precedent does it set if I'm not there at least fifteen minutes earlier than everyone else? And I told Ellie I'd see her there at four o'clock sharp. Technically Ellie is the co-owner—but let's face it, I'm obviously the one in charge. It was my idea to open a catering company. I'm the one with the viable business model. I'm the one who came up with the name Divine Foods. I have to be there.

I never would have thought of opening a catering company, but six months ago, I made an awful mistake, and Olivia Jackson was there to love every last minute of it. It was the Junior League's annual Atlanta Heart Gala Valentine's Day fund-raiser for the American Heart

Association. The Heart Gala is a formal ball with top-dollar tickets. It's a lot of fun, but also a notorious mathematical challenge, as half of the proceeds pay for the following year's party, while the other half goes to fight heart disease. I was in charge this year and knew I needed to hire a lot of help for very little money. I found the hotel ballroom and negotiated the rental fee down. I ordered the engraved invitations on cream cards six weeks in advance and brokered a reduced rate through one of Gerard's coworkers' wives. But I couldn't find a caterer who could give me what I was looking for—delicious, unique food with no hassle at a bargain-basement rate. I must have called every caterer in town before settling for Food Inc., who, despite their boring name, managed to create some interesting hors d'oeuvres during my tasting appointment. Unfortunately, they showed up two hours late to the gala that night. I had the cream of the Atlanta social crop teetering around the dance floor tipsy or worse because they had no food in their stomachs. And they overcooked the sea bass and used dark meat in the chicken salad. I could have died of embarrassment. Plus they had to set up in plain view while Olivia Jackson and her crew looked on and gawked.

As I signed Food Inc.'s enormous check that night, I knew in my gut I could have done a better job, and for less money. After all, I had the unique combination of skills that would make me a very successful caterer: I like to entertain, I have a knack for gourmet cooking, I'm organized, and I can write an award-winning business plan, thanks to my past life.

I had always intended to go back to work when Martha and Agnes got a little older, but up until that moment, I assumed that I would head back to the banking world. Once I got the idea for Divine Foods, though, it just wouldn't go away. I knew it was a good idea. I could feel it in my bones.

So the last six months have been a mad scramble. Gerard was supportive when I brought the idea to him, and I went to the bank where I used to work and applied for a small business loan. The more I thought about it, the more perfect it seemed. It's not like my banking career was really working out, once little Martha came into the picture. You can name your baby after Martha Stewart, but that doesn't mean she will conduct herself like a domestic goddess. My little Martha was never poised or in control, and she tended to spit up on Mommy's best new suit moments before I left the house. And then there was the day in the board meeting when I looked into my briefcase only to discover that I had accidentally grabbed Martha's diaper bag. When it came time for my presentation, the only handouts I had were baby wipes. After a year of struggling to make it all come together, I finally threw in the towel and decided to stay home, vowing to someday return.

But to have my own business? Would that be better? At least I could set my own hours and spend as much time as possible with Martha and Agnes.

And as far as I could tell, there was only one drawback. A minor one. A teeny-tiny one, I told Gerard. So I knew nothing about running a catering business. So what? And I don't even really know how to cook for large groups. And I certainly didn't know enough to make us the premier caterer for upscale Atlanta parties. But I prayed and thought of the solution. I ran an advertisement in the *Atlanta Journal-Constitution*. I figured I'd fix this problem like I always had. I would hire help.

The first person I hired was Daisy, the renowned pastry chef at Seeger's, a sleek modern restaurant just a few blocks from where I live. The desserts there were fantastic. In fact, I was a little too familiar with them, as my growing waistline could attest. I called Daisy as soon as she sent her résumé in. When she showed up to her interview, I was a little put off by her leather pants, and, well, by her thick accent. As a native Atlantan, I have a slow, even drawl, whereas Daisy, from a small town in rural Georgia, sounds like someone straight out of *Deliverance*. But her warmth and eagerness won me over. I decided to give her a shot.

Cate was the next to be hired, and I knew from the second I met her that she was right for us. Her background was in interior design, but she was looking to make a change. A quarter-life crisis, I suspected. But she was organized and her portfolio was impeccable, and I decided that she could handle booking the parties, decorating the tables, and developing themes. I hired her on the spot.

Ellie was another story. Ellie Howell-Routledge, that is. Within the first few minutes of our interview, I figured out who she was. How did I miss it when I first saw her name? I began to plan my exit immediately. I needed to get away from her, fast. But she was determined not to let me get a word in edgewise. She was tough, and normally I'd like that, but not with her. I said I'd be in touch.

A week later, she was in touch with me. I tried to put her off. We were still making decisions, I said. We weren't sure. The truth was, I couldn't do it. I couldn't face her every single day, make canapés together, and play nice. And what was worse, she seemed to have no idea about our history. I hung up the phone with a snap.

Two days later she showed up at my door.

I reluctantly ushered her into my living room, cursing good old-fashioned Southern etiquette. But the more she talked, the more I realized that she was exactly the sort of person I needed to hire. She was the wealthy daughter of the esteemed Howell clan of Atlanta, an African-American power family that has included a few state senators and even a governor over the years. They were always a good family to hit up for the Junior League fundraisers. And she was qualified: she studied for three years at Le Cordon Bleu, and even earned the coveted Grand Diplôme there. Then she met her husband, an old classmate of mine, and never got the chance to open the French restaurant she had always dreamed of. But now her twins were in kindergarten, and she was bored being home all day. She saw this as her big chance.

Then she handed me a check. How big? A Howell family kind of big. My jaw hit the floor.

"I like you. I want to be partners. I want to own half of the company. Is this check sufficient?" she said.

I swallowed. I could really give her an earful after what she did to me, and probably no one would have blamed me, and yet Divine Foods really did need more seed money. This would mean we'd be off to a great start. Should I let bygones be bygones? Stop playing the fiddle after all these years?

I almost told her I couldn't do it. But then I thought of my girls. I want the world for them, and I want them to know that they can do, and be, anything. I thought about what it would mean to my personal happiness to have a job again, to feel like I was doing something that mattered. I knew God was calling me to do this.

"This is plenty. Actually, make it out for five thousand less, and we'll have gone in evenly. That seems fair."

Ellie eyed me carefully. Her dark hair was pulled back into a sleek bun, and the tailored slacks on her thin frame made her look like a model. "You need me, you know."

"I know. You're going to be head chef," I said.

"I understand that. And all decisions are made with *both* of our approval. Got it?"

A small part inside me twitched. I hadn't envisioned sharing my dream with someone. Gerard let me run our household like my little organized kingdom. Could I really learn to work with someone fifty-fifty?

I looked down at the check again.

"Of course," I said, nodding. "We're partners now."

"I think we both need this. We'll work well together," she said, smiling confidently.

I forced a smile back. This woman had no idea what

she did to me. How on earth will this work? "I'm sure you're right."

It seems like hours later when Ed saunters back into the little shop. He walks right past me to report back to Sonny. I follow him into the shop to hear what's going on. Ed glances at me nervously and then whispers in Sonny's ear. Sonny's eyebrows reach for the ceiling and he whispers something back to Ed.

"Oh, brother," I say, rolling my eyes. "I'm right here. Just tell me what's wrong with the car." I put a hand on my hip and level my eyes at them. This used to make the men at the bank run for cover.

Sonny sighs and eases onto his feet. "Sweetheart, you got a real problem here with your car."

I flare my nostrils. Forget Emily Post. "I'm not all that sweet, actually."

"Pardon?"

"I'm not really a sweetheart."

Sonny eyes me like I'm a lunatic. "Well—"

"Or a darlin'. I'm Josephine Vann. And I'd just like to get my car fixed and go. I'm sure you understand."

He furrows his brow at me and stares at my hands, which are tapping out a nervous beat against the blue plastic counter.

"Ma'am"—he pauses to make sure I won't add this to my list of names I refuse to be called. I smile at him. "Ma'am, can I have your husband's number?" He gestures at my wedding ring. "You got a problem with your car, and I need to talk to him about it."

"You can tell me about it. It just so happens I know a lot about cars."

Sonny lets out a heavy sigh. Does he know I'm lying through my teeth? But really, there's no sense in his calling Gerard. He doesn't know a single thing about cars either. He "fixed" our ice dispenser with a paper towel last week, and now when the cubes in my glass melt, little pieces of paper float in my drink. I stare at Sonny, who is obviously not going to cave in on calling Gerard.

"I'm afraid I'm a widow," I say, hanging my head and sniffling a little. I peek up with one eye at the mechanic, who is wincing at his mistake. "I guess you'll just have to tell little ol' me."

Fifteen minutes later, Gerard has come to my rescue and I've got a new radiator on order. Of course, he nearly killed me when I said, "Thanks for picking me up, brother." On the drive over to what will be Divine Foods' headquarters, he treats me to a lecture about how old-timers don't understand that calling a woman "darlin'" and "sugar pie" is offensive, but I bought that car with my own money. It's just humiliating.

The small parking lot is empty when we pull up in front of the storefront.

"You're amazing." I give Gerard a quick kiss on the cheek and unlock my door.

"The best brother in the world," he says. I laugh. "Call me when you're ready to go home and I'll come back."

"Thank you." I glance in the mirror one last time, grab my briefcase, hold my head up, then walk into the old Burger Barn and flip on the lights.

I guess it is kind of out of the way, I think, as I look around. I'm a native and even I have never been to this part of Atlanta. It does smell a little funny. But we can fix that. And it's a bit dingy right now, I guess. But it's an off-brand burger shack in a run-down strip mall. It was never meant to be fancy. The important thing is, it's ours. I can't wait to rip down the fading Burger Barn sign and replace it with tasteful black letters spelling out Divine Foods.

I take a deep breath, whisper a quick prayer, and begin to set up the folding chairs around the plastic card table I brought in yesterday. I want to get it all set up before the others arrive.

I have enough time to arrange my papers and set out a pot of coffee and cups before Cate's blue Honda pulls up in front of the building. I watch as she slams the door and walks toward the storefront of the Burger Barn. She is wearing a knee-length black skirt and a pink silk shirt. Business casual. I look down at my overstarched business suit and smooth my skirt, biting my lip. Maybe I should have gone for the sweater set after all.

You're the boss, Jo, I tell myself as Cate walks through the front door. Co-boss, I amend, as Ellie's silver BMW pulls into the parking lot. I extend my hand to Cate, and she shakes it, smiling.

"Cate, so good to see you. And right on time. Just wonderful."

"Thanks, Jo." She smiles, looking around the dusty room. "So this is it?"

"It's a work in progress." I gesture to the chairs. "Why don't you take a seat? The others should be here shortly. Have some coffee if you like." She nods and places her purse down on the gritty floor next to her chair. She reaches for the coffee and pours it into a Styrofoam cup, carefully adding a splash of milk and one packet of sugar.

A few seconds later, Ellie opens the door and strides in, letting the door close slowly behind her. She's wearing chinos and a collared shirt, and her hair is pulled back neatly. I brush my hair back behind my ear and extend my hand to her.

"It's nice to see you, Ellie," I say. She smiles warmly, then turns to Cate.

"I'm Ellie. I'm Jo's business partner and head chef."

"Good to meet you," Cate says, shaking her new coworker's hand. They begin to chat politely, and I wander over toward the window to see if the final member of our team is coming. I do like things to start on time. I hear Ellie mention her twins, and I check my watch. I should just sit down and join the conversation. Get to know my coworkers. I wander over and take a seat on a folding chair.

"And are you married, Cate?" Ellie asks, leaning forward. I gulp. Can't she see Cate's bare left hand?

"No," Cate says, taking a deep breath. "Almost was, but

then the loser dumped me. Men, right? Can lead a horse to the altar but can't make him propose?"

Ellie laughs out loud, and I crack a smile too.

"I find that my husband, Mike, is a lot more like a stubborn old mule than a horse," Ellie says, nodding, "so maybe you made out just fine."

"I'm sure I did," Cate says, shrugging. "He had hairy feet anyway."

"And hey, you're only, what, twenty-five?" I ask. Cate is very pretty, with long dark hair and big brown eyes. I'll bet men are knocking down her door.

"I'm twenty-eight, which is to say I'm marital roadkill in this city, but I'm sure I'll find some nice septuagenarian who is looking for someone just like me."

"Breathing?" Ellie laughs.

"Exactly." Cate nods. I can tell these two are going to get along just fine.

I look at my watch again. "I can't imagine where Daisy might be." I dig into my purse, and find my phone buried beneath a bag of Cheerios. "Aha! I have a voice mail. I'll be right back. I'm sure this is her."

I walk into the kitchen, imagining how good it will feel to rip up the brown and orange linoleum and put in black and white ceramic checkerboard flooring.

I put the phone to my ear and listen. The message isn't from Daisy. As I listen my mouth falls open. My hands begin to clench into fists. I can't believe he has the nerve. . . . I slam the phone shut and storm back into the main room.

Daisy stands up from where she and Cate are chatting

like old friends. "Hi, Josephine. I'm so sorry I was held up. I've got a teenager, and they just have a mind of their own, you know."

I look at Daisy in confusion. What is she talking about?

"Are you okay, Jo?" Ellie asks, gazing at me with concern. "You look upset."

"I am upset," I say as calmly as I can. I glance around at their scared faces, then I look down at my phone. And I can't help it. I pitch my cell phone over my shoulder back into the kitchen. "I mean, why do I even try?" I ask as I watch it slide across the floor.

Daisy looks at me in disbelief and stifles a laugh. "Gosh, I'm real sorry, Josephine, um, Jo, um, may I call you Jo?"

"Oh, Daisy. Hi. Sorry. Sure. Call me Jo."

Daisy smiles, starts to speak, but I cut her off.

"Just so long as you don't call me 'sweetie' or 'sugar-cakes' or 'honey' or 'darlin'," I say, fuming. I begin to pace back and forth.

I know they're all staring at me, but I'm just getting started.

"Or 'little lady.' I better throw that one in there too. No 'little lady' either."

"Okay," Daisy says, lowering herself into her chair. She looks around, and Ellie and Cate shrug.

"No pet names, no condescension, no more! I can't take it anymore." I plant my hands on my hips.

"Jo," Cate says, "what happened?"

I stop and look back in the direction of the kitchen,

then shake my head and sigh. I sit down on the empty chair. "I'm sorry, ladies. I'm, I'm not myself today."

They watch me nervously.

"I just had a voice mail from the pastor at my church." I look up. Daisy looks interested, Cate looks sympathetic, and Ellie just looks confused. Okay, maybe this story doesn't exactly start off with the kind of catastrophe they expected. "There was an announcement in my church bulletin a few weeks ago that said they were looking for someone to handle the church finances. So I put in my résumé. I figured, I have a background in finance, and I could spare a few hours a week to help out. I'd be happy to do it, and I even had some ideas for how we could better allocate some funds to make our ministries more effective. So I called the pastor and volunteered. I just got his response," I say and point to my phone, now lying on the floor in the kitchen. "He thanks me for my interest and tells me that they have decided it was too much to ask of a mother with young kids. It would require too much time away from the home." I take a deep breath, looking around. "They gave it to this guy Walt, who knows nothing about finance. He's a landscape architect."

"Let me guess," Ellie says, leaning forward in her chair. "Walt has small children too?"

"Of course he does." I roll my eyes and pour myself a cup of coffee. "The pastor did tell me that they are looking for Sunday school teachers if I'm interested in serving."

Cate smiles wryly. "I'll help you toilet-paper his house."

Daisy laughs. "Me too. We'll TP the jerk. I'm always trying to get my daughter Tiffany to go TPing with me."

"Tiffany? Like the store?" Ellie says, her eyes lighting up.

Daisy lets out a loud guffaw. "Tiffany like the singer." She laughs. "I was so into her I thought about following her around on tour, but then I got pregnant, so . . ."

I cough. Three heads swivel toward me. "No," I say, shaking my head. "Toilet-papering his house lets him off too easily. I want real revenge."

I hear Ellie gulp.

"What do you mean by 'real revenge'?" Daisy asks nervously.

"If this turns into a murder-suicide thing, I'm out," Cate says.

I shake my head. "I am going to use my business skills in a whole different way. And then he'll see."

Ellie breathes a little sigh of relief.

"So, welcome, ladies, to Divine Foods. My vision—"

"Our," Ellie says, raising an eyebrow at me.

"Right," I say. "*Our* vision, that is, Ellie's and mine, is of a new kind of company." I look around and nod. "One that allows us to really balance work and family life. We will work hard, and we will be good. I want this to be the best catering company in all of Atlanta."

"I like the way this sounds," Daisy says.

"This is a different kind of company. This is a woman's company. Many of us have families." I see Cate shuffling her feet, and continue quickly, "And all of us have lives outside of work." I take a deep breath. "This is a company that will respect that. Rule number one of Divine Foods is that families come first. That means kids are welcome at work. Hours, except for actual parties we're catering, are flexible. We all understand family emergencies," I say, smoothing my hair with my hand.

"And we hope you're with us," Ellie says to Daisy and Cate.

I look around to see how they're reacting to this. Daisy looks like she's about to pee her pants.

"This is going to be so great. I'm crazy for food," Daisy says, wiggling in her seat. She must be one of those people who babble when they're nervous. "For me, it's just like Dolly Parton said. 'My weaknesses have always been food and men, in that order.'" She looks around, a broad smile on her face.

The room is silent. Ellie and Cate are looking at each other, and Ellie shrugs her shoulders slightly. Daisy doesn't seem to notice, and starts right on in with a story about an ex-boyfriend who loved her Snickerdoodle Salad. I remind myself that Daisy is a world-class pastry chef. We need her.

Cate raises her hand tentatively.

"Rule number two," I say, interrupting Daisy and looking at Cate pointedly, "is that there shall be no raising of hands. This is a democracy. We say what we feel. That's what women do."

"Amen," Daisy says, getting into the spirit of things. She is practically bouncing up and down in her chair.

"Um," Cate says. She waves a hand for our attention and then sits on it. She sighs. "In light of this being a cool, hippie commune and all—"

"This is so cool," Daisy says and claps a little. "We're going to change the world."

Cate looks at her and smirks. *World-class chef. World-class chef.*

"Right, well, I know I just met you guys and everything," Cate says, "but what do we think of the name of the company?"

I stare at Cate. "Divine Foods?" I look at Ellie. "It's, it's perfect, I think. Don't you agree, Ellie?"

Ellie frowns at me. "Not so much."

I feel my throat closing up. If Ellie had a problem with the name, she could have told me that at our first meeting. I told her the company was called Divine Foods. She didn't say anything about it. "Well, I just thought we had an agreement that, given our clientele . . ."

"It's kind of boring," Ellie says.

For a moment, I can see myself throttling her.

"What is your concern, Cate?" Ellie asks.

My face is turning bright red. Cate hesitates.

Ellie touches my arm. "Jo, I think we really have to listen to Cate on this. She has a background in interior design, which is the art of bringing concepts to life."

I take a deep breath and realize that I'm making a fool of myself. "Of course. Of course. It just took me off guard. I mean, we're a different kind of company. We should *all* be excited about the name. We should all agree. No manly-man proclamations here at Div—" I've been calling it Divine Foods for so long now that it's going to be hard to reprogram myself.

"So, Cate, what's your thought?" Ellie asks.

Cate bites her lip. "I wonder if it could be a little more distinctive. It feels a little forgettable. Our company's name has to be something that we can build an entire brand around."

"Yeah, let's think of something more fun," Daisy says. I see her start doodling names immediately. "I love to name stuff. My daughter has two middle names. I almost went for three, but then that seemed like overkill."

"But it needs to be classy," I say and eye Daisy warily. Do these two have any idea who we will be catering for? I could arrange for them to sit in on a Junior League meeting and then they'd see. Divine Foods is exactly the kind of name that would appeal to the Junior League ladies.

Ellie nods. "Cate's right. It needs to be more distinctive. Do we all agree?"

Everyone nods and then looks at me. I nod a little too. "Sure, of course. It's a democracy after all."

Ellie opens up a pad of paper and writes "Brainstorm" at the top. "Okay, let's just start tossing ideas out, and I'll keep track of them."

"Elegant Foods," I say and smile.

Ellie twirls her pen for a moment but then writes it down. "Um, Cate? Any ideas?" She looks at Cate desperately.

Cate gets up and begins pacing. "It's Atlanta. So maybe we should do something with the peach?"

I shoot her a look. "There are probably ten peach-named caterers in this city already. Somebody get me the phone book, and I'll show you."

Daisy leans forward. "But what if we made it La Pêche Catering. You know, *peach* in French. If there's one thing I learned at Seeger's, it's that food people love French words. It can't be a chocolate croissant. Oh, no. It has to be a *pain au chocolat*."

Ellie writes that down. "I kind of like La Pêche. It's easy enough to say and spell. And Jo, you have to admit, it sounds upper-crusty."

I wince and look at Ellie. I can tell she's kidding, trying to get me to lighten up, but calling me and my friends "crusty" isn't exactly the best way to do that. "Oh, um, yeah." Divine Foods is still better. "I like it just fine," I say. I feel myself coming around to it a little. It's French, at least. There's some cachet in that.

"No, no . . ." Cate says and sighs. She keeps pacing. "I usually have such a good sixth sense about these things. La Pêche is cute, but that's just not us."

Daisy screws up her face, thinking. "What if we tap into old Southern food traditions? My grandmother taught me practically everything I know in the kitchen. She was always shelling peas, boiling peanuts, baking biscuits, frying bacon, boiling greens, churning fresh butter—"

Daisy keeps going and going. I stare at her. She's in a trance. She'll keep talking if we don't stop her.

"—crackin' pecans, whippin' meringues, putting up preserves—"

"Daisy!" I say a little too loudly, and she stops. I can see that Ellie is relieved that she stopped too. Daisy shrugs like I'm crazy, and then Cate stops pacing.

"No, I think Daisy might be right," Cate says and sits down at the table. She takes Ellie's pen and paper and roughly sketches out an old-fashioned Mason jar while we all crowd around her. This is it? A jar?

"Okay, it's rough, right, but this is one of those iconic pieces of Southern cuisine. The Mason jar. You know, full of fresh preserves? Or jelly?"

I cross my arms over my chest. "We're going to call ourselves Mason Jar of Preserves?" La Pêche is sounding better and better. I can live with La Pêche.

Cate is expertly drawing a little calling card with a cute jar on it, complete with a checkered gingham scrap of fabric under the metal washer. "No. But we could do something with this. Look how cute it could be."

"I don't know. Mason jars are a little down-home," I say.

"Jelly Jar," Ellie suddenly says, staring at Cate's drawing. "Jelly Jar Catering. That's so cute."

"Yes!" Daisy says and gives Ellie a high five. "That's it!"

Cate is mumbling it to herself over and over again. "Jelly Jar Catering. It works, design-wise. We could specialize in Southern food. It's catchy. It's distinctive. We could have a lot of fun with it. Good work, Daisy," she says and smiles.

"And Ellie! Ellie thought of the name," Daisy says.

They all congratulate one another as I sulk. Jelly Jar

Catering? Are they kidding? That's a terrible idea. But they all love it so much. I pull at my bracelet. "Um, I'm not so sure that . . ."

They go silent and look at me.

"It's just that . . . are you sure you don't like La Pêche?"

Three heads shake vehemently back at me. I say a quick prayer for strength and force a smile. "Well, maybe if we go with Jelly Jar then we can always leave behind a jelly jar full of fresh peach preserves with our little label on it."

They stare at me with blank faces. Great. Apparently I have no good ideas.

"You know, like a calling card?" I squeak and then stare at my shoes.

"Josephine Vann," Cate says in a hushed tone. "You are a genius."

I look up.

"Simply adorable," Ellie says.

We all laugh, and the mood lightens. For the next half hour, we draw up fun sketches for our business cards and jelly jar labels and swap family recipes for peach preserves. I throw Mother's recipe into the running. We decide to do a blind taste test to decide the winner.

"Wow," Cate says. "That discussion went much better than I thought it would. I'm so used to having a boss tell me what to do. It's nice to have a vote for a change."

This warms my heart, and I say a prayer of thanks to God for helping me put aside my foolish pride. We are really doing something big here.

"Y'all," Daisy says, "this is amazing. I can really see this catching on. Who wouldn't want to work for a company like this? I wonder if other companies are going to see it and try it out too."

Before we leave that evening, Ellie draws up a makeshift document, showing our two rules. She writes it in her lovely, lilting handwriting, and I post it on a corkboard, which no doubt in its past life held the bathroom cleaning schedule for the fast-food joint.

After everyone else is gone, I walk around and take it all in. The space is hideous, but we'll fix it up soon. The business is new, but it will grow. The women I hired are strangers, but soon will be friends. What we are trying to do—start a new kind of business, one that caters to women with families—sounds impossible. But I know that nothing is impossible with God, and when he calls you, he equips you. I look at the list of rules and feel a tingle down my spine.

We're really going to do it.

The Jelly Jar Rules

1. Family comes first, and kids are always welcome at work.
2. This is a democracy. We say what we feel. That's what women do.

Cate

"HAVE I GOT A CATCH FOR YOU."

I don't recognize the number, but the thick drawl tells me it's Daisy calling. Jo made us all exchange contact information in case of an emergency, but no one has actually used it yet. I guess this is my first Daisy emergency. I brace myself.

"Hey, Daisy," I say and close my copy of *Domino* magazine. So much for spending a lazy Saturday afternoon researching color schemes and concepts for our new catering space.

"Cate, he works in the Publix near my house, and he's just the cutest thing you ever saw. Big blue eyes and this curly blond hair and dimples." She sighs. "I really think he might be perfect for you."

"Oh, um," I say, stalling. Am I so pathetic that people I barely know feel the need to find me a man?

"I'd date him myself, but we kind of look related. Although between you and me, I'm not really a natural blond. It's like Dolly says, 'I'm not offended by dumb blonde jokes because I know that I'm not dumb. I also know I'm not blonde.'"

I crack up. "Wow. Daisy. I don't know what to say," I stammer, stalling for time. How can I possibly answer her? Does she honestly think I'm going to go out with the man she ogled in the produce aisle?

"Now, I know you're still getting over what's-his-face, but you know any man who cain't commit ain't worthy of you. And Jared, that's the stock boy, he's just looking for someone, I can tell. He's ready. So what do you say?"

What do I say? That I don't date produce guys?

Okay, I also don't really date at all, but still. I barely know this woman, and she's already setting me up with random men. I've been single for only a few months now, and I'm not really over David. I'm not desperate . . . yet. I should never have told them about the breakup. Next time I have a quarter-life crisis because some mama's boy dumps me, I'll just take a Señor Frogs cruise to Jamaica.

But I can already tell that Daisy doesn't take no for an answer. And despite the completely ridiculous situation she has just presented me with, it actually seems like she genuinely does want to help.

"Daisy—" I don't know what I'm saying, but for some reason the words just come out. I swear God put them there, because it certainly wasn't me. "What are you doing tonight? Some friends are coming over for a junk food and movie night."

"Really?" she says slowly.

How stupid of me. True, Daisy is only two years older than I am, but she has a child. She's not some single girl who watches movies on a Saturday night. She probably wants to stay home with Tiffany.

"If you want," I say. "You don't have to or anything if that's weird."

"No, that sounds great," Daisy says, laughing. "Hooray. Anything to get me out of this apartment."

"Really? Don't feel pressured. I'll understand if you're busy or want to spend time with your daughter."

Daisy laughs. "Tiffany is fourteen." I swallow. I didn't know her daughter was *that* old. That would have made Daisy . . . Oh, my. "She wants nothing to do with me. We're like college roommates. If I don't get out of her hair every now and then, she'll probably kill me. Trust me, you've just made her evening. Now she can watch the Discovery Channel and IM her friends all night."

I laugh a little. "Okay," I say and then tell her how to get to my house in East Atlanta.

"I'll bring some slice-and-bake cookies. I don't bake off the clock," she says. I laugh and thank her, and we hang up. Then I say a quick prayer that I won't regret this.

I open the door nervously, peering around it as I take a deep breath. Frances and Beatriz are absorbed in a *Gilmore Girls* rerun and don't even look up as I pull it open to reveal Daisy, clad in dark blue jeans and a green silk top. I let the air out of my lungs. It's not that I actually thought she'd show up wearing fishnets and a bustier, but . . . well, okay, it didn't seem out of the realm of possibility, and my friends aren't exactly the cabaret type. They're more the coffee and bagels after church type. I remind myself that I've prayed about this and it really seems right, so it will be fine.

"Come on in." I smile. She holds up a tube of cookie dough and steps inside.

"Chocolate chip," she says, laying her studded white purse on the floor by the door. "They were clean out of plain old sugar cookies, but cookies are cookies, I always say." She smiles, tucks a lock of wavy golden hair behind her ear, smoothes her shirt down, and looks over expectantly at Frances and Beatriz, who are now watching her intently. It's weird, really. If I didn't know better I would say Daisy is as nervous about this as I am.

"Cookies?" Frances, my closest friend, is suddenly very interested in meeting our new guest. Even though she stands a mere five feet two inches, Frances has always been one huge ball of energy and can pack away more food than anyone I've ever met. She never gains a pound either, which is proof that God plays favorites.

"Daisy, I'd like you to meet Frances Kim," I say. Frances smiles warmly and welcomes Daisy. I silently thank God for Franny, who has this amazing way of drawing people into conversations. When I first met her in the dorms our freshman year at the University of Georgia, she was constantly organizing RA group brunch outings to the Five & Ten or coordinating intramural volleyball games. Just watching her tired me out. While I spent most of my time in the library hiding in the stacks, she was busy running Tri Delt without breaking a sweat. And though she never convinced me to rush, we were inseparable throughout college. She used to joke that she was praying about my non-Greek status. Now a pediatrician in a public clinic in Cabbagetown, she saves lives every day, while I . . . well, I'm really good at matching fabrics. She appears to still like me anyway.

Beatriz shakes Daisy's hand warmly and offers her the bowl of popcorn. Daisy takes a handful and smiles.

"And this is Beatriz," I motion, though with her right hand full, Daisy offers her left hand to my statuesque friend. Beatriz has waist-length brown corkscrew curls and is an MK—a missionary's kid—who was raised in Brazil. Franny and I met Beatriz at church, and instantly liked her, and not just because she was dressed like Cher for the Halloween party. Who knew Cher had a following in Brazil? Beatriz found her calling stateside, moving to Atlanta to become an ESL teacher after college. She knows what it's like to feel out of place, and her kids adore her. She quickly became a good friend, and the three of us hang out together almost every weekend.

"Pleased to meet you," Daisy drawls.

"And you," Beatriz says in her sexy Portuguese accent. It could be one funny night hearing the two of them converse. Only in Atlanta would you get a makeshift UN as a friend group.

"We rented *Pride and Prejudice*," I say, ushering Daisy into the kitchen so we can start baking.

"Have you seen it?" Frances holds up the box and wags her eyebrows up and down.

"Oh, yeah," Daisy says, nodding. "Matthew Macfadyen is so delicious," she says and rubs her hands together. She stops, looking around as if worried she might have just offended us.

"Very sexy." I laugh. "Though not as hot as Colin Firth in the BBC version." Daisy smiles, relaxing a little, while Frances and Beatriz debate the merits of various Mr. Darcys through the years.

Daisy and I go into the kitchen, leaving Frances and Bea to their heated argument, to make the cookies. I pull out a cookie sheet. Daisy slices the dough on a cutting board I place in front of her. We're both silent, and I find myself clearing my throat again and again. Why is it so awkward? I wrack my brain, trying to think of something more to say. Have I asked how she is yet? Wait, I did. Right?

"Nice place you got here," she says, finally, looking around my shabby-chic kitchen. I realize taking new things and making them look old isn't everyone's idea of practicality, but the warm distressed cabinets and the colorful tiles make the place feel comfortable and homey. I bought the three-bedroom bungalow in the up-and-coming (realtor code for cheap) neighborhood East Atlanta just over a year ago, when I thought David would be popping the question and moving in, and we would need space for a family. East Atlanta is going through a bit of a renaissance these days, with cute little cafés and bars and shops opening every other weekend, but it's still living down its days of high crime rates, which makes it afford-able. The price of my house was right, but it needed some work, so I put my heart and soul into refinishing the floors and peeling layers of wallpaper off the crumbling walls. A few coats of paint and a designer couch later, it's home, even if it's just a home for me—well, me and my very loyal goldfish, John the Baptist.

"Thanks," I say, then my mind goes blank. "Um . . . want a Coke? I've got Sprite, Diet Dr Pepper, and Jones Cola."

"Sure. Sprite?" She nods.

I pull a can of Sprite out of the refrigerator and hand it to her. "Ice?"

"Yes, please," she says.

I nod, trying to think of something to ask her as I get a glass and fill it with the lion's share of ice. It was Bea who told us that outside of the South, people don't usually drink everything swimming in enough ice to stop global warming. I hand the glass to Daisy. I smile, and she smiles back, and then begins to drum her fingers on the counter. I sigh.

This was a very bad idea. We have nothing in com-mon. Why did I ever think Daisy would fit in with my friends?

"Y'all, I was so embarrassed," Daisy says, fanning herself, as the rest of us clutch our sides and try to catch our breath. I take a sip of my margarita and try to compose myself. "I mean, there I was on the table, trying to get up, but they kept trying to tell me it would get better, which was a lie." She laughs.

"So what did you do?" Frances asks, gulping for air. "Did you let him finish?"

"No way!" she says, shaking her head. "I flailed my arms so much that he couldn't keep going, and I sat right up and pulled my pants back up and walked out."

"With it half done?" Beatriz screams, throwing her head back, tears streaming down her cheeks.

"What was I going to do?" Daisy shrugs, dipping a tortilla chip in the creamy queso and popping it in her mouth.

"So wait," I say, dipping a chip in the homemade guacamole. "Are you telling us that you have *half* a Tasmanian Devil tattooed on your butt?"

"More like two-thirds, but yeah," she says and shrugs. "He was really big back then." Daisy takes a sip of her drink while Franny takes deep calming breaths, trying to recover from a laughing fit.

After the inauspicious start to the evening, everyone relaxed during the movie, and we were chatting like old friends by the time we decided to pop into Cantina La Casita, my favorite little Mexican joint just down the block, for chips and queso. The open patio in back is warm and breezy on this perfect spring night, and Daisy has been regaling us with her nonstop anecdotes. "I always tell people I can't wear a bikini because of the stretch marks, but it's really that I don't want anyone knowing I chickened out halfway through Taz."

I smile, and we're quiet for a moment, enjoying the warm night air.

"So how do y'all know each other?" Daisy asks finally, taking a sip of her drink.

Frances and I look at each other, and then we both look at Bea, uncertain of what to say. I don't know Daisy all that well, but, well, she had a baby at sixteen. I doubt she's going to be too impressed with this answer. But I guess she wouldn't be the first person who bolted after I told them about my faith. Well, I'll still see her at work.

"Church," I say simply, hoping that will be enough for her.

"Really?!" she shrieks, her face lighting up. "What church do y'all go to?"

"Resurrection Community," Frances says, uncertainly. I can tell she's as confused as I am. Why is Daisy so excited? "Do you know it?"

"I've never been there, but I've heard of it," she says, nodding. "I go to Peachtree Presbyterian."

"You what?" I can feel my mouth hanging open in shock, but I can't make myself close it.

"Yeah," she says, smiling as if she's just discovered the cure for cancer. "Since last November." She laughs. "I didn't know y'all went to church." She shakes her head. "Isn't that something? My coworker is a sister in the Lord!"

Isn't that something, all right. I watch her, pure delight etched across her face, and I can't help but smile. I know that look. It's the look of a new believer. "That is pretty cool," I say, smiling at her, and then my face flushes. Here I was thinking God wanted me to take pity on poor Daisy and invite her over. Now I'm wondering if maybe he sent her to pull me off my high horse.

"Oh, my gosh, I didn't know it was so late," Frances says suddenly, startling me out of my reflection. I look at my watch and am shocked to see that it's almost one o'clock. "I have to work in the morning," she says, shaking her head. "And we've been having a horrible outbreak of poison ivy in the neighborhood."

"No problem," Beatriz says and signals for the check. The tired waitress drops it swiftly onto our table, relieved we're finally leaving.

Frances looks at it for a moment. She always does the tip. She's like a human calculator. "With tip, we should leave nineteen dollars," she says. "So, everyone put in five." I lay five ones on the table, and the others put their money on top.

"Now let's see," Beatriz says, flapping a single in the air. "Who has the most pathetic life?"

I roll my eyes. I hate this game, but we've been playing it for years. Whoever can convince the others that her life is the most pitiable gets to put in less on the tip. Like I need to be reminded of my pathetic existence.

"I have to work in the morning," Frances says, yawning as she takes the dollar from Beatriz. "And that guy Corey who lives on my floor never looks me in the eye after I asked him out for coffee last month, so I pay four."

"No way," Beatriz says, pounding the table. "I only have to pay four, because not only have I not had a date in forever, but my children this year are unteachable and one of them keeps swearing at me in Spanish. As if I don't understand Spanish. Plus my mother is coming to visit from Brazil," she says, crossing her arms over her chest.

"I don't know," Frances says, eyeing the extra dollar.

"My mother is coming to visit from Brazil and staying with me for two months," Bea says. Franny holds the dollar a little closer to Bea. "And I will have to help her cut her corns off."

"Ewww!" we all scream in unison. The table next to us turns to look. Frances hands Beatriz the dollar.

"I knew I would win tonight," Bea says, beaming.

"Nope," Daisy interjects without missing a beat. "I only have to put in four because I'm a single mom. Today my daughter told me I looked like a Vegas showgirl on crack, and the only date I've had in a year left the restaurant while I was in the bathroom when I let slip I had a teenager."

"Oooh," Frances laughs. Bea grudgingly hands her the dollar.

"Woo-hoo," Daisy says, pumping her fist as she tucks the hard-won dollar in her purse. "Finally that kid is starting to pay off." They all begin to pack up their purses to go.

"Hang on now," I say. "You haven't won yet, Miss Daisy." I take a deep breath.

"Oh, get out," Daisy laughs. "Didn't I just tell you I have half a Tasmanian Devil on my left cheek?"

"Here we go with the David card," Frances says. "At least once you could let someone else have a shot."

"We're getting you a date, Cate." Bea sighs. "I'm tired of losing."

"I only have to put in four," I say, ignoring them both as I dip a chip into the now-cold queso, "because two months ago, David, the man of my dreams, the man I dated for eight years dumped me cold. Why? Because God told him to break up with me."

"He didn't," Daisy says slowly, mouth open in shock. "God doesn't do that, does he?"

"That's what David said." I shrug.

"No, God doesn't do that," Beatriz says, draining the last of her drink. "It's the lamest excuse I've ever heard."

"It sure is convenient," Frances says, rolling her eyes.

"Yeah." I sigh. "I can't really argue with God, now, can I?"

"Oh, honey," Daisy says, shaking her head. "I'm sorry. That scoundrel. Here, take the dollar. You win."

"So how are you liking your new job? You must be so glad to have gotten away from Flaky Mollie," Franny says.

"Yeah." I take a sip of my coffee, stalling. The last thing I want to talk about is my madwoman of an ex-boss. I look around. "Good space. Score one for West Egg." Frances is on a mission to find the best brunch spot in all of Atlanta. The Flying Biscuit has been the heavyweight champion for six months, but we give them all a shot at the title. Today's restaurant of choice is a chic converted warehouse in West Atlanta famous for its egg dishes. The Sunday morning postchurch crowd fills the light, airy space with a sense of excitement.

Frances smiles. "Modern, clean. Points off for not taking advantage of the Gatsby reference. But still, I like it."

The waiter comes over and brings our order, and I'm relieved that Franny seems to have forgotten about her question. After five years of working for a boss who considered me her personal gofer and her business more of a hobby than a livelihood, I was ready for a change.

The waiter begins to walk away, but before he's really out of earshot, she says, "Our waiter is cute. You should ask him out."

I turn and look at him, then shrug. "You had me at 'May I take your order?' I don't think so."

"Fine," she says. "First the shuffleboard, now this. Don't say I never tried to help you."

"I am not entering a shuffleboard tournament," I say, grabbing the yellow flyer she took from the bulletin board by the door. "'Shuffleboard is an exciting game that is played by people of all ages for fun and for healthy outdoor and indoor exercise,'" I read out loud. "'It calls upon players to develop hand/eye coordination plus strategy and a competitive spirit.'"

She smiles. "Doesn't that sound fun?"

"Franny, you can't be serious." Frances, my so-called friend, is on a personal mission to pull me out of the depths of despair and into the arms of Mr. Right. Unfortunately, she's coming closer to Mr. Rogers. I take a bite of my black bean cake and muster my will to fight. "What men do you think we're going to meet playing shuffleboard?"

"Come on! How bad could it be?" Franny cocks her head at me.

"I just don't think shuffleboard is for me."

"That doesn't mean you shouldn't try it." She shrugs at me as if I'm crazy. "We'll show up, push a little thing with a stick, and meet some guys."

"My grandfather plays shuffleboard at the rec center. I don't think they're going to be exactly what we're looking for."

"Look at this guy." She points to a grainy black and white photo on the back of the brochure. "He looks like he could put up a fight."

I lean in and crane my neck to see the hunk of a man she's marrying me off to now. He has liver spots. "He's been state champion since 1973."

"See? He's way past his prime." She nods. "Ripe for a downfall."

"Franny, I cannot consider shuffleboard a competitive sport."

"That's just the problem." Frances stuffs a giant piece of sausage in her mouth. "You have this narrow definition of what constitutes a sport." She pauses to take a sip of orange juice, then plows on ahead. "For your information, in many places eating is considered a competitive sport. Witness the Black Widow."

"The Black Widow?" I should know better than to get her started on this, but at least she's momentarily forgotten about trying to set me up with an ailing octogenarian.

"She's the Dale Earnhardt Jr. of competitive eating."

"What are you talking about?"

"My hero. A hot Asian femme fatale weighing in at ninety pounds able to out-eat anyone on the planet."

"And what does this have to do with me?"

"I'm just saying you need to broaden your horizons," she says, shrugging. "Try a noneating sport if you must. But don't keep hiding. It's been two months. You need to get back in the game. And you need to cut back on the coffee," she says as I signal the hipster waiter for a third cup.

"There's nothing wrong with coffee," I say defensively, pulling my steaming cup to my mouth. "The latest studies show it's actually quite good for you."

"It makes your teeth yellow," she says flatly.

"Like corn!" I smile at her over the edge of my cup.

"It makes your pulse soar."

"Like an eagle!"

"It makes your neurons backfire and your—" Frances stops short and puts her orange juice down quickly, her eyes wide.

"What's wrong?" I look around quickly, scanning for a grease fire or a man with a gun.

"We have to go." She throws two tens down on the table and grabs her purse. "Come on, we'll go out this door," she says, pointing to the glass door that leads to the front of the building, away from the parking lot.

"Frances, what's wrong?" I haven't started on my grits yet. Frances knows better than to come between a lady and her grits.

"Just trust me. We have to go right now." I lay my fork down slowly and stare at her. She's dead serious. Frances is so rarely serious that I know she must mean business. I lean over and pick up my purse, then stand up slowly. She begins to walk toward the clear glass door, and I follow. What is going on? I turn to look behind me, and Frances catches me.

"Don't turn around," she hisses.

"Why not?"

"Remember what happened to Lot's wife?" she mumbles.

"What are you talking about? I'm going to turn into a pillar of salt if we stay here? I'm going to—"

"Cate!"

I freeze. I know that voice. Mrs. Gladwell.

"How are you, darlin'?"

I turn around slowly.

Mrs. Gladwell is coming toward me, arms outstretched, her frosted blond hair perfectly coiffed. I take a deep breath.

This is the woman I thought would be my mother-in-law. And next to her is . . . my breath catches. David. He towers over his mother and his broad shoulders stretch the fabric of his blue button-down. His close-cropped hair is perfectly messy, and he looks thinner and paler than last time I saw him. I can't breathe.

"I thought you were working!" Mrs. Gladwell says. "I wanted to see you, but David said you were working like crazy, isn't that funny? Is this one of your clients?" She leans in and gives me a familiar hug.

"Um . . ." I stammer. This is so strange. I look at David. He's looking at the ground. I haven't seen him since he unceremoniously dumped me, which makes this bizarre encounter all the weirder.

"You know, I'm only in town for the weekend, and David told me you were booked solid with your new job, but isn't this funny running into you?" She laughs and pulls back. "Now let me take a look at you." She eyes me up and down and beams at her son, who is cowering next to her. He won't look at me. "You look amazing, darlin'. Doesn't she look amazing, David?" She looks at her son, who nods noncommittally. "Now, you absolutely must join us for brunch. David was telling me that they have these great biscuits and gravy," she says, beaming.

"Actually, we just ate, er, uh, finished our breakfast meeting," Frances says quickly, grabbing my hand. I look from her back to Mrs. Gladwell, speechless. I can't believe this woman is acting as if nothing is wrong. What's going on? "Sorry, got to run. Client business, you know?" Frances smiles at her.

"Oh, now, that's too bad. I don't know when I'll make it back from Dallas again, sweetheart," she says, disappointment etched across her face. "But I understand. Work is work. Well, maybe next time."

"Yeah, next time," I say, looking at David helplessly. His mother seems so sincere. It's almost as if . . .

"Of course it won't be long now anyway," she says, winking at me. "I'm sure any day now this son of mine will get off his tuckus and get himself a ring, and then I'll be down all the time for the showers and . . ."

"We really have to go now," Frances says, pulling my arm. "Nice to see you." She pulls me out the door and closes it behind her, dragging me toward the car.

"Frances?" I manage to squeak out, stopping short. "What was that about? It was almost like . . ."

"She didn't know," Frances says, quickly. "That slime-ball didn't even have the guts to tell his own mother." She looks at me, taking a deep breath. "Are you okay?"

"I . . ." I look around me, confused. The air is warm and bright, and the breeze carries the slightest hint of jasmine. "I don't know."

"Come on," she says, pulling me. "Let's get out of here."

I follow her dutifully, unsure of what else to do. As we turn the corner toward the parking lot, I look back quickly. Through the large glass window, I see David watching me walk away.

A block and a half away from my house, I realize my mistake. I should never have let a blind date pick me up. I've read this in magazines, but they always warned about stalkers who won't take no for an answer and have weird obsessions with hunting knives. But this is a friend of Beatriz's cousin. I figured the connection, loose as it may be, made it okay, and he was so insistent that it was on his way from Decatur anyway. And Shawn doesn't seem like an ex-felon or the kind of person who has a Smurf figurine collection hidden in his closet or anything. But I can already tell this is not going to work, and now I am trapped.

"Yeah, I can't move out," he says, shrugging, "because I need somewhere to set up my telescope, and the backyard is just perfect." He shrugs. "Plus my mom makes the best barbecued chicken I've ever had, so there's that."

Really, I should have known better than to say yes to a guy who wanted to go to the Georgia Aquarium on a first date. I have nothing against aquariums. I like fish as much as the next person. But Shawn has been to the new aquarium fourteen times in the past year, and, as he said on the phone, he wanted to take me to his special place. Talk about a warning signal.

I sit in silence as he talks about his online astronomy club and drives his mom's old Dodge Caravan along DeKalb toward downtown. Mentally, I'm writing an angry letter to Beatriz demanding the next three hours of my life back.

We're standing in front of the stingrays, and he's still doing it. I can't figure out why Shawn thinks standing next to me and holding his hand in front of his mouth while he talks makes our conversation more private. It actually just makes it hard to hear him and makes everyone else stare. Didn't something like this happen on *Seinfeld*? I maneuver so I'm standing in front of him, hoping to get his hand away from his mouth and have him talk like a normal person, but he just walks over to my side so our shoulders are touching and continues his lecture on the stingray's predators. It's like being on a date with Rain Man.

"So what do you do?" Shawn asks, leaning in toward me, his hand on his face. I look at him, then look wistfully at the poisonous sea creatures.

"I work for a catering company." I sigh.

"The food industry has the highest failure rate of any industry," he says, nodding.

I take a deep breath and count to ten. The emergency exit lights beckon to me.

"How did you decide on catering?" Shawn continues, oblivious. "Surely you knew."

"I don't know." I take a deep breath and shake my head. "I think I'm just having a quarter-life crisis or something."

"You're twenty-eight, according to Beatriz."

Thanks, Bea.

"Yeah. I can't even have a quarter-life crisis right."

Shawn takes his hand down away from his face, and he squints at me in the dim light. The fluorescent bulbs in the tanks make his eyes look purple. "Do you like the work at least?"

"I don't know." I squint back at him. He is looking at me intently, as if he actually cares what I'm saying. Did David ever look at me like that? I turn and face the stingrays. "It's weird." Out of the corner of my eye, I see Shawn nodding, and I don't know what else to do, so I babble on. "My coworkers are all moms, so they're always talking about sippy cups and Boppy pillows and Baby Einstein and the Tooth Fairy and . . . it just gets boring." I glance at him. He smiles.

I cross my arms over my chest. Suddenly, I don't know what I'm saying. "Not only that, their kids are everywhere. I can't think because there are always kids around, and we haven't catered a single event yet. I thought I'd be doing party concept planning and execution, but instead I'm just sitting through one meeting after another about menus, who will come let the electrician in, marketing ideas . . ." I stop and put my hand over my mouth. Did I really just say all that to this stranger?

A man next to Shawn taps on the tank, and Shawn glares at him. A stingray resting near the front of the tank darts away. "This is a new job?"

I nod. "I was kind of happy working with my old boss, Mollie. She was flaky. She took credit for my good ideas. She once called me from Bali when she was supposed to be finishing up a house in Marietta." I take a deep breath. "My 'office' was really just the spare bedroom in her house, and I had to put up with her little yappy dog, who hated me, all day. But it was creative, and I was good at interior design."

Shawn is nodding, watching me closely. "And you're wondering if you made the right choice?" he asks.

I nod. "I was ready for a change. I needed a clean break from . . . my old life. But now I'm not so sure."

The smooth green algae on the rocks moves gently with the current. He clears his throat. "Do you know the reason people always hit deer on the highway?"

I turn to look at Shawn. This guy is like a human Animal Planet.

"When a deer is frightened, its instincts always tell it to return to where it was safe. So when it sees a car coming, instead of just running across the road, it doubles back. And most people try to swerve behind the deer to miss it, assuming it will run forward."

I give him a look. "What?"

"You're the deer."

I roll my eyes. Lovely. You're the odd duck, then.

"You're going to get hit by a car."

I stifle a laugh, but he seems totally serious. I look back at the stingrays, gliding smoothly through the water. They're so peaceful, so free. It's really kind of amazing how well equipped they are for their habitat. So perfectly suited for their station. So beautiful in their simplicity. So . . .

So now I'm jealous of a stingray. I really need to get out of here. I pull myself away from the oddly mesmerizing tank and turn toward the door.

"Trust me," he says, cupping his hand over his mouth and leaning in. "No one wants to clean up deer guts."

I glance down at the map. Maybe we can skip the River Scout section and head straight for the giant shark tank and get this over with. But as I see Shawn's eyes light up at the sight of the upcoming coral reef, I get the feeling I'm in for a very long afternoon.

I slam the door behind me gratefully, vowing never to return to the cursed aquarium. Why bother? I already know everything there is to know about sea life. But Shawn might have had a point about the job thing. I shake my head, place my purse down on the counter, and wander into the kitchen to get a glass of water. Never again. I put my glass under the Brita spout and take a grateful gulp. I pull my phone out of my purse, dial into my voice mail, and put it on speakerphone while I feed John the Baptist.

"Hey, John," I say to my goldfish. He just *glub-glubs* back. I look at his fish food and notice that it still has "Locusts and Honey" scribbled over the preprinted "Fish Flakes." That was David's favorite little joke. He loved to relabel stuff around my house so that I would find it later and laugh. He also loved to tuck little love notes in drawers, in the coffee canister, in my favorite magazines, in . . . I shake my head.

Is it really only two months since he called it quits? After dating for eight years, it's such a small amount of time, but it feels longer than all those years put together. We were juniors in college when he transferred to UGA. We met at a kickoff picnic for Campus Crusade. I noticed him right away, with his penetrating blue eyes and dark hair. I introduced myself, he made a joke about C. S. Lewis, and I was a goner. He smiled at me, and we spent the evening laughing. When the sunlight slipped away, we went for a walk through town, over to the golf course, where we sat on the hill by the sixth hole and talked until the sky started to brighten again. I'd never met anyone who could go from deep theological discussion to quoting lyrics from pop songs in a single breath. He challenged my preconceptions and made me think. I knew this was the man I was going to marry.

Looking back now, I can't help but laugh. We were so young. What did we know?

"Enough of that, right, John?" I swear he nods at me. I press my password into my phone.

"You have three unheard messages. First message," the Verizon woman says.

"Catie. It's me again. Call me back, huh? I can explain about my mom and everything else. I want to see you. We need to talk. It's important. Call me." The message clicks off.

This is the third message David has left on my voice mail since I saw him at West Egg. Why does he keep doing this? I want to accept that it is God's will that we not be together. I really do. But how can I if he keeps calling all the time? I force myself to erase the message.

"Next message."

"Hey, Cate. Me again," says David's familiar voice. "I'm not stalking you. I just wanted you to tell John the Baptist hi for me. I miss him. Tell him to watch out for Salome." I smirk in spite of myself and roll my eyes.

Fine. I'll call him. How could a call hurt? He can't actually reach through the phone and attack me or anything. Just a friendly call.

"Next message."

"Hey, Cate. It's Bea. I heard from Franny that Dave the Plague has been calling you every day and that you haven't called him back. Just wanted to congratulate you on the willpower. My mom is coming at me with nail clippers, so I have to go. Bye."

"End of new messages."

I stand still with the phone in my hand like a deadly weapon.

To call or not to call, that is the question. Bea's probably right. I shouldn't call. We all know I can't control my-

self around David and I'll only end up going back to him if
he asks me to, especially now that I know what else is out
there. In a word, Shawn. And even if David doesn't want
to get back together, hearing his voice will make me remember how much I miss him and then I'll feel worse. I
throw my phone on the couch across the room and keep
my back to it. There. Okay. Don't call him.

I walk back to my bedroom and change into some
comfy clothes. I'll just pop a bag of low-fat popcorn—get
crazy, single girl—and watch some reruns of *Buffy the
Vampire Slayer.* Or maybe there will be an eighties movie
on. I come back into my living room, plop down on the
couch, and take a deep breath.

It's so nice and quiet when you live alone. No one to
move your stuff around, no one to eat the last of your
food, no one to clean up after, no one to talk to, no one to
laugh with . . .

I pick up the phone. David owes me an apology, at the
very least. I'll just call, let him say he was sorry about the
other day, and then go.

I open up the contacts and scroll down past the *D*s. I
had him under *D* for David for years, but recently I had to
move him to a new location so that I wouldn't be tempted
to call him.

"You Idiot," my phone's screen says. I smile as it starts
to ring.

Ellie

 T'S NOT THAT I LOVE TO BE RIGHT, IT'S JUST that, okay, fine, never mind, I *love* to be right. But really, Jo almost makes it too easy. I arrive at The Glenn, the sleek boutique hotel in downtown Atlanta, a full hour before Jo asked us all to be there, which at four o'clock is still three hours before the event tonight, as a kind of experiment. I toss my keys at the cute valet at the hotel, take the elevator from the lobby, and blow out onto the rooftop bar area, swinging my tote bag at my side like I don't have a care in the world. And I catch her.

"Ellie, why, I didn't expect you so early," she stammers. Jo is still digging in her purse for her sunglasses, which makes me think she has just arrived herself. I smile at her and snap my own sunglasses onto my face. "Early bird gets the worm, I always say."

The look on her face is just priceless. And maybe I'm being a little mean, but she had it coming. I've served on every board, committee, and organization in the city of Atlanta, and I can sniff out someone trying to co-opt leadership a mile away. If she thinks she can do that on my watch, simply by arriving early, she's wrong. I'm co-owner of this business, and though I doubt she's ever had anyone challenge her on anything in her life, Josephine Vann is just going to have to learn to like it.

"Let's get to work, then," Jo says, recovering. "I'm going to go find the hotel manager to discuss how to get guests efficiently through the lobby and into the elevator. You can just do, um, something else, maybe."

I take stock of the rooftop restaurant. It is minimalist, cool, and modern, and tonight we will have one unbeatable view up here of the downtown city lights. But there is just one little thing I'm concerned about. Okay, a big thing.

"Jo. How well do you know the bride-to-be?"

This is our first catering event, and Jo landed it through her Junior League connections. I didn't think we were ready yet, but I got outvoted. Personally, I feel we shouldn't be accepting work when Cate has half of the floor of the Burger Barn torn up for remodeling, and Daisy and I agreed on a menu only two nights ago. But here we are, and I figure I'll probably live through this too. It can't be as bad as giving birth to twins, right?

"I know her very well. She's the younger sister of a sorority sister of mine." Jo checks her watch. "I should really be—"

"And she's from the area?"

"No. She's from Macon. Conservative small-town family. Salt-of-the-earth kind of people."

I look around at the roof. "Did she request this specific location for her wedding shower?"

"No, it's a surprise bridal shower. Look, Ellie, what's this all about? I told Catherine's mother I'd handle everything."

I smirk at her. "Did you notice that these are, let's see, how do I put this delicately?" I walk around to one of the large pieces of furniture on the roof. I sit down on it and recline a little.

Jo looks around at the rooftop with her head cocked to one side. "What?"

"They're beds, Jo."

"What?!" she shrieks. She stares at me in horror.

"Didn't you know the rooftop restaurant is run by B.E.D.?" I ask, putting my hand on my hip.

"What is B.E.D.? I mean, who on earth has ever heard of such a thing?"

I hit my head. "Gracious, Jo. You never watch *Sex and the City*?"

Jo shakes her head at me. "Of course not. Not even on TBS with all the dirty parts taken out."

I laugh a little.

She just shakes her head frantically. "This is not happening."

"You eat and drink *in bed*. That's the theme."

"This is all wrong," she says and walks over to one to inspect it. Each bed has throw pillows and gauze curtains hanging from an overhead chrome frame. "I just thought they were big ottomans or something. The latest craze." She tries to shove one of the giant padded platforms but can't make it budge. She kicks it. "Ouch, ouch," she says and starts hopping around, clutching her espadrille. "Oh, fudge bunny."

"Jo, just calm down," I say, fighting back a snicker.

"I can't calm down, Ellie. Catherine's mom is going to kill me." She goes over to another of the offending beds to study it. "You think they would remove them for the evening?"

"With a crane? After they unbolted them from the floor?" I check my watch. "All in a few hours? I don't think so."

I watch her pacing back and forth and then begin to worry that in her frenzy she might flip over the edge of the roof. I walk over to her and make her stop pacing. Once she is still, I let her go again.

"I wondered if you knew, but you kept saying you had it all under control."

"How was I supposed to know?" she asks, biting her lip. I nod. Mike and I never get out to places like The Glenn anymore. We do better at the boring Marriott, where I don't have to worry about my children breaking the crystal paperweights or grinding Play-Doh into the lambskin throw rug.

"This is so frustrating. All my research said this is the spot of the moment. And we sent Daisy and Cate to check it out. They loved it. You remember."

I give her a look.

"Those two are no longer scouting locations, that's for sure." She places her hands on her hips, shaking her head.

"To be fair, it would have been fine if it was an event for one of their friends," I say.

Jo throws herself down on one of the beds. "We're over, and we haven't even catered our first party yet."

I lie down next to her and look at the clear Georgia sky. "We're not over yet, Jo."

"Yes, we are. And you know what makes it worse? It's a *bridal* shower. The accidental innuendo is almost more than I can bear."

I snicker. "It could be worse, you know."

"How?" she says and looks at me. "There is no possible way it could be worse. These people have a grandfather on the board of the Southern Baptist Convention. They're personal friends with Billy Graham. It, I assure you, could not be worse."

I wait for her to finish. "It could be a baby shower," I say and smirk.

Jo looks at me, stone-faced, for a moment, and I know I've pushed it too far. I gulp. Can she fire me? But then she bursts out laughing. Hearing her loud, unladylike howling sets me off too, and we both laugh hard until Jo has tears running down her face. Finally she sits up, wipes her eyes, and fans herself. "I feel like Nero playing the fiddle while Rome goes up in flames."

I sit up too. "If we're going to fail, let's at least go out in style," I say calmly. "You go find that hotel manager. I'll stay up here with the beds and try to figure out how to downplay the 'harlot boudoir' theme we've accidentally got going."

An hour later, Jo has terrified the hotel manager into pulling a valet from the garage and assigning him to greet the guests at the hotel lobby door. Shower attendees will be escorted through the lobby directly to the elevator and up to the party. For my part, I sweet-talked two men on the custodial staff into unbolting the chrome canopies on each bed so that we could take down the sheer Scheherazade curtains. We even removed all the throw pillows. Then I retrieved large rectangular bamboo serving trays from the restaurant manager and put one in the middle of each bed with a small jade plant, which we'd brought along for table decorations, on top. They really don't look like beds anymore. And besides, while the bride's friends might figure it out, it is the old Southern biddies we're worried about, and they probably would never even think of such a preposterous thing as a rooftop full of beds.

Jo walks around and inspects my work. "Very impressive, Ellie."

I smile and look around. "I guess it doesn't say 'Congratulations, you hussy anymore. So that's good."

Jo and I smirk at each other, just as Daisy walks up carrying a huge tray of cookies.

"Hey, y'all, here are the macarons I made, not like the American coconut ones, but like those little French sandwich cookies. I really think they should just call them something else. Or maybe we should call ours something else? They might have had the idea first. Hey, wait," she says and puts the tray down at the long table where the food will be arranged for tonight. "Where'd all the beds go?"

I stumble in through the garage door at two in the morning, rubbing my eyes. Even though the roads were clear at this hour, the drive to Druid Hills still took twenty minutes, and I'm about ready to collapse. I open the door to the kitchen and sneak inside in the darkness. "Ouch!" I howl as my foot lands squarely on something hard and plastic. I remember that Sophie and Seth are asleep upstairs and try to contain myself.

"Ouch, ouch, ouch, ouch," I whisper. I flick on the kitchen light and see what I stepped on. Below me is a purple cell phone, lighting up. "Hello? Do you want to come to my party? I would love to have you," it says to me, singing a little tune.

"Shhh." I switch it off. I pull off both of my flats, inspect my wounded arch, and then put the little cell phone on the counter. The twins love this crazy thing, though I'm highly dubious that they're actually learning good manners from it like the box promised. But you know toy companies. They can charge twice as much if it's deemed "educational." Of course "educational" is practically code for "annoying."

I walk over to the fridge and open it. There must be something to eat.

"Aren't you out past your curfew, young lady?"

I sniff the expired milk carton and turn around. "Hey. Did I wake you up?"

"Hello? Do you want to come to my party? I would love to have you," Mike says in a dead-on mimic of the phone.

"I'm sorry. I didn't see it. I stepped on it."

Mike comes over to me, shuts the fridge, and gives me a big hug. "I feel like I haven't seen you in years. Go sit down, and I'll fix you something to eat."

I hobble over to the kitchen bar and smile at him while he takes out a Tupperware container.

"You're okay with leftover mac and cheese?" Sophie and Seth eschew all foods that are not Easy Mac, and though a few years ago I would have sooner gotten the mail in my bathrobe than voluntarily eaten microwaved macaroni and cheese, now I think it's actually kind of good. I know pregnancy can make your feet get bigger. Do kids make your standards die?

"Anything you've got. Those Macon ladies ate even the radish garnishes tonight." I stare at the counter, dazed, running over the party again in my head. We made it. It probably couldn't have gone worse, but we made it. And, from what I understand, they didn't even dock our pay. Sure, it was probably because Jo is a personal friend of the bride's family, but still. We made it, and we got paid. Next time will be better.

"Sophie slapped Seth tonight, and he's got an ugly scratch on his face now."

I roll my eyes. "That's your daughter."

"And she spent half the night in time-out for it. And

then later Seth decided that he wanted to say the *S* word. We really need to start monitoring him."

"The *S* word?" I look up in shock.

"*Stupid*," my husband says, and slides a paper plate of steaming-hot Easy Mac in front of me. I haven't eaten on a real plate in years, and my wedding china is lost forever in the attic.

I pick up a red plastic spoon with a monkey curled around the handle and shove some macaroni in my mouth. "Oh, *that S* word," I say between bites. Wow. I had no idea how famished I was.

Mike slides a glass of water over to me. "I don't think he'll do it again, though. He just heard it at school or something." He walks back toward our bedroom. "I'm beat. Good night, Angel."

I stop chewing for a moment and look at him. There are bags under his blue eyes, and his face is pale. His dark brown hair is starting to gray around the temples. "Wait," I say and take a swallow of water.

He locks the garage door and peeks his head back into the kitchen. "Yeah?"

I stare at him, incredulous. "Well . . ."

He scratches his right sideburn, a nervous habit, and then shrugs. "What, Ellie?"

I squint at him. "Don't you want to know how it went?"

He screws his mouth up and kicks at nothing on the tile floor. "Um, okay. How was it?"

I tuck another bite of the macaroni into my mouth. "You had better come and sit down for this because it was awful." I take a long drink of wonderful, cool, refreshing water. Mike looks at the wall clock and then comes around the bar and sits down next to me. I'd better make it quick. He's fading fast.

"These people were Jo's friends. You remember which one Jo is?"

Mike scratches something off the counter. "Huh?"

"My partner, Jo. She is like this crazy Martha Stewart person. Anyways this client was a friend of hers so it was probably okay, and I think they still paid us, but it was a catastrophe."

Mike looks at me. "Oh?"

"It was so embarrassing. My No-Miss Salmon Puffs not only missed, they completely struck out. They were so salty you couldn't eat them. The only thing I can figure is that I did something wrong when I multiplied the recipe to feed seventy-five." Mike nods a little and then presses his fingers into his eyes hard.

"And then it turns out that the bride-to-be had a severe nut allergy that no one told us about, and she had to break out her epinephrine pen after a bite of Daisy's baklava, which actually did turn out just fine, aside from nearly being the instrument of the intended's death."

"Hmmm," he says.

"And Cate had to take over the dj table after the college kid who was manning it kept playing some kind of weird music with a loud beat, synthesizers, and a person blowing a whistle in the background."

"Wow." Mike turns the word into a mumble.

I wait to see if he has anything else to say, but he just

stares across the kitchen in silence. I put my hand on his back and rub it for a moment.

"And you know the three of them just won't stop talking about God ever since they found out they are all Christians."

I look up at Mike, who has his eyes closed. We used to go to church when we were first married, to Druid Hills Methodist just down the road, but ever since the twins came we can't get our act together to get there on Sunday mornings. They're twins. Mobilizing them for anything is hard, and especially for church. Sophie isn't the kind of little girl who relishes knee socks and lacy dresses. And Seth unclips his clip-on tie and tries to leave it all over the church.

Mike sighs. "We should really get back to church. If my great-grandmother knew I wasn't going, she'd rise from the grave to haunt me. She was a founding member of our church. It looks bad that we don't go."

I look down at my Easy Mac and frown. I wasn't exactly raised religious. The Howell family is Christian, of course, because Southern politics demand it, but we didn't go regularly. And when we did go, we went to a simple African Methodist Episcopal Church where I felt like I belonged. No women in designer dresses and men with Rolex watches.

"The kids are really old enough to appreciate it now," he says.

I feel like a twig has been thrust in my stomach. There it is. The guilt. We need to go for the twins. Everyone here goes to church on Sundays. We're probably depriving the twins of their necessary spiritual instruction by not going. "I know. And their friends go. They'd like it better now."

"And my mother is always after me about it." Mike runs his fingers through his hair.

I bite my lip hard so I don't speak. When Mike and I met in Paris, he was pretty religious, and we both agreed that we would raise our kids in the church. And I really want to, just like I said I did. But I don't want to do it just because his mother will disapprove of us if we don't. It's not like she's some kind of shining example of Christian love.

"This Sunday, we'll get organized and do it."

Mike nods slowly in silence. "Do the, uh, other women know that you're Christian too?"

I take a bite, thinking back. "No. They haven't decided about me. I haven't piped up either way."

Mike rolls his eyes ever so slightly and stands up. "Okay, I have to go to bed. We can talk about this later."

"You're tired, huh?" I ask, unable to keep the disappointment out of my voice. I could use a little reassurance right now, that he doesn't blame me for not going to church with him, that I've made the right decision with this catering adventure.

He stands up and shakes his head. "Yeah, Ellie, I'm tired." He stretches and runs his palm down his face. "Come to bed soon?"

I sigh, and nod as I lift another forkful to my mouth.

———

It's only ten-thirty, but I've already downed two large mac-
chiatos and a handful of Advil, and I'm afraid there may be
another dose in my future. We have to get this place in
shape to pass our health inspection, and since we're doing
most of the work ourselves, things are a little tense. We
have to stay focused and not let anything distract us.

I hear a loud crash and wince. We could start our own
kindergarten.

I brought my five-year-old twins, Seth and Sophie,
today. Their identical OshKosh denim overalls were filthy
before they'd even made it to the kitchen. They are ob-
sessed with Bob the Builder, and so they haven't stopped
tapping on everything with their Playskool plastic hammers all morning. Every couple of minutes, I hear Seth or
Sophie sing, gleefully, "'Bob the Builder: Can we fix it?!'"
I'm ready to take their tool kits and shove them into the
Dumpster behind the store, but then I'd just have to find
something else to keep them occupied.

Jo's girls, five-year-old Martha and three-year-old
Agnes, are the picture of wholesomeness. Their blond
curls gleam, and their bright blue eyes are wide and clear.
Today Agnes is wearing a pink shirt featuring Belle from
Beauty and the Beast over her little pink skirt, and Martha
wears Aurora from *Sleeping Beauty.* They are both shod in
perfectly shined patent-leather Mary Janes and acting like
little princesses, quietly coloring within the lines in their
matching Disney coloring books.

Perhaps I should have let Mike take the twins today instead of bringing them to work, but with the big golf tournament coming up, he wanted to get some practice shots in, and, well, this is supposed to be a family-friendly company. Making work a place where children are welcome is a great idea, and the future of the modern workplace and all that, but if Seth takes apart my cell phone one more time, I may have to reconsider this whole motherhood thing. Surely the hospital will take them back, right?

"Hey, Mom?" The improbably named Tiffany looks up through her thick smudged glasses. Her long dark hair is greasy, and her jeans are loose and dirty on her pale, rail-thin frame. Daisy has the music up too high in the other room to hear her.

At first I refused to believe that Tiffany was actually Daisy's daughter. How could this serious math student be the offspring of someone as flighty and free-spirited as Daisy? But Daisy swore up and down that she was, in fact, her daughter, so what can we do but believe her? Daisy brought her here so she wouldn't be by herself all day, though I get the distinct impression that being alone would have suited Tiffany just fine. Tiffany appears to be in that angry-at-the-world stage and has spent most of her time silently playing games on her graphing calculator.

"Whoa," Jo says and scoops up Sophie as she runs by. "Let's not chase people with the, um . . ."

Sophie looks at her, her brown eyes wide. "Screwdriver."

"Right, with the screwdriver. Let's not chase people with the screwdriver," she says, putting her down.

"Why?" Sophie asks.

"Because you might fall and hurt yourself or someone else," Jo says, smoothing her perfectly coiffed hair that does not need smoothing.

"Why?" Sophie says again.

Jo looks over at me. "It's a vortex." I laugh. "Don't keep answering her. She'll just keep asking why." Jo pats Sophie on the back and smiles at her. "She almost reduced their babysitter to tears the other day."

Jo laughs. "Thankfully, we pretty much skipped that phase. But biting is Agnes's new thing, so watch out."

I laugh and shrug.

"Mom?" Tiffany calls, a little louder this time. She peers around the door to where her mom is theoretically painting the reception area. Daisy, dressed in short jean cutoffs and a tight white tank top, her hair covered by a red bandanna, is holding a paintbrush like a microphone, dancing around the gallons of paint as she sings along with "Sweet Summer Lovin'," which is blaring from a small radio at her feet. Occasionally, Daisy applies some light lemony-green paint to the walls in between bursts of the running man.

"Daisy," I echo, but she doesn't look, just dances along with the beat. I shrug at Tiffany and she sighs, turning back to her calculator.

Cate is supervising the installation of the cabinets. She has been on the phone most of the morning arguing with the manufacturer, who has apparently sent flat panel when she specifically ordered beadboard. She did a fantastic job laying out the space. We planned for a comfortable reception area out front for meeting with clients, a small office for managing the business, a large storage area for equipment and supplies, and a professional-grade kitchen in the back for food prep. The only indication that this used to be a Burger Barn is the persistent smell of grease that we can't get rid of, no matter how much Lysol and Febreze I spray. We decided to cut costs by doing much of the renovation work ourselves, hence the chaos we find ourselves amid now.

I wipe my hands on my old jeans and look around slowly, fanning myself with a plastic saw, making a mental note to get an air conditioner in here, stat. The floor is ripped up. There is dust everywhere from our sanding. The pantry door is off the hinges. We're never going to make it.

Tiff sighs and gets up to show her mom something on her calculator. They talk quietly and Tiff gestures toward the kitchen, and Daisy nods absently and points at Jo, then goes back to her dancing. Sophie is dancing with her and tottering near the paint.

"Careful, Sophie," I say, trying to let Daisy handle it, trying not to be that mom who micromanages her children even when other moms are around. Sophie shrugs and walks away.

Tiff rolls her eyes and walks back to the kitchen.

I'm about to check the master task list when Martha comes running up to Jo, who is unpacking the floor tiles. "Mom, Fluffy Makeup needs to go potty." She holds up her Build-A-Bear.

"Ellie, would you mind taking over here for a bit?" Jo asks. She takes Martha's hand and walks toward the bathroom and as she passes me she says in a low whisper, "Fluffy Makeup always gets hungry, thirsty, tired, and needs to go potty at the exact same time as Martha." Jo chuckles to herself and leads her little girl away. "Okay, c'mon, Martha. Let's go potty."

I crouch down over the tiles she's unloaded and begin to arrange them on the floor. Tiffany walks over, scrunching up her face.

"How many boxes of tiles did you order?"

"I don't know," I say, reaching for the purchase order. "Check this and see." She nods and hunches over the pink paper, punching numbers into her calculator.

"That's what I thought. Not gonna work."

"What?" I say, turning to face her. She won't look at me, but begins to mumble.

"I've been trying to tell my mom," she says, rolling her eyes, "that you don't have enough tiles. It's simple math."

Could she possibly be right? She's only what, fourteen?

I look at Jo nervously. She waits outside the door to the bathroom while Martha sings the theme song from *Sesame Street* inside. As soon as the little girl comes out and runs back to her coloring, I signal to Jo.

"Jo? I think we have a problem here." Jo's hair is pulled back into a neat ponytail, and her crisp white shirt and khaki pants make her look cool and put together even in this hot den of chaos. I start counting tiles. Jo takes a deep breath before making her way toward me.

"What's wrong, Ellie?" She sits down next to where I'm crouched on the floor and lays a hand on the cool ceramic tiles in front of us. Tiffany, her long dark hair falling in her face, is mumbling to herself as she scribbles on a piece of paper.

"Tiffany just discovered that we don't have enough tiles here to cover the whole kitchen," I say.

"What?" she asks, rubbing a hand across her forehead. "That can't be right. I calculated it myself. Did they deliver the whole order?" I scan the invoice and nod, my lips pursed.

Tiffany crosses her arms across her chest. "I know I'm right."

"Two hundred tiles, half white and half black." I nod again. "So that should work. The kitchen is two hundred square feet, and we don't even have to tile under the island, so if each square is twelve inches per side, we should have more than enough."

"That's the thing," Tiffany says. She pushes her glasses up on her nose. "If they were each one square foot, you'd be fine, but each tile is only ten inches. So to cover two hundred square feet, you need 288 tiles. You don't have to tile under the island, but it's only fifteen square feet, so you would still need 266 tiles at this size," she says, holding out a diagram she's drawn.

"What? No," Jo says, leaning her head against the wall. "I ordered the twelve-inch tiles. This can't be right."

"Sorry, Jo," I say, grimacing at the invoice again. "The tiles that were ordered were ten inches." I hold my head in my hand. Where's that Advil?

"I'll call the manufacturer," Jo says, grabbing the invoice. She wanders outside to call, and Tiffany, Cate, and I wait silently in the kitchen. I can hear Daisy singing out in the front room. A few minutes later, Jo comes back in, shaking her head.

"They're backordered for two months."

"Two months? We can't wait two months," I say. I know it sounds whiny, but we have to pass our health inspection next week to get certified to actually begin catering for real clients. I hear a loud crash, and Sophie cries out. I turn in panic at the sound of my daughter's cry.

"Everything's fine," Daisy yells from the other room, but somehow that's not comforting.

"Are you sure?"

"Promise!" Daisy yells. I frown. If I go in there now to check on Sophie, does it look like I don't trust Daisy?

"This isn't working," I say, covering my face with my hands.

"We'll figure something out with the tiles," Cate says.

"Huh?" I say and look up. "Oh, no. I'm sure we'll figure that out. *This* isn't working," I say, motioning to the chaos of four children under the age of six running around. "Why did we think this would work? It's all fine and well to say that you can bring your children to work, but we can't actually get any work done with them here." My voice is thin with desperation. Daisy has done a wonderful job entertaining my twins and Martha and Agnes, but she also hasn't gotten anything done all day.

Jo is frowning. "But it has to work."

I look at Cate for her opinion. "I might have to agree

with Ellie. Tiff is fine." Cate looks at Tiff, who looks at the floor. "Actually, Tiff is a big help. But work is no place for anyone who still eats Play-Doh."

Jo bites her lip. "Okay, we'll fix it. We'll hire someone to help during Jelly Jar meetings. Today was just a trial, and there's going to be a learning curve, of course. We can fix this. Maybe we can pay Tiff to do it? Would you like to earn some babysitting money?" Jo smiles from ear to ear at Tiffany.

Tiff scowls at her.

"Right. Not interested," Jo says.

"I know someone," I say. "Seth and Sophie have a great babysitter named Lauren who's in college. I'll bet she'd be interested. Even if she could just watch them here at Jelly Jar during our weekly meeting, that would help, I think."

Jo's shoulders relax. "Perfect. Problem solved. Just talk to Lauren, and we'll pay her out of the Jelly Jar money. Now, onto our tile problem. You see? There's nothing we can't fix."

Cate takes a deep breath and looks around the kitchen helplessly. I scan the invoice, thinking.

"If you don't tile the pantry," Tiffany says, pointing to the corner of the kitchen where a large closet stands next to the space for the Sub-Zero refrigerators, "it will work."

"What do you mean?" Jo asks. Tiffany begins to sketch the space on the back of the pink paper, and Jo nods.

"No one will really see in there anyway, so I guess it wouldn't matter if the floor is different," Jo mumbles. "Cate, what do you think?"

"Do what you have to do. We have some extra tile left over from the bathroom," Cate says, gesturing toward a stack of small cool blue tiles against the reception area wall. "We can get more of those and finish it off that way."

Tiffany watches us, sucking on the end of her ponytail. Jo and I look at each other, and I shrug. "Fine with me."

"All right, then. We'll get started on the checkerboard tiles for now. You ready to grout, Tiffany?" Jo laughs, but the sullen teenager shakes her head.

"Thank you, Tiffany," Cate says. "If you hadn't discovered that mistake, we'd have been in a world of trouble." Tiffany doesn't say anything, but looks at her feet and blushes.

"Hey, Daisy, your daughter's a genius," I yell.

There is no answer. I look around the kitchen wall toward Daisy and the children, but don't see anything either.

"It's too quiet," I say nervously.

"Agreed," Jo says and starts walking.

The three of us dart around the corner and come to a screeching halt.

"Daisy!" I gasp, staring at my twins.

"Oh, my," Jo says.

I look from Daisy down to the kids, and nod, my mouth hanging open.

"How in the world did you get them to do that?" Cate asks, shaking her head.

There, in the middle of the room, the four young children are quiet for the first time all morning, working very diligently on painting the empty cardboard box the dishwasher came in. Each of them has taken a side and is carefully applying green paint, and not one of them is screaming or crying or acting out.

"I just asked 'em if they could help me paint this very important box." She shrugs. "They were all over it."

"Mom, look!" Sophie squeals, pointing proudly to her half-green wall. "I'm helping!" She smiles, her brown eyes sparkling with delight.

"Daisy, I see where your daughter gets it," Jo says, shaking her head.

"Kids are just little people." Daisy twirls around. "They want to feel like what they're doing matters."

I look around at our company, taking shape before my eyes, and my beautiful children in front of me, and somehow I know exactly what she means.

My back aches, my arms ache, heck, even my fingernails ache. But we made major progress on the Jelly Jar space today.

I walk over to the kitchen area to admire it one last time. I bend down and run my fingers over the smooth, flush tiles. They look perfect. I stand up and look around the gleaming kitchen. The space is completely quiet.

Daisy and Jo went home a few hours ago, and Mike picked up the twins, but I decided to stay and help Cate until the bitter end. Just because she's a single girl doesn't mean she should always have to pull the late hours. And late it is. We just finished and it's almost midnight.

I roll my head in circles, cracking my neck. Cate left just a minute ago, and I'm supposed to be locking up, but for some reason I can barely tear myself away from this place. It's just so beautiful. And we did it all by ourselves. And the kids were here.

I walk over to shut the bathroom door and turn off the light. As I walk back into the kitchen, I pass the new corkboard. Something catches my eye. The rules we made at our first meeting are tacked up there, along with everyone's phone numbers, but now there is also a ripped piece of soft, brown coloring book paper with a little princess on it. At the bottom, someone has written in crayon:

3. Kids at work are a blessing—never forget it!

I guess that's a new rule. I smile, thinking about Daisy today. I'll never underestimate her again. I click off the lights, punch the alarm on, and slip out into the night, feeling reborn.

It's during my fourth reading of the Health Codes and Inspection Self-Prep Packet 23-FG for Fulton County that I begin to wonder how this became my job. That Jo is a clever one. She passed this huge doorstop of a booklet to me this morning and has been in the back cleaning ever since. I have another sip of coffee. *This is important, Ellie. Focus.* We can't fail our health inspection this afternoon because we have a birthday party signed up for next week. And this time, we want to have a dress rehearsal before the big day. I reapply myself to the booklet.

"In accordance with the Sherman Act, as ratified by the Environmental Health Services Division of Fulton County, Georgia, all commercial food retailers must use approved utensils and equipment which have been in-stalled properly and meet applicable standards. (114065, 114090)"

I sigh. We'd better hope that the health inspector is just as confused about the codes as we are. I look around the kitchen. It really is an amazing space. The giant gleaming stainless steel sink, warm maple cabinetry, under-cabinet lighting, and sleek range and oven with fume hood all look like a magazine ad. Plus, the new energy-saving AC unit has really cooled the space down, and the two professional-grade freezers and three refriger-ators were delivered yesterday. We came in a little over budget, but hey, what project doesn't? There's no way we can fail. We've thought of everything.

"What do you mean we need three sinks?" Jo spits. We have one hour before the inspector arrives, and my eye-sight is blurred from going through this book for the thousandth time. But this time, I caught something.

I clear my throat and begin to read, "'Three sinks are the minimum any food retail store may have. One located in the bathroom, one for proper and safe food handling in the food preparation area—'"

"Yeah, yeah," Jo says. "We've got those."

I give her a look, and she shuts up. I continue. "'And one separate from but near to the food-prep-area sink for employee health and maintenance.'"

"Huh?" Daisy says, fussing with her bun and hairnet. We are all dressed in new, crisp white aprons, our hair pulled back neatly for the inspection.

"It means hand washing," I say. "We have to have a separate sink for hand washing."

"Who ever heard of such a thing?" Jo says, pacing. Here she goes again.

I look at Cate, who leans on the counter as if she might collapse. "We have to get a sink in here in one hour or we're going to fail?"

I shrug. "It seems pretty easy to notice the missing sink," I say. "Maybe we can reschedule?"

"We can't reschedule." Jo sighs. "This was the only appointment they had free all month. We need to pass this one."

"Well, then," Daisy says calmly, sitting down on a high bar stool. "Where are we going to get a sink?"

Jo looks at her. "Daisy, what are you talking about? We can't get a sink now. It's too late. We'll just have to hope they don't notice or just give us a citation."

I sigh. Jo's right, unless . . .

"Hey, Cate, if we had another sink, where would you put it?" She gives me a funny look but begins to walk around the kitchen.

"The regulations say it has to be near the food-prep sink?" she asks. I nod. She bites her lip. "Well," she says, taking a deep breath, "we could carve out a hole in the counter here," she says, tapping on the Formica counter down a few panels from the main sink. "And I could probably splice and run the plumbing down this way so that we could have a very basic working sink."

"Okay." I nod. "Get your saw and start cutting." I flip open my cell phone.

Thirty minutes later, Mike arrives with a very basic, very small sink from Lowe's. Cate is just finishing up the hole we'll need in the counter. We won't be able to get the plumbing working today, but if the inspector doesn't actually turn the sink *on*, we just might pass.

"Ladies, the sink you ordered," Mike says, straining to hold the heavy porcelain bowl.

"Hi. Thank you. Right this way," I say and lead him through the kitchen to the hole Cate cut. He sets it down in the hole, but it is a little too small. He takes it back out and puts the sink on the ground.

"Mike, this is Cate," I say, gesturing to my coworker who is picking up the saw to enlarge the hole. Mike nods at her.

"And Daisy." Daisy pats her hairnet self-consciously and smiles.

"And, this is Josephi—"

"We've met," Jo says and extends her hand to Mike. They shake hands for a long moment and study each other. They've already met?

I look at Mike, trying to figure out the connection. "Jo and I are old friends," he says, finally.

Jo sniffs, drops his hand, and walks away. "What?" I mouth at him.

"I'll explain later," he whispers.

Cate makes a few passes with the saw and pronounces the hole perfect. Mike hoists up the sink and sets it in the wonky hole. It does fit, barely. We all cheer.

"Our hero!" Daisy says, pretending to swoon.

Mike dusts off his hands. "I should get back to work."

"Thank you," I say, leaning in to kiss him on the cheek.

"Bye," he says, dodging me, practically running for the door. It slams behind him, and I shake my head. What's with him?

Daisy comes over and bumps me with her butt. "Cute hubby, Ellie. And a real hero too."

I look around and nod distractedly. Maybe it's my imagination, but I could swear Jo shot me a dirty look before she started wiping down the counter for the third time.

The inspector is a small, prim man with wire-rimmed glasses and short brown hair. He wears a blue tie over his short-sleeved dress shirt, and he is holding a clipboard and scribbling on a stack of forms as he walks around, mumbling to himself about different codes. The four of us are standing in a straight line, not daring to breathe or move.

I squint and try to make out his name tag. I think it says "Mr. Jordan."

He strolls over to the Viking range and peeks behind it. I really hope we got it connected right. He begins to turn on each one of the gas burners and scribbles something down.

"This is going to take forever," Daisy whispers to me.

I shrug back at her, hoping that she stops talking, but instead I hear her clear her throat.

"So, um, Mr. Jordan," she says. "I'm Daisy." She walks over to him and shakes his hand. She giggles. Is she flirting with him? "Should I call you Mr. Jordan? Or something else?" she asks, batting her eyes.

The inspector looks over his glasses. He stands about as high as her shoulder.

"My first name is Michael. You may call me that if you wish," he says in a perfunctory manner.

"Oh, gosh," she says, giggling. "Well isn't that a hoot, honey? You're famous!" The inspector glares at her. Daisy seems to think he doesn't understand her so she begins to dribble an invisible basketball.

I look around. Jo is shooting daggers at Daisy, and Cate is trying to stifle her laughter. I don't know what to think. What is she doing?

"I'm six months older than the basketball star. I had the name first," the inspector says flatly. He scrunches up his face like he's about to sneeze, but nothing comes out.

"Oh, I guess you get that all the time," Daisy says, laughing. "You know, my first name is Daisy, and I always kind of wished my last name was Duke, but it's not." He looks at her and pauses, then looks up and down. Daisy doesn't seem to notice and just continues. "I own a lot of short shorts so you might think it was but—"

"Daisy?" Jo's tone is firm. "A word with you?"

Daisy shrugs and follows Jo into the front room while Cate and I exchange a look and chuckle. Poor Daisy. She was just trying to help in her own way.

Mr. Jordan goes over to the big sink and turns on the water. Cate and I bore holes in his back, and I begin to sweat. If he goes to the new sink and tries to turn it on, we're toast. He turns off the faucet and then begins to walk toward the next one, sliding his hand down the countertop. C'mon Ellie, think. Do something.

"Mr. Jordan," Cate says. Whew. She'll save us. "Catherine McCoy. I'm a licensed interior designer and the engineer of this space. Let me know if you have any questions at all."

Mr. Jordan stands directly in front of the bogus sink but turns around to face Cate.

She walks up to him, puts a hand high on his back, and guides him away from the sink. "Have you seen what I did to update the ventilation? I'm really quite proud of it. So much more sanitary," she says, ushering him far away from our sink.

Half an hour later, it's all over and Mr. Jordan has barely made a peep, which I think is a good thing, though he's been scribbling on his stack of papers the whole time. We all huddle around him for his pronouncement.

"Ladies, I am very impressed with the space you've created," he says, finally. We all visibly relax a little. We'll be officially licensed and even get to keep on schedule for our party next week.

"This is a clean and well-designed environment for a catering operation. I see no blatant violations of our county health code, though I would advise you to make sure to replace the bar of soap in the bathroom with a liquid, as they are preferred by the health board."

We all smile and nod, and then Daisy hugs Jo.

"So, without further ado, I'd like to—"

He stops and stares down in horror. I look down in time to see a giant white rat scamper across the kitchen and right over the inspector's gleaming black shoe.

Pandemonium breaks loose.

"Eeek! Eeek!" Jo screams and jumps on a stool.

Cate freezes in fear, her eyes wide. I take a deep breath and try to shepherd the little rat out the back door. Ugh. He's so gross. Just look at his little rat nose and his thick rat tail.

"Vermin! Vermin!" Mr. Jordan squeals and runs for the door. "Automatic failure. You automatically fail," he screams as he runs out the front door.

Daisy, however, does something curious. She watches the rodent, unmoving, studying it with her hands on her hips.

"Archimedes?"

Mr. Jordan stops outside the door just long enough to post a bright pink slip on our front window notifying the public of our shame and humiliation before running to his car.

I'm still trying to take stock of what happened when Tiffany comes running in through the back door.

"Mom! Help! Archimedes got out of his cage!" she says, her face red, her eyes wide.

Daisy scoops the rat up off the floor and hands it to her daughter. Tiffany coos and holds it like a kitten while we all stare at the two of them. No one says anything. Daisy looks at the ground.

"Unbelievable," Jo says and crosses her arms across her chest, leaning against the counter. She glares at Daisy.

"I'm real sorry, y'all," Daisy says slowly, looking around. She bites her lip and clenches her hands. "This is Tiff's pet rat, Archimedes." She coughs. "He must have gotten out."

"Daisy, we just failed our health inspection." Jo looks at her sharply.

"I know," she says, her drawl thicker with the emotion in her voice. "I am so so sorry. Tiffany was supposed to wait in the car, and . . ."

Tiff looks like she's about to cry. "I'm, I'm sorry. I didn't know he was out." She takes a step back and looks around anxiously.

"Why were Tiffany and her rat waiting in the car?" Cate asks calmly, taking a deep breath.

"We were going to go see my math team partner Roger later," Tiffany says, a tear leaking out of her eye. "He has a rat too. They were going to do a maze."

"Why would you bring a rat on today of all days?" Jo asks, staring at Daisy.

"Jo, she didn't mean . . ." I start, but am cut off by Daisy.

"I'm sorry," Daisy says. "I asked her to wait in the car so she would be out of the way. She didn't mean for Archimedes to get out. Next time—"

"Don't you see, Daisy," Jo asks, throwing her hands up. "There won't be a next time. If we can't cater this party next week, we're done. We needed to pass this inspection, and now . . ."

Daisy looks down at her feet. "Are you going to fire me?" Tiff stares at her mother's profile.

"What?" Jo asks, raising her voice.

"I'd understand," Daisy says, nodding. "I can take it."

"Daisy Johnson," Jo says, putting her hands on her hips. "I am surprised at you."

Daisy looks at Jo, her head cocked to one side.

"We're not going to fire you. Men fire people," Jo says. "Women," she says, crossing her arms over her chest, "work through their problems."

"I'll fix it," Daisy says calmly, setting her jaw firmly. She glances at her daughter and takes her hand.

Jo nods, then looks away. "Do it quickly, please."

"I'll fix it," Daisy says again. "I'll take care of it. Tiffany, let's go." She puts her arm around the bawling teenager, and they walk silently out the door.

After they leave, I raise an eyebrow at Jo. The big softy. So now we know her bark is definitely worse than her bite.

"I like what you said," Cate says to Jo.

Jo blushes and shrugs.

"Me too," I say, digging for a pen in my purse. I find a Sharpie and stroll over to the corkboard. "I think we have a new rule."

"I just hope she figures this out," Jo says quietly.

The Jelly Jar Rules

1. Family comes first, and kids are always welcome at work.
2. This is a democracy. We say what we feel. That's what women do.
3. Kids at work are a blessing—never forget it!
4. We don't fire people. Men fire people. Women work through their problems.

Daisy

TIFFANY IS HUDDLED OVER THE KITCHEN BAR doing her homework when I burst into the apartment. She looks up listlessly, then, bored by me already, looks back down at her calculator.

"Guess what?" I sing as I drop my purse on the granite counter and walk toward her. I still can't believe I have granite. But granite comes standard in the lofts at Atlantic Station, the new development that's a mishmash of stores and apartments and restaurants. It's called mixed-use development, whatever that means, and it's apparently the future of urban planning, but I just think it's cool to live right above a Starbucks. My poor, practical grandmother would have fainted. A Johnson in Atlanta? In a high-rise loft apartment with not even a half acre of land? I've come a long way from Plainsville, Georgia, that's for sure. I lean over to give Tiffany a kiss and she freezes up, but despite all the Butterfingers that girl can pack away, I still out-weigh her, so she knows better than to try to resist.

"What?" She wipes pink lipstick off her cheek and looks down again, her long brown hair falling like a curtain, cutting her off from me. I resist the urge to tell her it's time to wash it again. Hygiene isn't high on her list of favorite things right now. I try to look on the bright side. At least she's not boy-crazy. Though if she were, I might be able to relate to her better. What kind of fourteen-year-old girl isn't boy-crazy?

"What are you doing with that thing?" I ask, walking back to the kitchen, and pull a can of chili out of the cabinet. "Bisecting angular circumferences? Cosine tangent vectors?" Tiffany, my alleged daughter, is the star member of Covenant Christian School's Mathlete Team. I don't understand where that brain of hers comes from. It sure wasn't her father, who, as I recall, had an IQ that matched the number on his football jersey. I pull a block of Cheddar out of the fridge and begin to grate it mindlessly.

Tiffany rolls her eyes at me. "It's precalc, not trig." She looks back down in disgust. "I'm studying the binomial theorem."

"Oh, the binomial theorem!" I laugh. I made it through the tenth grade, but I was mostly studying the backsides of the football players, which explains how I managed to get pregnant before I got my driver's license. "That's way easier than the trinomial theorem, and once you start getting into the gizoogular theorems, watch out."

She shakes her head at me without looking up.

Sometimes I wonder if there was a mix-up at the hospital. This is hardly what you expect to get out of an evening that was two parts tequila and one part post-football-game one-night stand.

"Did you have some news?" Clever girl, trying to change the subject.

"I've found a way to fix our little problem." She watches me, waiting. I know she still feels terrible about letting Archimedes out and accidentally causing us to fail our health inspection. I need to fix this for the business as much as I do for her. Mom to the rescue.

She grunts in response and looks at the floor.

"I'm taking the inspector out to dinner tonight." Her eyes widen with shock. "Isn't that great?"

"Mom!" she gasps. "That's a horrible idea."

"No, it's not. It will fix everything. I'll explain the situation, everything will get resolved, no harm done."

She shakes her head at me. "Why don't you just go back to your job at the restaurant? Didn't you say it made more money?"

Suddenly, all the air is gone from my lungs. It's no secret we've struggled financially. As soon as I turned eighteen, I took my infant daughter and moved out on my own to Hot-lanta, where I was determined to make it and leave my whole sordid past behind me. Those were lean years, to be sure, waitressing nights and picking up extra shifts whenever they were offered while Tiff was staying at a neighbor's house. We clipped coupons to make ends meet and had very few luxuries, but I am proud to say that

Tiffany never lacked anything she needed. And as I slowly worked my way up at Seeger's, our living conditions improved too. We're not doing half bad, in fact. And now, my only daughter, the light of my life, has the gall to . . . I take a deep breath and say a little prayer in my head.

"Why, is there something you need?" I ask calmly, pulling an onion from the fridge. I begin to chop, slowly, methodically.

"I was just asking," she says, shrugging. "That's all."

"Honey, I took my new job," I say, cutting the soft onion into thin slices, "so I could be home nights now." She doesn't say anything. "You're growing up so fast, and you'll be gone soon, off to some fancy school where that big brain of yours will be right at home, and, well . . ." I take a deep breath. I knew I was missing out on Tiff's life, and I wanted a change. And as Dolly says, "If you don't like the road you're walking, start paving another one." So I prayed about it, and the Jelly Jar job fell into my lap. Why can't she see this is good for us? "I just wanted to take the job."

She grunts. I guess I should have known better than to expect her to be excited about this. She's a teenager, after all. Armageddon couldn't get her excited.

"Tiff?" She looks ups at me blankly. "This company means a lot to me."

She watches me as I take the bag of Fritos off the top shelf.

"Are you making Frito pie again?" she asks, rolling her eyes. "Aren't you like a famous chef or something?"

So I don't cook at home. My dirty little secret. Cooking is my job, and I'm thrilled to be able to make a living doing what I love, but when I come home, the last thing I want to do is whip and frappe. Besides, I grew up eating Frito pie and any salad whose main ingredient is Jell-O, and I turned out fine.

"I'm a pastry chef." I sigh. "Not Emeril."

"Gross," Tiffany says, closing her book. She storms off into her room.

An hour later, she sneaks into my bedroom while I'm getting dressed for my date with Michael Jordan.

"You're not really wearing that, are you?"

I straighten my clingy red shirt and adjust the buckle on my red strappy sandals. I decide to deflect her question. She's wearing a men's extra-large cable-knit sweater. I am not taking her fashion advice.

"Don't forget that field hockey practice starts on Monday, honey." I twist the tube of my Juicy Melon shimmery lipstick and pucker.

"I'm not trying out for field hockey."

I take a deep breath. She may act hostile, but it was her choice to sit here on my bed while I get ready. I'm not holding her prisoner.

"It will be good for you." I try to affect a light tone. "You'll meet some nice people. Get your blood pumping a bit." I flex my biceps and make a funny face, but she doesn't even look at me.

"Math club keeps me busy." She sniffs. "And your skirt is too short."

I pull the hem of my black velour skirt down as far as it will go. "You can still do math club, honey. I'm not sayin' you can't. I'm just sayin' it would be good to try some new things too."

"I don't want to try new things," she says, sticking out her bottom lip. "I'm good at math." She pulls at a loose thread on my blue silk bedspread.

"And who knows? Maybe you're good at field hockey too," I say, sucking my cheeks in and running a cream blusher over them. "You need to give it a try. Just give it three weeks, and I'll get you that new game for your PTP."

"PSP," she says and rolls her eyes. I never get that silly thing right. "I need the new Sims," she says.

I frown. She loves that video game. You simulate a whole world, creating people called Sims. I can't help but think some real friends would do her a little better. Is that so wrong?

"I was legendary at field hockey when I was your age," I say, smoothing my hair down against my scalp. The humidity sure does a number on the curlicues I straightened into submission this morning.

"I'm not good at field hockey," she mumbles. "Did you know that in the new version of Sims, you can control your Sims throughout their entire lifetimes?"

I pretend to hit the ball with my stick. "We went to state. They called me 'Deadly Daisy.'"

"The Sims even pass on their genes to their children. It's supposed to be amazing."

"If I'd gotten to play my senior year, I probably would have gotten a scholarship."

She looks at me, biting her lip. Oh, no. Maybe I shouldn't have said that. I'm just trying to encourage her to branch out a bit, make the most of her teenage years, but . . .

She looks down at the bedspread and tucks the end of her ponytail in her mouth.

But we both know what happened to my teenage years.

I try to catch her eye, but she won't look at me.

"Yeah," she says quietly, looking down at her hands.

Michael Jordan is actually a wonderful man, just like I thought. Sometimes you just got to give people a second chance. That's something I've been learning at Bible study recently. Turns out Jesus himself hung out with people most folks wouldn't really choose. Michael is like that.

He picked me up right on time and has been a total gentleman all night—pulling my chair out for me, holding doors, and ordering the most expensive bottle of wine. He is wearing a stylish, if suspiciously new-looking, long-sleeved striped shirt, and he drives a black Audi Roadster, of all things. Not at all what I expected.

In fact, this whole evening has been a surprise, a lovely, pleasant surprise, considering how nervous I was about pulling it off. I mean, it's not really a love connection. He's not my type, and I do feel the slightest bit guilty about the pretext here. But if nothing else, I've gained a new friend.

"Michael," I say, looking at him over my glass. "I really love this restaurant. Excellent choice." I dip a bit of my breadstick in the pool of olive oil between us and wink.

He smiles shyly. "It just passed my health inspection." He blushes. "I try to stick to the high scorers."

"That's very smart of you. You never can tell—"

"I'm so sorry about the other day," he says, interrupting me. "I had no idea it was house-trained."

I reach across the table and pat his hand. "Don't you worry about that one bit," I say, laughing. "You had no way of knowing that was my daughter's pet."

"Vermin is an automatic failure. It's right in the book," he says. "A pet is something different, of course."

"Well, of course it is," I say, laughing. "Innocent mistake. No harm done. And now look at us here. Looks like it worked out all right to me."

"I feel just horrid about it, Daisy. I'm calling Jo first thing Monday to reschedule the appointment."

"Oh, she'll be able to work you in, I'm sure." I nod.

"Just a simple walk-through is all I will need and then you guys can get your official license."

I smile and pat him on the hand. "Aren't you sweet?"

That's the other thing I've been learning lately at my Bible study. Sometimes when a man don't see things the way he ought to, a woman of the Lord can talk to him and make him come around. There are loads of women like that. Look at Ruth. She just stuck with old Boaz until he got so turned around that he thought getting hitched was his idea. And Esther changed the king's mind with her bodacious curves and saved an entire race.

"I'm really glad you called me," Michael says. He winds fettuccine around his fork and smiles.

"I am too," I say, dabbing my mouth daintily. "I'm having a great time. And don't forget about the potluck on Sunday. You gonna come? It's just after the second service, and I'm makin' my famous Ding Dong Soufflé."

He smiles and then looks down at his plate. He'll be there. I can see it in his eyes. A lot of women in my Bible study ask for prayer about being bold in inviting their friends to church. I know we all struggle with different things, but I guess I just don't understand that one very much.

After a four-course dinner, Michael takes me for coffee at a little café that got an excellent rating on their health inspection. But when he suggests we split a piece of cheesecake, I decide it's time to make my excuses and leave. I have a teenager, after all. Who knows what kind of trouble she could be getting into.

He drops me off at our apartment complex, and I boogie upstairs, but when I unlock the door I see that the apartment is dark, except for the light from the television, tuned to Animal Planet on mute. I creep inside and see that Tiff is asleep on the couch, our cat Richard Simmons asleep on the pillow next to her. I sit down and begin to stroke her hair gently. The only sound is the squeak of Archimedes' wheel in the corner.

On screen, a kangaroo and her joey cuddle. I remember those days. Now we seem to butt heads a lot, but there was a time when I could make my daughter's face light up with just a smile. I sigh, watching the screen, mesmerized.

Tiff rolls over in her sleep and puts her head in my lap. I know I should wake her up, that we should both go to bed, but as I twine her hair around my finger, I thank God for my little girl.

The doorbell rings, and I look at my watch. It's already nine-thirty. I'm in a smidge of a panic. "Tiffany Belinda Debbie Johnson," I scream to her closed door. "If you don't get out here this instant, there'll be no computer time later." Okay, I'm more than a smidge panicked. I hear the doorbell ring again, and I run to answer it. Why does Tiff always do this to me?

I open it quickly, and Lillian strolls in.

"Darling, how are you?" she says. Lillian, my neighbor and dear friend, is a true Southern belle. She went to brand-name schools, married a blue-blooded man, and raised three perfect children, and then, as soon as her dear Henry was cold in the ground, chucked the house in Buckhead and moved downtown to recover the youth she never got to have. We're kind of kindred spirits in that way. Lillian was also the first person to welcome me into the building when I bought our loft. And now we get along like peanut butter and marshmallow fluff. She's the one who led me to the Lord last year, and for that I will be eternally grateful. I'll never tell her I know about the face-lifts.

Lillian is seventy-five years old, but tells people she's sixty-five. Today she is wearing a tasteful black suit and the most ridiculous hat you ever saw. Two words: pink feathers. She always wears a Sunday hat, as some weird vestige of her former life, I guess. All I know is she actually likes them, and I will never again put a breadbasket on my head in mock solidarity.

"Lillian, I'm so sorry," I say, pointing at Tiff's room. "She's still not ready."

Lillian just holds up a hand, strolls into my living room, and perches on the edge of one of my chocolate-leather sofas. I couldn't resist going with the leather.

"The Lord will wait. Let the child primp a little." She pats my hand. "And please give me a twirl so I can check out that outfit."

My mother always hated how I dressed, but I just so happen to agree with the great Dolly, who once said, "Yeah I flirt, I'm not blind and I'm not dead!" I twirl around for Lillian to show off my short jean skirt, gold-bangle-and-chain mesh belt, and alligator heels.

"Honey, you look ravishing," Lillian says.

"And I like that hat," I say. "Haven't seen that one yet."

"Gift from my son. I want to try to sit in front of some stuffy old ladies so they can't see today."

I look at my watch again. "Okay, I'm breaking out the big guns," I say. I walk over to Tiffany's door. "Tiff, Lillian and I were just thinking that if you came out right this moment, we'd still have time to get coffee and Cinnabons."

Tiff practically falls out of her bedroom, and we hurry

off to Lillian's red convertible, another present to herself when poor Henry died.

I pop in my favorite Dolly album and Lillian and I sing along to "Coat of Many Colors" at the tops of our lungs as we cruise down the road. I used to be more of a "9 to 5" or "Jolene" kind of girl, but now that I understand what Dolly's talking about in the song, I love it. It's about Joseph and the love behind his coat of many colors. I wonder if the Lord was workin' on my heart all along with Dolly as his guide. It's possible. Stranger things have happened. After eating her Cinnabon in almost one gulp, Tiff glowers out the side of the car, desperately trying to hold her hair down, watching the cottonwoods zoom by along Peachtree.

Sure, there are churches closer to our development, but when you don't start going to church until you're almost thirty, you don't want to go to a converted warehouse or one of those megachurches in a brand-spanking-new complex complete with a coffee shop. You want a real church. With stained glass and wooden pews. Clapboard walls and a steeple. A pipe organ. Once I found Jesus, I thought nothing could make me happier, but some Sunday mornings I would swear that organ is the most beautiful sound in the world. And Peachtree Hills Presbyterian Church has close ties with the school I enrolled Tiff in this year, plus Lillian goes there, so it's our happy little home every Sunday morning. Well, my happy little home. It takes the promise of one Cinnabon roll and sometimes the threat of cutting off the cable (that girl is addicted to Animal Planet) to get Little Miss Sunshine here each week. She's not exactly sold on the whole God thing yet.

"What are you so cheery about this morning?" I ask playfully, punching her arm, as I sip from my Caribou Coffee travel mug. I like the coffee just fine, but mostly I carry the mug because I love the cute little moose on the side.

"Everyone at church hates us." She doesn't pull her eyes away from the scenery.

"Hates us?" I say, laughing. "How could they hate us? Have you seen my new shoes?" I point to my awesome new alligator heels.

"Your shoes are part of the problem," she mumbles.

Lillian looks in the rearview mirror at her. I can see that she's wondering if she should intervene or leave us to our family business.

"Honey, we're going to *church*." I laugh. I mean, sure, we're not your typical Peachtree Hills members, but just because I don't drive a Lexus and wear pearls to play tennis doesn't mean we're not welcome in God's house. Even I know that. "They have to like us at church. Jesus said so." I take a breath, waiting for her to crack a smile. No reaction. I try a different tactic. "These are God's people, Tiff. We may be different, but we're still family."

"Whatever," she mumbles.

Lillian can't help herself any longer. "Besides, honey, when you're my age you realize that if people don't like you, they can just get in line. Life's too short not to have fun," she says. Tiff at least smiles at her. Lillian, she likes. Her mother, not so much.

"I heard the youth group is organizing a campout this summer," I say, checking my lipstick in my compact. I wipe a little off my teeth. "It might be fun to go." I turn around and hold the tube of lipstick out to Tiff, who stares at it like it's a snake. "You might meet some neat people."

"I have friends, Mom," she says. "I don't need these stupid church people to be my friends."

I don't know much about youth groups, never having been a member of one myself, but it sure looks like a lot of fun to me, lots of singing crazy songs and wacky games and fun trips and cute guys. I wish someone had told me there were cute guys at church when I was a teenager. My whole life probably would have turned out differently.

"It could be fun, honey. When I was your age, I would have done practically anything to get away from my parents for the weekend," Lillian says. Tiff gives Lillian a sideways glance. That got her attention.

Lillian pulls us into the wide parking lot and drives right to the front to nab one of the handicapped spots. She has her handicapped ID hung on her mirror. She says she is just too cute to park in the back anymore. We all climb out of the tiny car, and I take a moment to straighten my control-top hose. Pesky buggers. Always climbing up places they ain't supposed to be. Tiffany stands impatiently in front of the car.

"Can we just go?" she whines.

"Well, if you're all that anxious to get to church, okay."
I laugh, walking toward the big red doors at the front of
the building. I link arms with Lillian and try to link with
Tiff, who dodges us, as we walk toward church.

"Hey, isn't that one of the girls from your class at
school?" I point to a slim blond girl walking in front of us.

"Yes," Tiffany mumbles. She doesn't look up. We follow the girl, who clutches her Bible tightly as she sashays
toward the building.

We open the doors and walk into the sanctuary. "Wait,
don't all those girls go to your school?" I ask, as the blond
girl slides into a row near the front with several other
shiny-haired girls. "Why don't you go sit with them?
Make the first move?" I just know Tiff, who must share at
least some of my genes, would get along well with these
girls if she just got over her shyness.

"Mom, can we just sit down, please?"

"Fine, fine," I say, and the three of us slide into a pew.
Betty Flowers begins pounding away on the organ, and I
start to fold my bulletin into a fan. The thing about old
churches is that they have old wiring, hence patchy AC.
Next summer we may become Baptists. I grab a prayer request slip and start filling it out. Lillian leans over to read
my handwriting, but she doesn't see so well. Tiffany takes
it out of my hand and reads it.

"Mom, no!" she hisses at me. She shoves it into her
jeans pocket. "You cannot put in a prayer request for
Richard Simmons. People are going to think we're nuts."

"We had a little accident involving the cat and the

dryer this morning," I explain to Lillian. "And Tiff, prayer requests are anonymous."

She gives me a withering look, and I throw my hands up in surrender. Guess we'll pray for him at home.

At the pastor's signal, we all stand, and I begin to belt out "Great Is Thy Faithfulness" like it's the last song I'll ever sing. After all, you never know. I was in the children's choir at the church my family went to when I was very little, and I can actually sing quite well, if I do say so myself.

We get to the part about pardon for sin and a peace that endureth before I hear the snickering, and we're on to the chorus again before I figure out that it's coming from the pew of high schoolers behind us. I turn, ready to hiss that some of us are trying to worship here. But I stop cold when I realize that they are pointing and making faces at my daughter, who is crying silent tears beside me.

The theme is Classic Pooh. Annabelle Madden was very clear about that. New Pooh is passé, old Pooh is back, I guess. Or something like that. I feel a little wilted because Ellie and I were up at the Jelly Jar all last night cooking and baking for our second catering event. We really wanted this one to go better than the last, especially now that we are a legitimate, licensed caterer. Michael Jordan pushed our paperwork right on through and even came to church and ate himself two big platefuls during the covered-dish supper. We've become big friends, though our dating days are over. I need a man with a little spunk to him.

I press my hands into my eyes and feel like I'm ready to keel over, but when I open my eyes, I see my Classic Pooh birthday cake, and that makes me smile. It turned out perfect. He's sitting up, two feet high off the table, with a hand on his big tummy. I even muted out the colors so that he looks like the older Pooh. And that's all that matters. My contribution looks great.

I place a jar of peach preserves on the counter. Jo says it's good advertising. Whatever it is, those preserves are amazing. I wipe the cake display one last time as if I were still at Seeger's. It's just a bunch of four-year-olds and their mothers. It's not like little Shelby Madden is going to care about smudges. She's just going to take one look at Pooh here and put her hand right in the frosting. At least that's what Tiff always did.

"Daisy, you're a genius," Jo says as she scurries by. She's in hyperwarp, again. I don't think I've seen that woman stand still yet. Guess that's why she's got that fancy house on the hill and those two perfect little girls.

A slim woman comes into the kitchen and cocks her head to one side. She is wearing tan slacks, a white collared shirt, loafers, and a headband. "Hi, Annabelle Madden," she says and extends her hand. The birthday girl's mom looks me over and nods.

I shake it. "Daisy Johnson. I'm the pastry wench." I laugh, but not everyone appreciates humor.

Annabelle smiles at me. "Um, Daisy? Listen, Shelby and her friends were wondering when the clown was coming."

"I'm sorry?"

"I know. I don't like clowns either, but you know kids."

"I'm with the caterers," I say. "I don't think we have any clowns coming. You could ask Jo. I just made the cake."

She cocks her head to the side again. "Oh, and isn't he precious? Don't you love Classic Pooh? Each of my kids has a theme. Shelby is Classic Pooh. Her sister, Anika, is Noah's Ark, and Jacob, our son, he was Le Petit Prince. You know, like the children's book?"

I look around the professional-grade kitchen that shows no sign of use. I have no idea what this lady is talking about. As long as Tiff wasn't aspirating peanuts, we called it a good day. Her nursery had more of a "kitchen casual" theme, as that's where it was . . . in the kitchen of our studio apartment. "Sure."

"Listen, would you be a dear and get some games going?"

An hour later, Cate and I have played every single game that both of us can remember, including Red Rover; Duck Duck Goose; Mother, May I; Good Morning, Judge; Simon Says; and Down by the Banks, and the twenty-five four-year-old girls are still screaming for more. It seems that our employer assumed we were a full-service party-planning company, not just a caterer.

"What is Jo doing?" Cate asks, a smile plastered on her face. A little girl is wrapped around each of her legs as she tries to walk. I have one on each of my legs, squealing with joy.

"She said she just needs fifteen more minutes. You can't think of even one more game?"

Cate looks down. "I can't even think, much less remember some game from childhood."

I wrack my brain, trying to recall when Tiff was a child. There was one more. You danced in it. What was it? Think, Daisy. Oh, yeah!

"Girls," I say, peeling a lacy dress off my leg. "Girls, come here." They stop chasing one another around the yard and follow me. "I have another game. Has anyone ever played Sally Walker?"

One little girl raises her hand, but when I look at her, she puts it back down shyly. I chuckle. She just wanted to raise her hand. I love kids at this age.

"Okay, hold hands and stand in a circle," I say. Cate and I arrange the girls in a roughly circular shape. "Now, here is the song we sing." I sing the catchy tune: "Here comes Sally Walker, walkin' down the street." During this part I walk around the inside of the circle while all the girls watch me. "Don't know where she's going so she stops in front of me." I stop in front of the birthday girl and begin to dance like a jumping bean. "Hey, girl. Do that thing. Do that thing, and stop!" I stop dancing and grab Shelby Madden's shoulders. "Shelby, now you have to repeat the dance I just did," I say and they all laugh. I sing again. "Hey, girl. Do that thing. Do that thing, and stop!" Shelby does a pretty good job mimicking my crazy dance. I pull her into the middle and take her spot. "When the person in the middle stops in front of you, they do a dance and then you have to repeat it. Okay?"

The girls nod. "Okay!" I say and we begin. After a few turns, the girls have the game down pat and are loving trying to one-up each other with wild moves. Twenty minutes later, just when I am beginning to think very evil thoughts about Miss Sally Walker, Jo finally calls us all in for cake and presents time. Saved by the bell. The little girls run for the house, their fancy party dresses flowing behind them like a giant tide of lacy foam streaming across the manicured lawn.

"I vote that in the future we only cater for people who don't eat paste and know what the word *cappuccino* means," Cate says.

I lean my back against the double-hinged door and push through to the kitchen, careful not to spill any canapés on the hardwood flooring. Annabelle Madden and her friends are huddled around the countertop gabbing away. My first impulse is to go over and visit with them, but then I remember the talk Jo had with us this morning about being professional. I should just keep working quietly and try to remain unseen. I dump the remaining canapés in the trash and begin rinsing off our platter. Jo would be so proud of me. I've been on my best behavior all day and the party has been quite a success, much better than the engagement party fiasco, though I still say those old harpies just took the whole bed thing too hard.

"And do you know that she just whipped it out right there in Seeger's and started feeding the baby?" Annabelle says. My ears prick at the sound of my old workplace.

"No!" her friend says.

"Yes. I'll bet you she was one of those lactivists," Annabelle says. "You know, like the ones that were after Barbara Walters because she dared to suggest that there is a time and a place for feeding."

"Some people!"

"Hey, Daisy?" Annabelle says and I groan to myself. If I get accused of goofing off and chatting, I'm gonna tell Jo that they talked to me first.

I turn around. "Yes." I wipe the excess water off my hands on my white apron.

"Listen. I wanted to know if you could teach me that adorable little game you were playing with the girls out there. The one with the dancing? It was just so darling. I must have snapped up a whole roll of film. How on earth did you ever learn such a thing?" she asks.

I laugh. "I remember it from when my little girl was young."

The women cock their heads at me. "What?" Annabelle asks. "Oh," she says, nodding. "Your stepdaughter."

I chuckle. It's kind of fun to look so young. Of course, no one knows my little beauty secret is teenage motherhood. "No, the doctors say she was all mine. I had to trust them because I was high as a kite when I had her."

They look at me, appalled.

Uh-oh. Better tone back the jokes. "Um, because of the epidural, you know," I say.

"Oh." Annabelle laughs uncomfortably. "I had mine naturally."

"You're a tougher woman than I was." I turn back around and try to begin washing again. I'm much too tired to maintain appearances right now. I glance at my watch. Okay, only one more hour including cleanup. I can do that. But I can feel Annabelle still staring at my back.

"You know, Daisy, I'd say that *you* are definitely the tougher woman. Why, I just don't know how you can manage working when you've got a child. I couldn't even dream of it."

I stop washing, and I shut my eyes. I'm so tired I want to cry, my heels ache even though I am wearing sneakers, and I haven't had any quality time with Tiff in a week, to say nothing of the fact that her childhood feels like it's going by too fast. I decide to change the subject. As Dolly says, "We cannot direct the wind, but we can adjust the sails."

"My daughter did the most amazing thing on our computer the other day." I look at Annabelle, who watches me carefully. "She got it to recognize her voice so she can type without even touching the keys. I barely know how to turn the thing on, but isn't it amazing how much kids can do with technology these days?"

"Oh, but Daisy must have stayed home when her daughter was young," Annabelle's friend continues as if she hasn't even heard me. "She couldn't have done all of this with an infant."

"Oh," Annabelle says, nodding. "You must be right."

Okay, Daisy. Think of a Bible story like this. Stay calm and think about how Ruth would handle it. Or Mary Martha.

"Is that right, Daisy? Is this your 'comeback career'?" Annabelle asks. "I so admire comeback moms."

No good Bible story comes to mind, so instead I think of how Dolly Parton might handle it. I turn around. "This is a new job," I say evenly, "but I definitely had to work my whole life, even when Tiffany was a newborn."

The women recoil in horror, and I bite my lip, hard. I want to scream at them that sometimes staying home with your child is not an option. Even if they think I abandoned Tiffany, I did the best I could.

"In fact," I continue, "I think it made her much more mature and independent than the other kids." I cross my arms on my chest as Ellie enters the kitchen with a tray of leftover crudités. I can hear Cate and Jo helping the girls with the Pooh piñata in the next room.

"I'm sorry?" Annabelle says and looks at me intently. "But you can't be suggesting, why, I'm sure you're not at all, that it was better for her." I take a deep breath.

Ellie comes over to the group, and I give her a panicked look. I don't normally lose my temper, but when I do, it can be a bad situation.

"Um," I squeak.

"Daisy? Are you okay? You look a little weak," Ellie says.

"I'm fine," I muster, keeping my teeth clenched tight so that no errant words slip out.

"Oh. It's all my fault, I'm afraid," Annabelle says.

I sigh. At least she admits it. Okay, I can forgive her. Give her the other cheek. It's my better side anyway.

"I was just saying how very shocked I was that Daisy chose to work when her child was young." Annabelle fusses with a piece of fuzz on her slacks.

Ellie studies my face. My eyes are welling up with tears.

"You know this is a different kind of company," Ellie says, clearing her throat. "Designed for women with kids. We put families first."

"How *progressive*," Annabelle says with mock admiration in her voice. "That should be an, ahem, interesting little experiment."

"What?" Ellie stares at her.

"I guess I'm just a traditional old fuddy-duddy. I still believe motherhood is the highest calling." She shrugs. "God calls us to train up our children, and I take that to mean raising them myself, not handing them over to someone else to raise." She coughs into her hand and looks at her friend who is nodding at her solemnly. "It's just a little preposterous, acting like you know more than God, don't you think?"

"What about the Proverbs 31 woman?" I ask. Now that I'm studying the Bible in my women's group, I'm finding out that there are all kinds of interesting tidbits in there that no one ever talks about. "She planted a vineyard and bought real estate. The Bible says her trading was profitable." Wow, where did that come from? I pat myself on the back a little. "That sounds like a working mom to me."

Annabelle puts her hand on my shoulder, and I resist the urge to shirk it off. "Daisy, I take my call to stay home from Titus 2:3–5. And I take it seriously." Annabelle crosses her arms over her chest. "I just don't want my life to be a pile of paychecks. That's all," she says, almost, but not quite, apologetically.

I think Ellie might actually choke our client. "I have five-year-old twins," she says, taking a deep breath. "Are you suggesting that I'm hurting them by working?"

"You're certainly not helping them," Annabelle says, placing her arms on her hips. Ellie and Annabelle are squared off face-to-face.

"Many studies show that a working mother has such a positive impact on young children that it is worth all of the sacrifices. Kids begin to understand that they are not the center of the universe. Not only is the mother happy and fulfilled, but the kids grow up knowing that women and men are equal and that women are capable of anything men are," Ellie says, then takes a deep breath of air.

Annabelle smirks at Ellie and then nudges her friend. "Guess somebody is a little touchy about this."

"Apparently, *someone* is," Ellie says, nodding at Annabelle's friend.

I stare at Ellie, shocked. She always seems so calm, so controlled. I didn't know she had it in her.

"I'm sure we all have our own little 'theories' about it," Annabelle's friend says. "I just don't want to miss seeing my children grow up."

Jo peeks into the kitchen and looks at the four of us squared off. She gives me a confused look and I shake my head subtly, trying to tell her not to get involved.

"Daisy, Ellie, can you come and help me with the, um, thing?"

I walk away quickly, but Ellie does not follow. I look back, and she is staring down Annabelle and her insipid little friend. Finally Annabelle looks at the floor, and then and only then does Ellie come too, head held high.

When we get into the other room, Jo pulls me aside into the hallway, leaving Ellie and Cate to run the piñata.

"What happened in there?" she asks.

I give her a brief synopsis of what Annabelle Madden and her friend said to us, and Jo is about ready to go and throttle our client by herself.

"She can't even make her own kid's birthday cake and she's pointing a finger at us?" Jo whispers through clenched teeth.

"I know," I say, shaking my head. "That's why I made up a new rule for Jelly Jar, just now."

"Oh?" Jo says.

"The customer ain't always right," I say and then lean in to Jo and nudge her, "especially when she's just plain wrong."

Jo laughs and gives me a high five, and I can't help but wonder if it's her first.

Jo

"HONEY, WHERE DO WE KEEP THE STARCH?"
Gerard calls from the bedroom.

Honestly. We've lived in this house for ten years, and
he still hasn't found the starch? It's not like I hide it from
him.

"It's in the hall closet," I yell, checking to make sure the
bathroom door is locked in front of me. "On the top shelf.
Above the towels."

I hear some faint rummaging noises, then a soft thud.

"I found it," he yells, slamming the door to the cabinet.
I know I should go help him, or at least clean up the mess
he's just made, but I can't yet. I have two more minutes.

"Mom?" Martha cries from the kitchen. "Where is
Abby Caddaby?" It was big news in our house when *Sesame
Street* finally came out with a likable female monster, but

that doesn't mean I want to hear her high-pitched squeal right now.

"I'll help you find her in a minute, sweetie," I yell through the closed door, burying my head in my hands. Can't they manage for three minutes without me?

I tap my fingers on the marble counter and take a deep breath. It doesn't matter, I tell myself. Either way is fine.

"Jo? Do you know what happened to my red tie?" Gerard calls, from the bedroom this time.

I take a deep breath. "It's at the dry cleaner's." I try to be patient with him, really I do, but why can't he see that I need these few minutes to myself? Isn't that what going into the bathroom and locking the door means? I look around anxiously. We really need to repaint in here.

"Oh, okay," he calls. "I'll wear the green one, then."

"Good." I let my breath out slowly.

I look at my watch for the hundredth time. Thirty more seconds. I look at the box again, just to make sure I have it right. I don't want to waste precious seconds fumbling to read the instructions. Even as I do it, though, I know it's ridiculous. I sprang for the deluxe digital brand that literally spells it out for you. No messing with ambiguous pink lines for me.

My watch beeps and my hands shake as I pick up the plastic stick. I whisper a quick prayer, take a deep breath, and turn it over.

"Honey?" Gerard calls through the door. "Are you going to pick Martha up from school today, or am I?"

The words are there, unmistakably final. Mocking me.

Not pregnant.

Again.

"I will," I manage to squeak.

"Okay. I'm off, then," he calls, whistling as he pads away toward the garage.

"Okay," I whisper.

Buck up, Jo. It wasn't the right time anyway. You know that.

I pull a tissue from the box behind the toilet and begin to blot my eyes.

You know you can't have another baby right now, I tell myself. Not when it's all about to take off. I rock back and forth on the toilet seat, hoping the repetitive motion will calm me down.

"That's okay, God. All in your time," I whisper.

And then I burst into tears.

When the doorbell rings, the girls squeal and run to the front door. Martha is working on turning the lock before I make it there myself to stop her.

"Now, Martha, we don't just open the door," I say, trying to smooth her hair down as she wriggles out of my grasp. "What do we do?"

"Who is it?" Martha yells, jumping up and down.

"Who dis?" Agnes screams, clapping her hands.

"It's Gigi," Mother calls through the door. I roll my eyes. Mother refuses to be called Grandma. She says she doesn't "feel" like a grandma.

"Gigi, Gigi," the girls scream. Martha tries valiantly to turn the heavy lock on the door. I help her, and she swings it open. Instantly, my mother has both girls in her arms, their legs wrapped around her tightly.

"Okay, girls," I say, ushering her through the door. "Let Gigi go."

"Don't you dare." She laughs and hugs my daughters tighter. "My two favorite granddaughters can hang on me as long as they want." She smiles at me and walks into the living room, dragging them along with her. I sigh as I notice that she's wearing her Ugg boots again. Her hair is an even lighter shade of blond this week. What's next, platinum? Refusing to grow old gracefully is one thing. Taking fashion advice from the teenyboppers in *People* magazine is quite another.

"How are you tonight, Georgia?" Gerard asks, turning off the television and standing to shake my mother's hand.

She gives him a big hug instead. "Very well, thank you."

"How's your golf game coming along?" Gerard asks with a twinkle in his eye.

Mother flashes her ultrawhite smile, nearly blinding me from across the room. She knows nothing about golf, but has been dating a widower over at the club recently and is suddenly interested in every aspect of the game. Poor Daddy would roll over in his tastefully manicured grave if he knew about Mother's exploits with Howard. It's like she's living in an episode of *The Golden Girls*.

I take a deep breath and recenter myself. I really can't complain too much. She is a dear old woman who is filling her life in whatever way she can and loves her two grandchildren more than anything. I don't know what Gerard and I would do without her coming over while I'm at work and every Friday night to be with the girls so that we can go on a date. Date night is very important for relationships. Everyone says so.

"They've already had dinner and their baths, so you shouldn't have too much to do tonight." I motion toward the girls, clad in matching pink nightgowns and fuzzy slippers.

"Uh-huh," Mother says, nodding, though I know better than to believe she's actually listening. She leans in and whispers something to the girls. They immediately run over to the duffel bag she has dropped by the door and rip it open.

"Ice cream!" Martha screams, hauling out a tub of Breyers. Agnes digs through the bag, pulling out containers of sprinkles and a bottle of chocolate sauce.

"Mother, you know they aren't supposed to have ice cream now," I say. "They're too wired to sleep if they have sugar in the evenings."

"Pish-posh," she says, waving away my concerns with her hand. "You never let those girls have sugar. That's why they're so excited when I bring it."

"I limit their sugar intake because it's bad for them," I say. "Especially before bed." I look at my mother, who is looking around distractedly. "You *will* put them to bed at eight, won't you?"

"Of course, dear," she says absently, walking toward the table. She pushes on the top, resting her weight on it. "This should be fine," she mumbles.

"What are you doing?" She ignores me and turns to the girls, who are pulling a two-foot section of plastic rain gutter out of the bag.

"Gigi, what dis?" Agnes asks, her eyes wide.

"That's our trough," she says, winking at me. "We are going to fill this with ice cream and whipped cream and chocolate sauce, and then we'll eat straight out of it!"

"Like a pig!" Martha says, delight registering on her little face.

"YAY, YAY, YAY, YAY," Agnes sings, jumping around in a circle, unable to contain her joy at being allowed to eat like an animal.

"Mother, you can't be serious." I glare at her, and she smiles at me innocently. "I laid out some fruit that they can have, and then they should go straight to bed."

"Sure. Whatever you say, boss lady." She smiles, then walks over to help Martha carry the gutter to the kitchen table.

"Mother," I say loudly, putting my hands on my hips. "Look at me."

She throws a glance my way, then goes back to the task at hand.

"You cannot do this," I plow on ahead. "This goes against every rule I have set for the girls." I gesture to the full-page document I hung by the phone, listing the house rules. "You can't just—"

"Go on your date, dear," Mother sings. "Have a wonderful time."

I turn to Gerard, who is laughing at Agnes, who

has unscrewed the lid to the chocolate syrup and is licking the edge of the bottle. Over my clean floor. I turn away.

"Gigi gets to break the rules," Martha sings at me. The phrase is so perfectly practiced that I can only assume she has heard it many times from my mother's mouth. I look from Gerard to Mother, standing defiantly by the table, where even now Martha is starting to scoop ice cream out of the container and launch it onto the floor, to the faces of my children, who are in heaven.

"Honey, we'd better go. We don't want to be late," Gerard says as seriously as he can.

I sigh. Gerard and I really need this time to ourselves to reconnect, especially if we're ever going to be able to have another baby. And this week isn't just any old date night. This is a retirement party Gerard's company is throwing for one of the founding partners, and I wanted to take notes on the catering presentation. As Martha spills ice cream down the front of her clean nightgown, I make a decision.

"Okay, let's go," I say, picking up my purse. It's hopeless. My mother is slowly destroying any modicum of structure and decorum I have drilled into my daughters, but I don't have to watch it happen.

"Have fun!" Mother says, spraying whipped cream haphazardly into the bottom of the gutter, as we march out the garage door. I just pray she'll have the mess cleaned up by the time we get home.

———

"It's just preposterous," Bruce, Gerard's boss, says, taking a canapé off the passing tray.

"We'll fight it," his wife, Emily, adds, her sleek, unnaturally dark hair pulled back tightly against her head. Her Chanel suit is perfectly tailored and pressed, and I feel a bit frumpy in my standard black dress. "There's no way they can possibly get away with it. It's a private club, for heaven's sake." She takes a sip of her champagne and shakes her head.

"The right of eminent domain is intended to take land for the good of the masses. Those people aren't the masses. They're the money-hungry, polo-hating, young-wine-drinking nouveau riche." Bruce takes a bite of his canapé.

"So wait," I say, slowly, looking at their faces. Step gingerly, Jo. This is your husband's boss. "The city of Atlanta wants to seize your world-class private golf course and turn it into a world-class public golf course?"

Now, I know Gerard is fond of his club, and he and Bruce often enjoy a good game of golf after a hard day at the office. And I'm not advocating letting in just anyone off the street. But it does seem that they're taking this whole exclusivity thing a little too far. I take a sip of sparkling cider and nod. Sure, I could have had champagne, but I'm feeling lucky about our chances tonight. If my thermometer charts are right, I should be ovulating.

"Accessible to anyone who lives within the town limits." Emily nods, confirming the horrors that lie ahead.

"But they still have to pay the fees, right?" I say, looking at Emily carefully.

"It's not a question of money, Jo, it's the principle of it," Gerard says quickly. "There are thirty-five golf courses in Atlanta. They can use any of them. There's no reason we should have to turn ours over."

"That's right," Bruce says. "This golf course has been part of a very exclusive club for two hundred years. They can't just take it over and demand we let in everyone who brings their own sand wedge."

"I see." I suddenly feel like I'm trapped in a *New Yorker* cartoon. I take a bite of shrimp from my plate so I have an excuse to not say anything more.

"If you'll excuse me, I have to go check on the chocolate tartlets," Emily says, gesturing toward the kitchen. "I want to make sure they don't bring them until they are finished passing around the savory hors d'oeuvres." I nod and smile, and she walks away. Gerard and Bruce launch into a discussion of the new Titleist five-iron, and I tune out and look around.

Springer, Hunt, and Lansing has rented out the grand ballroom of the Georgian Terrace Hotel, and I have to admit the room is stunning. There are flowers everywhere, and a twelve-piece band is playing swing music, which is a huge hit with the retiring lawyer and his contemporaries. This is one of the older hotels in Atlanta—it's where the opening reception for the premiere of *Gone With the Wind* was held—and it feels historic and elegant without seeming stuffy. I'll remember to suggest this space to the Millers when they come in for their appointment for Stacy's wedding next week.

"How are you doing?" Gerard says, wrapping his arms around my waist. I look up to see that Bruce is gone, and I smile.

"Better now." I sigh, leaning into him as he rests his head on my shoulder.

"So what do you think?" Gerard is wearing the cologne I got him for Christmas, and I breathe deeply to inhale his scent.

"I think Bruce is pompous and you can see the scars from his wife's face-lift," I say, smiling.

"Agreed. Though I meant about the catering." Gerard pulls back and twirls me around to face him.

"I have to admit I was dubious about the idea of having dozens of kinds of appetizers and cocktails instead of a full sit-down dinner," I say, nodding. "But I kind of like it. No endless meal seated next to the insufferable wife of a coworker I've never met. We'll have to try this idea some time. If we ever get the chance, that is." I roll my eyes, thinking about our grim financial prospects.

"I'm so proud of you." He takes a sip of his champagne and smiles at me over the rim of the glass.

"What?"

"I really am. You did it."

"We haven't done anything yet." I shake my head. After the little blowup at the Madden birthday party, I'm afraid we're the laughingstock of Atlanta. "We have yet to cater a successful party, we can't even pay our bills. I thought we'd have a full roster of parties lined up by now. If we don't nail this bridal shower next week, I don't know if we're going to make it."

"You'll make it," he says. "Josephine Vann can do anything." He pulls me close.

"I don't know," I say, leaning my head on his shoulder.

"You can. And you seem happier these days," he says, nodding. "I'm glad. You're doing what you want, and it's working. You'll do it."

"I sure hope so." I sigh, and remind myself to just enjoy the night.

"Hey, Catie girl, where do you want me to put this?" Daisy sings, and I actually see Cate tense up. Daisy walks in carrying the most exquisite cake I've ever seen—three layers in light blue and chocolate brown—on a large serving platter, and though I am in awe of her talent, I definitely understand Cate's reaction. It's seven AM. No one should be this perky at seven AM.

"Over there," Cate mumbles, jerking her head toward a stark folding table in the corner of the Fellowship Hall. Mary Ellen O'Connor's bridal shower starts in four hours, but we're going to need all that time to make this plain beige multipurpose room attached to my church look like the rose garden the mother of the bride has requested. Why she didn't just have the shower in a real rose garden, I have no idea.

"I just had the darndest time getting this fondant to be smooth," Daisy says, oblivious to the look of death from

Cate, who, I'm learning, is not a morning person. Ellie is still at home getting the twins dressed, but I feel confident that she would know better than to try to engage us in conversation this early. "You know, buttercream is so much easier to work with, but fondant just looks more professional, so I went with it, and, oh my, it was a task. Anyway, it turned out okay. What time does this thing start? I know that the cake probably didn't need to be here so early, but I was up anyway, since I had to take Tiff to her Mathlete competition, so I figured I'd come over and see if I could help set up. What do y'all need?"

I look at Cate, who is pressing her hands against her eyes. Her face was pale when she came in this morning, and her eyes looked sunken. She mumbled something about a late call with an ex-boyfriend, and I knew better than to press her for more, so we've been working in companionable silence up until now. Even to a modern, independent woman, matters of the heart are still hard.

"Are you okay?" Daisy asks, walking toward Cate with concern etched on her face. "You look like you're in pain. Can I help—"

"Just stop talking," Cate says desperately, keeping her eyes down. Daisy looks like someone has just smacked her across the face, her eyes wide. Uh-oh. Time for damage control, Jo.

"How about a coffee run?" I say quickly, smiling at my coworkers. "Daisy, why don't you come with me?" I smile at her, and she nods, looking at Cate in confusion. Cate does not look up, and Daisy and I leave her to arrange the potted rosebushes around the drinks table.

"What was that all about?" Daisy says as soon as we're out of earshot. "Did I do something wrong?" She looks hurt, the poor thing, and utterly confused.

"You're fine." I take a deep breath and picture the rich dark coffee that will soon be infusing my veins with much-needed caffeine. "She didn't mean anything by it. She's just tired."

"I guess," Daisy says, shaking her head.

I can't believe it, I think, as we unload the last of the trays from the back of the rented van and bring them into the Jelly Jar kitchen, but it appears to be true. Mary Ellen O'Connor's bridal shower went off without a hitch.

After the rough start this morning, everything really came together. Cate turned the Fellowship Hall into a virtual garden, bringing in blooms from her own yard as well as from some of the best florists in Atlanta. And Ellie made so many hors d'oeuvres that we have two trays of leftovers, even though all fifty Steel Magnolias gorged themselves. It was flawless. It really was.

Daisy and I cover and store the leftover food, as Ellie's cell phone begins to ring. She wipes her hands on a dish towel, steps away from the sink of greasy pots, and walks into the main room. Cate comes in, bringing back tablecloths and napkins to be washed, and begins to sort them into piles. Jelly Jar has completed its first successful event. There may be hope for us yet.

"Jo?" Ellie says quietly, walking back into the kitchen. "Could I have a word with you?" She smiles sheepishly, and I know this can't be good. I follow her out to the front room. She opens and closes her cell phone, biting her lower lip. The fading light coming in through the front window casts a cheerful glow over the Jelly Jar reception area.

"That was a call from Lauren," Ellie says, taking a deep breath.

"Tell her that I set up an automated monthly pay-check for her. Did she not get it?" Lauren has been a godsend. She comes to watch the kids once a week during our official meeting so that we can all focus and get work done. Other than that, we have evolved into working in shifts because everyone has very different schedules. So beyond the weekly meeting, there is rarely a time when all five kids are in the building at once. And when they are, Tiffany has been helping us with the younger ones. I think Daisy might have talked to her, or maybe she's just warmed up to them now. But event days are sacred. Those are the only days that we can't have the kids around and every woman must make her own child-care arrangements. Gerard is at home with my munchkins, and Ellie uses Mike and Lauren to pinch-hit.

"Oh, I think she did. What I mean to say is—"

I wipe my brow. "She's a lifesaver. The meetings are so much better now that she's watching the kids. Don't you think?"

"Yes," she says and puts her hands on my shoulders. "But Jo, Sophie pushed Seth at the playground, and he hit his head on the slide."

"Oh, no!" I say. "Is he okay?"

"Lauren says it's not bad, but, well, I told her to take him to the emergency room just in case. I need to go," she says calmly, though the terror in her eyes belies her outer calm. I know that look. When Martha was three, she choked on a Lego that Mother had brought over, and I would have torn a grizzly bear limb from limb to get to her. I glance back at the pile of dishes still in the sink. "Go." Somehow, we'll take care of it.

"Thank you," Ellie whispers, then takes off her apron, grabs her purse from the floor by the kitchen door, and walks out. I see her walking quickly to her car, and I sigh. I whisper a little prayer that all will be well.

I break the news to the other girls, and they accept their extra tasks with graciousness. No one can argue with a mother going to see her injured child, even if it does mean some extra dishes to wash.

By five o'clock, we're done. The kitchen is clean, and we're all tired. But we did it. I walk to the hand-washing sink one last time, and the bulletin board catches my eye. Someone has posted a new rule.

The Jelly Jar Rules

1. Family comes first, and kids are always welcome at work.
2. This is a democracy. We say what we feel. That's what women do.
3. Kids at work are a blessing—never forget it!

4. We don't fire people. Men fire people. Women work through their problems.
5. The customer ain't always right, especially when she's just plain wrong.
6. No one talks before coffee.

I can't help but laugh as I run my hands under the warm water.

I add tampons to the grocery list and sigh. I'd better get going if I want to stay on schedule. I have to run and pick Martha up from kindergarten and drop both girls off at Mother's, then I'm supposed to meet Ellie in forty-five minutes for some pre-prep. It was her idea to cater this family reunion, and it will be something new for us. We're finding that often people would like to use a caterer for smaller functions, since no one seems to know how to turn an oven on anymore, but the full catering service is too expensive. So we developed the "No Muss, No Fuss" package, and it's much cheaper than the full service. Ellie thought it might be a way for us to find more clients, which we desperately need, by diversifying our price range. We just plan a menu for the customer, cook everything over at Jelly Jar, and then deliver it in disposable trays two hours before the event starts. The clients can warm and serve the food themselves. Easy as pie. Easier, in fact, since piecrust is deceptively difficult to get right.

"Come on, Agnes," I say, poking my head into her

room, where she is happily playing with her dollies, telling them all, "No, no!" She smiles and stands up, then follows me to the car. As I buckle her into her car seat, I check my watch. We'll make it. I walk around to the driver's seat and turn the car on, tuning the radio to my favorite praise station, then back the car out of the garage and down the driveway. It's a beautiful fall day, and I drive down the wide streets of our little neighborhood on autopilot. I like picking Martha up from school. It makes me feel better about dumping her with Mother some afternoons, and I get to talk with her teacher, which makes me feel like a very involved parent.

I arrive at the school just as the bell rings, and after a moment of chitchat with Martha's teacher, I hustle her into the car. I ask her about her day and listen as she tells me about their upcoming Halloween parade. She wants to be a princess, naturally. I make a mental note to look for patterns the next time I'm at the fabric store. I'll have to arrange some time to be at the sewing machine in the coming weeks. As I turn onto the freeway onramp, though, I gasp. The traffic is backed up halfway down the ramp. There's no way to turn around. I'm stuck. This is going to take forever. I try to stay calm, but as the minutes tick away, we inch forward only a few car lengths. I'm not going to make it. I flip the radio to a news station. A few minutes later, and a few inches farther, I dig my cell phone out of my purse and call Ellie.

"Mommy, using a cell phone while you're driving is dangerous," Martha says, parroting the information she's heard me say hundreds of times. Busted.

"I know it is, sweetie, but this is an emergency." I smile at her in the rearview mirror.

"An emergency?" she asks, creasing her brow. She looks at me with fear in her eyes, then bursts into tears. "I'm scared of emergencies," she says, her voice shaking.

Uh-oh. I forgot that we just had a family talk about what to do in case of a fire last weekend. Gerard stressed to the girls how important it is to get outside because fires are really dangerous.

"Martha, this isn't an emergency like a fire," I say as Ellie's phone rings in my ear. "This is a different kind of emergency. An emergency where no one is going to get hurt."

"But emergencies are scary," she says through her tears. "We have to get outside." She begins to reach for her door handle, and I click the child safety locks, which only makes her cry louder.

"Hello?" Ellie says breathlessly.

"Hey, it's Jo," I say, smiling at Martha in the rearview mirror. She looks out the window and continues to cry. "I'm stuck in traffic, so I'm afraid I'm going to be late."

"No problem," Ellie says. "I'm here and ready whenever you are."

"It looks like it might be a while," I say, scanning the road ahead to look for signs that it may be letting up.

"We have an emergency," Martha wails.

"An emergency? Are you okay, Jo?" Ellie asks.

"We're fine," I say as Agnes, disturbed at her sister's tears, begins to cry too. "I'll be there as soon as I can. I'm sorry."

"No problem. But I have to take Seth for a follow-up visit to the doctor at three," she says. "Lauren has a study group later, so she can't do it." After her aptitude in handling Seth's (ultimately minor) injury, Lauren has practically been elevated to a member of the Howell-Routledge family, and her skills at handling four rambunctious kids at once at our meetings has made her an honorary member of Jelly Jar to boot. I flick my eyes to the dashboard clock.

"I'll be there as soon as I can," I say, shaking my head at the waterworks in the backseat.

I'm near hysterical by the time I drop the girls off at Mother's. It's almost two o'clock, and I have to use the ladies' room like nobody's business.

"I'm so sorry," I say over and over and I usher the girls into my mother's cool house. They run off toward the playroom, where "Gigi" has set up a whole world with play kitchen, dress-up clothes, Polly Pocket collections, and everything else a little girl could want to play with. It's no wonder they'd rather come here than hang out at Jelly Jar.

"It's no problem," Mother says, waving her hand at me. "Would you like some tea?" I shake my head as she takes a pitcher from the refrigerator and pours a glass for herself.

"I had a schedule," I say, trying to catch my breath. "This wasn't supposed to happen."

"Traffic happens," my mother says, nodding as she

pours another glass. "You can't control everything, Jo." She hands me the glass, and I gulp the tea gratefully.

"It won't happen again." I place the empty glass on the counter. "I just need a better plan."

"Sure, it will," Mother says, shrugging her shoulders. "But it's okay." She empties a packet of sweetener into her glass. "You can't do it all, Jo."

"I have to run," I say, ignoring her. "But I have to use your bathroom first. Gerard will pick them up later." I turn toward the hallway.

"I could pick Martha up from school every day," she says, taking a sip of her icy drink.

"I can do it, Mother," I say, turning back to her.

"It would be no trouble."

"I can handle it." Why doesn't she just drop it? Am I not allowed to be late once without hearing a lecture? It wasn't even my fault.

Mother watches me, then closes her eyes briefly and nods. She looks at me with pity.

"Sure, you *can*. But why?"

Ellie totters up to the glass doors at Jelly Jar, and I run to let her in. She's hauling her KitchenAid mixer from home, again. Ours still hasn't come in because Cate insisted that we get the pistachio-green color that is hopelessly back-ordered. That silly thing had better "tie the whole kitchen together" like Cate keeps promising every time I grab the phone to change our order to a simple black one.

"Thank goodness you're here," Ellie says and makes a beeline for the counter to set the anvil-like mixer down.

"I'm so sorry." I clear a space for her on the crowded countertop. By the time I made it here yesterday, it was time for Ellie to take Seth to the doctor, so we postponed our party prep until today. I did some on my own yesterday, but then spent most of the afternoon trying to balance the books while I kicked myself for letting the schedule get thrown off, so now we're a full day behind on the reunion prep.

Ellie shakes out her arms. "Don't even think about it," she says. "Things happen." She watches me for a second, then turns toward her KitchenAid. "If that mixer doesn't get here soon, I'll . . ." She fumbles for words.

"Tell everyone that Cate wears Target underwear?"

"Exactly." Ellie smirks. I have to admit, it was a great moment. The other night, when we were all up here working on the reunion gig, Cate bent over, and a bit of the elastic from her panties peeked over the edge of her low-slung jeans. Daisy saw them and exclaimed, "I have those underwear too!" Cate's face went beet-red as Daisy continued, "Target makes the best kind." Apparently Target is not the cool spot to go clothes shopping, a fact that was lost on us mothers.

But after the joke passes, a silence hangs in the room, and we both know why. Cate and Daisy seem closer and closer every day, which leaves Ellie and me together a lot. Sure, we have some things in common—husbands, young children, families that live nearby, and, heck, a business we co-own. But we aren't exactly best friends. Never mind the awkwardness of what she did to me so long ago. We just don't click. I can't quite put my finger on what it is.

Ellie finds my typed-up list of tasks to complete today and reads it silently. "Okay," she says. "We might as well get started. I'll work on the pumpkin bread."

I nod and reach for a handful of dough. I'm making the pastry for the Pigs in a Blanket. At first I balked at serving such a retro food, but Lucy Renshaw demanded them. At least I'm making them with puff pastry and sopressata. There is a line.

"So," Ellie says, as she slides her rings off and places them in a bowl behind the sink.

I take a deep breath. I had forgotten how beautiful it was.

"Yes?" I look away from the ring to Ellie, and she's smiling kindly.

"Um, so. How are things?" She reaches into a drawer and pulls out a metal measuring cup. I watch silently as she dips it into the silky flour.

The only ring I've ever seen her wear is the slim gold wedding band, but of course she would have the engagement ring too.

"I'm a little nervous about the Pigs in a Blanket idea," I say without looking at her. "But apparently Great-grandfather Renshaw loved them, God bless his dearly departed soul."

She cocks her head at me. "Oh. Yeah. But I meant, how are *things*?"

I look down at the bowl of pastry, blinking back tears. I will not let her see. "Good," I say casually and continue to work.

I finish the batch, roll it into a ball, enfold it in plastic wrap, put it in one of the fridges, and get to work on the next one. These Renshaw people are sure planning on eating a lot of these horrid little things.

I clear my throat. "And, um, you?"

She looks at me. She seems tired.

I try again. "How are things with you?"

Ellie takes a deep breath. "They've been better."

I turn and look at her. She pushes a strand of hair off her face with her forearm. Her hands are covered in pumpkin pulp. "Let me ask you something. Does your husband have any problem with this?"

I look at her, confused.

"No?" she asks.

I shake my head.

"That's what I thought," she says, her shoulders sagging. "Mike is really struggling with it. I mean, well, that isn't exactly fair. He hasn't said anything just yet, but you know how men are. He's walking around our house all glum, and he's really cranky. And when I ask him what's wrong, he says, 'Oh, nothing.'" She shakes her head and starts on the next batch of pumpkin batter.

I don't know what to say, but I should say something. "I'm sorry." There. That was something.

She looks over at me and smiles. "Thanks."

I look back at my puff pastry quickly. I can't ask her about it, can I?

"Well, thanks for listening, anyways," Ellie says. I look at her, and then we both turn back to our projects. I know I shouldn't say anything, but I just . . . want to see.

"Hey, Ellie?" I say timidly. She glances up at me. "Is that your engagement ring?" I point to the rings in the bowl. My ring. A gorgeous Victorian piece made of rose gold with a garnet stone surrounded by seed pearls.

"Yeah," she says, laughing. "Have you ever seen such an ugly old thing?"

I keep staring at the ring.

"I have to tell you, when he gave me that thing, I thought about saying, 'Okay, I'll marry you, but only if I get a new ring.' It's so tacky, right?" She rinses her hands, wipes them on her apron, takes the ring from the bowl, and hands it to me to investigate more closely.

I stare at her for a moment and then mumble something. Tacky? It's the most beautiful ring I have ever worn.

"But then he went on and on about how it's been in his family for generations and how important it was to him. Blah, blah, blah. So what could I do?"

I think back to those six short months that I wore this ring until Mike broke off our engagement to go to Paris for work, where he would later meet Ellie. Mother told me I didn't have to give it back, but it was an heirloom. I knew it meant everything to his family.

"I'm just glad this job gives me an excuse to never wear it. I'm terrified of dropping it down the drain. His mother already hates me. I don't need to lose 'the ring' and make it worse."

Edith Routledge. Mike's mom.

Ellie looks at me. "Jo? Are you feeling all right? You look weak."

I close my hand over her ring for just a moment.

"Jo?" I don't even need to look up. I know that voice.

"Hi, Mike," I say, standing up slowly. He leans in and gives me an awkward hug, and I pull back quickly. Let's not make this any weirder than it has to be.

"It's good to see you," he says. "Can I get you some coffee?"

I motion to the coffee I'm cradling in my hands, and he nods, then walks calmly to the counter to order one for himself. He brings it back, black like always, and takes a seat across from me. He takes off his suit jacket and drapes it over the back of his chair. I run my hand over the smooth surface of the table.

"Look, Mike . . ." I start. I picked a Caribou Coffee on the other side of town, and even though I know Ellie is at Jelly Jar right now, I can't stop myself from looking around nervously. "I know this is weird, and I appreciate your taking the time to meet with me today." I keep my voice level, though I'm shaking. I had forgotten how his eyes have those brown specks in them.

"Jo." He takes a sip of his coffee and sighs. "How are you?"

"I . . ." Why is he asking me how I am? This is a business meeting. Short and sweet. "I'm fine." I take a sip.

"Thank you for coming all the way out here on your lunch break. I know it's a pain. But we have something we need to discuss."

"Jo, we're old friends." He cocks his head. "How are you?" I search his face for a sign of malice, for the joke to be up. We're not here to chitchat. He smiles.

"I'm fine." I sigh. "Life is good. Busy, but good."

He nods. "You look great."

"You're looking well too," I say, nodding. The corner of his eyes crinkle. His handsome face is smooth and tan, and his dark hair is just starting to gray around the edges.

"Your family is good?" He takes a sip.

"They're great. Two girls."

He nods. "Ellie mentioned that."

"Of course." I clear my throat. "Look, Mike. About Ellie." He looks down at the table. "You have to tell her."

"I didn't know, Jo." He takes a deep breath. "When she came home and told me she was going to start working again, I had no idea it was with you. There are a lot of people named Josephine in Atlanta and your last name has changed."

"I married a man named Gerard Vann. I knew him at Emory, and we reconnected later."

"And didn't I hear you moved away? I thought after I, um, after we broke up that you went north to work for a bank. I didn't even think you were living here anymore."

I nod. After Mike broke up with me, I accepted a transfer with my bank. I needed to get the heck out of Atlanta and away from all those gossiping old biddies. "I was in Boston for a few years, but I missed my family and the South too much and came back. That's when I ran into Gerard again."

He laughs. "When I saw that it was you, really you, that day at the catering place I nearly . . ." He smiles at me. He's still so charming. "I blame my mother, personally. Isn't it her God-given job to keep me up on local gossip, like the fact that Josephine McCleary has moved back home?"

I look at my coffee and pray. "Mike, you have to tell her." I play with the sleeve on my cup to keep my hands from shaking.

"She doesn't even know I was ever engaged to anyone else. To find out now would only hurt her, Jo."

"It's not fair to her."

He looks at me, then looks down.

"Or me."

His phone begins to bleat from his pocket, and he pulls it out and looks at the screen. I see it flashing the word "Ellie."

"Mike?"

He takes another sip, then places his cup down on the table carefully.

"I have to go," he says, standing up. He takes his jacket from the chair and strides across the room and out the door.

"And she's wearing my ring," I say to no one.

Cate

WHEN MOLLIE CALLS, I ALMOST DON'T ANSWER.

For one thing, I have my arms up the chest cavity of a bird. Somehow I got talked into testing out a version of Ellie's turkey with cornbread stuffing. As an extension of Ellie's No Muss, No Fuss drop-off package, we're now cooking Thanksgiving dinner for people who are too lazy to cook for themselves. And the four of us are responsible for figuring out which of the recipes Ellie has used in the past are best for us.

But the main reason I almost ignore the call is that any moron knows it's never good news when your old boss decides to get in touch. Though I still feel kind of bad for leaving her in the lurch when the Jelly Jar thing came up. Mollie found Angela, a new designer straight out of FIT, to take over my projects, but that doesn't lessen the guilt of leaving the woman who gave me my first real job with only two weeks' notice. I pick up the phone gingerly, cradling it between my chin and collarbone.

"Cate?"

"Mollie? How are you?" I turn on the tap and run my hands under the warm water. The smell of turkey flesh is hard to get off sometimes.

"Oh, you know." She laughs, her nasally northern twang identifying her as a transplant to the South. Mollie grew up on Long Island, but she went to UVA and fell in love with a real Southern boy, then moved on down to Georgia when they got married. She has a great eye and has managed her own design company for ten years, but in truth, decorating is more of a hobby than a career for her. Her husband, Barry, is a bigwig at a brokerage firm, and in between vacations to Provence and Argentina, Mollie occasionally takes on some clients. Of course, the trips to Thailand and South Africa to look for pieces also meant that she always had the best stuff, and I got some great experience redecorating some of Atlanta's best homes. "Busy. How are you? How's the new job?"

Mollie and I got along well enough, especially considering she took all the credit while I did most of the work, but I have a hard time believing this is just a social call.

"It's good," I say, more optimistically than I feel. I wipe my hands on the dish towel. "A new experience, you know? I'm learning a lot," I say, and almost believe it.

"Good." I hear the click of a keyboard in the background. "Look, I was wondering if you're available for some freelance work. I got a contract to do some staging, but it's for fifteen apartments, and I just don't see how I'm going to have the time to do them all with my trip to Borneo coming up next month. Do you think you could help out?"

"Isn't Angela working out?" I walk into the living room, sit down on the couch, and switch the phone to my other hand.

"She's fine," Mollie says absently. I hear more typing. "But her aesthetic is more modern, and the agent is looking for comfortable, livable designs. And you're so good at that, so I thought . . ."

"Things are pretty crazy at work right now, Mollie." I sigh. Things are crazy. We're catering a big party for the diamond industry next week and doing this Thanksgiving thing. Besides, the point of taking the job at Jelly Jar was to get away from doing interior design and into something with a little more variety and challenge.

But staging is different. There are no fussy clients or wealthy mavens who change their minds about the color scheme three-fourths of the way through the project. Staging is taking an ugly old apartment and redesigning it—repainting, bringing in furniture, hanging tasteful art, and adding personal touches—so that it will be more desirable to potential buyers. Working for realtors is easy. They just want to make the place look good so they can sell it, which means lots of freedom for the designer. I miss that kind of freedom. And doing something for Mollie would mean sophisticated designs, which would be a nice break from the endless garden themes I've been working on lately. Why does everyone want her party to be a pastel paradise? Plus, if I know Mollie, she'll make it worth my while.

"Okay," I say, picking at a stray thread on my couch. "I'll do it."

"Catie," David says, walking up to me with his arms outstretched. I know this is what he calls me when he's trying to pacify me, but it feels good to hear it nonetheless.

I suggested that we meet in Piedmont Park. He insisted that we talk in person, and I thought meeting in public might neutralize his effect on me. It's fall, after all. The park will be so beautiful that I won't even be able to concentrate on what David is saying. But as he strolls up to me, my stomach turns over.

I give David a quick hug, then pull away, though he tries to pull me back.

"Hey," I say, as nonchalantly as possible.

He smiles at me, nonplussed by my little routine. "You look so great," he says.

"You wanted to see me?" I ask. I have to get this over with fast or I might crack. And if Franny and Beatriz even knew I was here, I'd be in serious trouble.

"C'mon, let's stroll. It's gorgeous outside today."

I look at Atlanta's crown jewel and can't say no. David and I used to picnic here on lazy summer days after we graduated from college. We begin to stroll toward Lake Clara Meer and I realize that God has blessed us with one of those knockout autumn days. My city is definitely in the Deep South, but, unlike all points south of here, we get all four seasons. Our summers are hot and sultry, but then the fall comes and cools the whole city off and the colors burst forth in the trees and you could swear that you live in Vermont.

"So how's your new job going?" he asks.

"Fine," I say. C'mon David. Don't toy with me. Get to the point.

"You guys have clients beating down your doors already?"

I snort a little. "Sorry," I say and shake my head. "This whole thing is an experiment, and so far it's been kind of weird."

"What happened? That doesn't sound like my Catie." He watches me. David has a way of making you feel like you are the only person in the world when you're with him. He was never the kind to smile at a passing girl. When he was with you, he was all there.

I swallow. "Long story. But basically we're a small start-up, and we're trying to be a different kind of business, so we're still working out the kinks." We walk past a playground filled with laughing children on this beautiful Saturday afternoon, and David smiles. He always loved kids. He was never happier than when he was playing with his nephews.

We reach Lake Clara Meer, and begin to walk along the path at its edge. "Different, how?"

I shrug. "Some kind of thing about being women-friendly. You don't want to hear about it." It's been a rough few months with Jelly Jar. I know the others think that our business will save their souls and answer all of their mommy-related issues, but what about me? My interior design degree is languishing on the side while I develop birthday parties for four-year-olds and wedding themes for spoiled brides. Not exactly what I had in mind. And what do I care that I can bring my kids to work? Talk about a benefit that doesn't profit me.

"I think it's a great idea, but I'm beginning to wonder if it's actually doable."

We find a park bench facing the lake, and we sit down. "Cate, I know it's a hackneyed thing to say, but if you're serious about the new company and what it stands for, then it's worth it, no matter the cost."

I stare at the ducks swimming in the lake.

"Hey, why didn't we ever get over here and do Shake at the Lake?" David asks.

Piedmont Park does outdoor performances of Shakespeare in the summer at Lake Clara Meer. Every year, David and I swear that this summer we're going to check it out, but every year the summer comes and goes before we know it.

"Too busy, I guess," I say and shrug. Usually it was

David who was too busy, first with business school, and then, more recently, with the job.

"I regret that," he says and takes my hand. I let him hold it. I shouldn't, but forgive me, Lord, because I do. "I regret a lot of things, Cate." He looks away. "Do you think we're doing the right thing?"

I look at him out of the corner of my eye. What is all this "we" stuff? Does he mean "God and I"? Because I was not consulted about our breakup. I was *told*. I was told that God and David felt that we were better off apart.

David looks at me in the eyes. "I miss you, Catie. I'm so sorry about the thing with my mom, but I guess I feel like if I tell my mom, then we're really over. I just haven't been able to do it."

I take my hand back in a quick snatch. I thought we were really over. What is he talking about?

"Do you miss me too?" he asks.

Too? I stand up. My first thought is to flee. I have the uncontrollable desire to start running and not stop until the pain is numbed and my brain is quiet. He can't do this to me. He doesn't mean it. I start to walk away, but David catches my hand.

"Wait," he says. I whip back around and face him with my hands balled up into fists.

"David," I blurt. "Just stop it."

"But—"

"No, just, stop it. Okay?" I walk toward my car, I have to get out of here immediately. Soon I hear steps behind me, and I turn. He is jogging to catch up with me.

"Catie," he says with arms outstretched. He makes a teddy bear face.

"Look, David," I say, stopping. "If this is what God wants, then let's just try to accept it."

He stares at me with his mouth hanging open a little.

"Don't call. Don't write. Let's just let go," I say and walk away. This time, he lets me leave.

I walk to my car, praying all the way. But I'm still mad as I drive away. It may be God's will, but I don't have to like it.

"And so I give you, Richard Yarby," Melissa says and gestures at the goateed man in the front row. We all clap politely as Richard ascends the little stage and takes the podium. I look around, nodding. This was the perfect night to bring Daisy. Usually the Sunday evening group is only about thirty hard-core regulars, but tonight there are about forty people here, and a couple of them are kind of cute. And the speaker Melissa brought in has quite a list of credentials. This should be a good night.

"Thanks, guys," Richard says and grips the podium. When Daisy mentioned that she was having trouble meeting other Christian singles at her church, I practically begged her to come with us to the next small group. This group needs a little shaking up. Plus, if I can get her to come regularly, I guarantee she'll soon be out recruiting for us. And we could sure use some fresh blood, I think, as I see Paul the mechanical engineer raise his hand to ask a question already. I force my eyes to sit straight in my head. They have a tendency to roll when Paul talks in his nasally way.

"Um, yes? You in the front now?" Richard asks, no doubt a little baffled that someone as old as Paul is raising his hand.

"Are you going to be handing out an outline?" Paul asks, tapping the end of his pen against his leather Bible. I groan. Some of the speakers we've had have done this, and while I think it makes the whole thing seem too rehearsed, Paul and his cohorts love to make sure they get every word.

"Of course." Richard smiles as Melissa moves to hand out the white sheets of paper he pulls from his briefcase.

Okay, Lord. I can take notes. After all, dating is something I apparently need help with. I pull a couple of pens out of my purse and hand one to Daisy, who looks at me as if I'm crazy.

"Is he serious?" she asks. I nod solemnly, and she takes the pen in resignation. I take a paper and look up to see that Paul is already scribbling away. Is it wrong to ask why the people least likely to go on a date are always the most interested?

"Hello, Resurrection Community Singles Group," Richard says.

Paul in the front row raises his hand again. He's going to correct him. Typical.

"This isn't a singles group, per se. Most of the church is single, sir. This is just a fellowship event."

The speaker's eyes light up. "Is that so? Most of the church is single?" Many of us nod. The speaker cracks his knuckles on his left hand and chill bumps rise on my arms. I hate that sound. "The Lord sure works in mysterious ways," he says, smiling.

I look at Frances. She is looking down at her feet.

"I've been giving this speech at colleges across the nation, and it's really striking a chord. I hope that tonight it will touch your hearts and lay a heavy burden on your consciences. Because brothers and sisters in Christ," he says, gesturing to us, "I have come to talk about the *sin* in *single*."

I gasp and clasp my hand over my mouth. I look at Beatriz, at Franny, at Daisy, to see what they are thinking. Franny glares at Richard, who is now writing "SIN" and "SINGLE" on the dry erase board behind him. Beatriz has her arms crossed on her chest, and Daisy just looks confused.

But all around us, I see my fellow singletons taking notes. I glare at a cute freckled girl sitting behind me, happily writing. "There is sin in being single."

Okay, Cate. I take a deep breath. He might have a point. Maybe he's just being provocative to get our attention. Don't fly off the handle yet. Hear what the man has to say first. You can always write him angry e-mails later.

The four of us sad, wilted schlubs trudge into Caffè Intermezzo and get a table. The hostess puts us in the back, near the bathrooms. After all, we're single women. We should be hidden from society.

With its long hours, free wireless Internet, and more than fifty kinds of desserts flown in from around the world every day, Caffè Intermezzo might just be the best place in all of Atlanta. Plus the owners based it on old world café houses in Vienna and Prague, and it looks every bit the part. It has huge antique chandeliers, beautiful hardwood flooring, and lots of private nooks for conversation, as well as a full waitstaff and serious baristas. It's the best way to feel like you've flown abroad for the weekend without breaking your pocketbook. But that doesn't make us feel any better as we slide into our chairs.

"I can't believe that I actually feel worse, but I do," Bea says, propping her head on her hands. "I thought after my mom left, my life was going to turn around. No more foot care. But his words are still ringing in my head." She grips her head like it hurts her.

"What a creep," I say. I am too tired to care about playing nice, turning the other cheek, not looking at the speck in my brother's eye. Blah! Tomorrow I can go back to trying to be a good person. I've had enough tonight. I'm spent.

"When he said that it was our fault that we were single, I thought I was going to sock him," Franny says.

Daisy laughs. "I'd like to see that." She puts her hands in front of her face and throws some air punches.

Franny turns to her. "He looked like one good pow to the kisser and he'd topple over."

Bea slaps her hand loudly on the table. "He was so full of it. He got married at twenty to the only girl he ever dated. How does that make him the authority on the single life? He has no idea what it's like out there." I hold back a smile. Poor Beatriz. The madder she gets, the cuter she sounds. It's just something about her accent.

"I can't believe he said we should let our fathers choose husbands for us." Franny rolls her eyes. "If I let my father choose, the guy would be a better mate for him than for me. You know, Married Asian Man seeks husband for daughter. Must like kimchi, the Atlanta Braves, and long walks on the golf course."

I shake my head. "There needs to be a term for people like him in the church. Bridget Jones had her 'smug marrieds,' but this is worse. This is judging in the name of God."

"Smug churchies?" Frances says.

"Marisees?" Bea suggests. We all look at her, confused. "You know, like Pharisees? Married Pharisees?" I shake my head, and she shrugs.

"Breedvangelicals?" Daisy suggests, laughing.

"Finger pointers?" I say. "Wrong-headed, unsympathetic, mean-spirited, self-righteous, male-centric, arrogant jerks?" Hmm, that last one doesn't exactly roll off the tongue, but I don't have the energy to care. And for all of this to come on the heels of my little chat with David is almost more than I can bear. I don't even want to be single. Richard made it sound like we were all wild hedonists, young fillies refusing to be corralled and branded with a wedding band. I'm not some label-obsessed dye-job in designer jeans. I'm a person. And I'm lonely. And that's not my fault.

"What can I get you girls?" We look up to see a tiny waif of a waitress, holding a small pad of paper. The diamond on her left hand sparkles in the candlelight.

"Coffee and turtle cheesecake, please," Franny says. That's her standard order. Bea and I usually split a fruit tart while Frances polishes off a giant piece of gooey chocolate and caramel cheesecake all by herself. "With extra whip, too."

"You're all by yourself tonight, Bea. I need my own dessert," I say. "I'll take a coffee and a piece of brownie chocolate cake."

"We're not sharing?" Bea asks, looking stricken.

"I'm too sinful to share, Bea. Haven't you heard I'm a selfish single woman who only cares about herself?"

Daisy and Frances laugh, but our waitress looks at me like I've lost it.

"Fine," Bea says, scouring the huge menu. "In keeping with tonight's theme, I'd like to have the Deadly Chocolate Sin, please."

"Ooooh," I say and raise my water glass in a toast to her.

"And a coffee?" the waitress asks.

Bea nods.

"Oh, y'all. I just can't decide," Daisy says, looking at the menu. "I think that nasty man made me lose my appetite."

I look at her and feign shock. "Daisy Mae. You *have* to get dessert. They're amazing here, and we've all had a rough night."

Daisy scrunches up her face, thinking about it.

I turn to the waitress. "Can you take her over to the case of desserts? Don't let her leave until she chooses something."

The waitress looks at Daisy. Daisy shrugs and gets up.

"Don't come back until you've ordered some sugar, sinful creature!"

Bea, Frances, and I dissect the painful talk until Daisy plops down again at our table.

"You find something?" I ask.

"Tiramisu and a coffee."

"Good. And I'm treating you. It's the least I can do after subjecting you to that horrible little man," I say.

"I had fun anyway." She shrugs. "My next-door neighbor Lillian wanted to spend some time with Tiff, so it worked out really well for me to come along. Even if I didn't really agree with him."

I smile at her. She doesn't have a mean bone in her body. I may have been a Christian since I was born, but I have a lot to learn from Daisy.

"I just want you to know that it isn't normally like that at our church."

She nods.

The waitress arrives with our desserts and coffee and sets everything down on the table. I grab my fork and am about to plunge into the stack of sugar on my plate to erase the memory of tonight, but Frances clinks on her coffee mug with a spoon.

"A toast," she says. "To my single girlfriends."

We all raise our mugs in the air.

"You guys are the least sinful bunch I know," she says, smiling, "and no matter what 'Richard' says, we are okay."

We all clink mugs and take big swigs of our coffee. The warm liquid is soothing as it slips down my throat. It's sweet, a little syrupy. A little different than normal. A little . . . well . . . tastier.

"Hey, wait," Beatriz says. "There's something in my coffee!"

"Mine too," Frances says, raising her mug in confusion.

I look over at Daisy. She is giggling like a child.

"What'd you do?" I ask. She cracks up.

"I told the waitress to throw some Kahlúa in all of our drinks," she says, taking a sip. She smiles and rolls her eyes in delight. "I thought we could use a little zing in our coffee tonight."

We look at one another, and I raise my glass again. "And to our new friend Daisy," I say, smiling at her. "May the good Lord continue to bless her with infinite wisdom."

I get home late and unlock the door to my empty, dark house.

"I'm home," I call to John the Baptist. I flip on some

lights and kick off my shoes at the door. Normally, I keep my house neat as a pin. But really, what does it matter? John doesn't care. I walk over to his tank and find him sleeping on the bottom of the bowl, his eyes open. Great. Even my goldfish doesn't wait up for me.

I trudge to the bathroom and wash my face with skin-firming cleanser and then inspect the two creases across my forehead. When they first appeared, I told myself it was from the stress of my job at the interior design firm. But they haven't gone away. In fact, unless I'm crazy, they're getting worse. I lean in to get a better look at them. They are twin ravines.

I dab on some new rejuvenating serum that I found at the fancy skin-care clinic in the Virginia Highlands. They promised miracles with this stuff, and, well, I just hope they're right.

I scrub my teeth with Ultra-Brite toothpaste (voted most whitening by *Consumer Reports*) and then put in my retainer. Last time I was home my mother pointed out that my teeth were moving back and asked if I had been wearing my retainer. Even though I hadn't noticed it, she was totally right. Moms have a way of cutting right to the quick of things.

I flip off the bathroom switch and slip into my comfy pajamas. I grab my laptop off the couch and trudge back to my bedroom. I have a study and a spare bedroom too, though I never get any use out of them. As I pass the study, I decide to go in there and sit on the couch out of principle. This house is not empty. See. I use the study. Why, I practically *need* this study.

I open up my e-mail, praying that it contains an uplifting letter from a friend. I have two e-mails from Jo, with the frantic subject lines "MANDATORY MEETING TO-MORROW" and "RE: RE: DIAMOND FUNCTION." I stifle a yawn. I am not even surprised when I see that one of the e-mails was sent just an hour ago, at one in the morning. She really never sleeps. I decide to open her e-mails tomorrow. I'm too tired for Jo. But I do have an e-mail from an old friend from high school. I click on it. Natalie and I were in all the same art classes in school, and last year I even flew out to Texas for her wedding. We aren't as close as we used to be, but she's known me since I was in pigtails and I always love to hear from her. But my heart sinks when I open the e-mail.

It's in a mass e-mail. With a sonogram attached. With a message:

It's a boy! We're so excited!!!!

I turn my head to one side and then another, trying to make sense of the sonogram. What is this thing, an inkblot? I hold my laptop upside down. Did she paste it into the e-mail wrong? But it looks no better upside down. I look at it right side up again, and finally, slowly, an image does appear. Only, it's not a darling baby boy. It's an alien. It looks just like the weird cone-headed, green, bug-eyed monster in every horror film.

I snap my laptop shut. This isn't good. I just failed the inkblot sonogram test. Maybe that guy was right.

———

As I trudge into Jelly Jar on Monday morning, all I can think is: *What was I smoking?* Between testing recipes for Thanksgiving, brainstorming for the big diamond event, sketching ideas for the new apartments, and wallowing in my sorry single misery, I have hardly slept, let alone prepared myself mentally for this big mandatory meeting Jo is all excited about. And when I see that Ellie's twins are running around the room tapping on things with their godforsaken hammers again, I am ready to scream. Sometimes I miss working at a place where the word *pee-pee* isn't part of our everyday vocabulary. At least Lauren is here. I can't imagine what she's majoring in that gives her this much time to babysit.

"Hey," I call to Jo and Ellie, who are hunched over some papers on the counter, as I pour myself a big cup of coffee from the pot in the kitchen. They nod, and I walk into the main room and pull out my notes about the diamond party and begin to review them.

Jo and Ellie come out of the kitchen and sit with me, but neither of them says a word. Jo looks around and sighs. Daisy is late. Again.

I look back down at my notes, and Ellie gives Lauren a stack of coloring books for the twins. Lauren sits them down on the floor, and they take the crayons in their greedy little hands and start to work. Coloring is their favorite thing these days.

We all flip through some papers for a few more minutes, until Jo finally clears her throat.

"I have to take Agnes to a doctor's appointment at

eleven." She takes a sip from her coffee and glances toward the door. "I guess we should just get started. I'm sure Daisy will be here any minute."

"The good news is, we have eight Thanksgiving dinners signed up, and we have two more families considering. The bad news is, one of the families wants a vegetarian Thanksgiving meal." She laughs. "Does anyone know how to dress up a Tofurky?"

"Bacon?" Ellie says.

"I'm pretty sure dressing up a Tofurky is actually impossible." I shake my head, chuckling. "I'd just focus on the side dishes."

"Okay. Just do your best. Now, for the Diamond Commission party." Jo looks down at her notes. "We've put together a preliminary menu, and Anna Rogers is coming in Thursday for the tasting. Now, Ellie, were you going to—"

The door bursts open, and Daisy stumbles into the room, unwinding a long brown scarf from her neck. "I am so sorry, y'all," she says, walking over to where we're sitting. "Tiffany was impossible this morning, and when I finally got her in the car and to school, the principal stopped me and went on and on about how worried he is about her social situation. As if I don't know my daughter is shy. I tried to get him to shut up as quickly as possible, but"—she looks around and shrugs—"I'm sorry."

I don't even have to look at Jo to know she is mad. I've never met a more punctual person in my life than Josephine Vann. But I also know that Daisy has pulled out an ironclad excuse. With Jo's own children practically partners in this business, she can't say anything about Daisy's parenting woes.

"That's okay, Daisy," she says, taking a deep breath. "Next time, please try to get here on time." I smile at Daisy, who grins weakly at me. "As I was saying, the diamond party—"

"Oooh, I had a brilliant idea for that," Daisy says, bouncing up and down in her seat. "One of Dolly's best lines is 'It's hard to be a diamond in a rhinestone world.' So I was thinking, what if we made that the theme? We could write that on the invitations and stuff. Everyone wants to be the real thing, right? I think it could really work."

"That's not a bad idea," Cate says, nodding. "We would have to get rights to use the lyric, but—"

"Cate, I'm afraid that's not going to work," Jo says. "We have to cut our budget on this, so we probably won't be able to do that. And we won't be able to use the wall of plasma screens like we wanted either."

"What?" I look down at my sketches. I had five televisions screens lined up, each playing a favorite diamond commercial throughout the years: *"A diamond is forever," "Diamonds that make a statement," "I forever do," "Every kiss begins with Kay," "Old maids don't get to wear sparklies."*

Okay, so maybe designing for this party wasn't the healthiest thing I could have been doing at this point in my life, but that doesn't make it any easier to see all those hours of work go up in smoke. Sure, the wall would have been a little pricey, but the profit from the Right Hand

Diamonds campaign alone should have been enough to cover the screens.

"Why are we cutting the budget on this? Are you giving them a break of some kind?" The moment De Beers starts needing our financial assistance, I'm done.

"No." Jo sighs. "Nothing like that. We just . . ." She looks at Ellie helplessly. "We have to cut costs where we can." Jo looks around and smiles, and we all fall silent. Something isn't right.

"What do you mean—" I start, but Jo cuts me off.

"So what's the deal with your whole Dolly Parton obsession anyway?" Jo says quickly. She nods at Daisy, who flushes a little. Clever Jo. Change the subject. "I mean, I like country as much as the next person, but you're a really big fan." She pastes an innocent look on her face.

The question seems to throw Daisy off. She flushes, gathering her hands in her lap.

"She came along at the right time, I guess." She shrugs.

We all watch her, waiting for her to go on. Daisy looks around at us, then sighs.

"It was a bad time in my life," Daisy says quietly. "I was broke and Tiff and I were living in a rat-hole apartment with a guy who . . ." She lets her voice trail off, then takes a deep breath. "Anyway, I was home one day, doing endless loads of laundry on my day off, and Tiff wouldn't stop crying, and I was starting to lose it, when I heard 'Light of a Clear Blue Morning' on the radio." She shakes her head. "The song was talkin' about getting through a bad time, and waking up and seeing that everything is going to be all right. It was so hopeful. And

I looked around at my life, and I didn't see any light, except for Tiff. Dolly was singing about a life so far from where I was, and I wanted to feel that optimistic about the future."

Ellie reaches out and takes Daisy's hand. I study her face. She's so young, and she's lived through so much. Suddenly my problems seem small and silly.

Daisy laughs a little. "As Dolly was just singin' her heart out, Tiff finally quieted down and went to sleep. I plopped down on the couch and right then and there knew I had to make some changes." Daisy clears her throat. "Get out of Plainsville. I had to do it for me and for Tiff."

It's so quiet I can hear the coffeepot gurgle in the corner. Jo fusses with the hem of her skirt.

"Anyway," Daisy says quickly, "with my next paycheck I went and bought myself an old tape of her songs, and they were all kind of like that." Her face brightens a bit. "Even the ones that were sad felt true somehow. I listened to that tape until it broke. It was kind of a turning point for me, I guess. I pulled myself together, broke up with the jerk, and bought a bus ticket. I realized that if I wanted a better life, it was up to me."

Daisy reaches up and pulls her thick hair up into a ponytail, her eyes focused somewhere beyond us.

"It spiraled out of control from there. I bought all her albums. I even bought an autographed picture on eBay. The woman's got style." She gives a weak laugh, and it echoes off the tile floor in the quiet room. "She's not afraid to be who she is. I guess it helped me come to the point where I wasn't either."

"You should write her a letter," Ellie says quietly. "Let her know how much her songs mean to you."

"Yeah." Daisy clears her throat. "Maybe I will. Dear Dolly, I just wanted to tell you, you probably saved my life."

"Hey, you look familiar." I groan. People tell me I look familiar all the time. Nine times out of ten, I've never met the person before, and half the time people conclude I look like their cousin Allison. Apparently I have the most generic face on the planet. I look up, ready to explain that no, we haven't met, and isn't that funny that I look like his cousin, but when I see him, I freeze. He seems familiar too. I retract the tape measure in my hand and look at him carefully.

I came to check out the apartments I'll be staging in the new section of Atlantic Station this morning, only to find that they're not *quite* finished, a fact that Mollie neglected to mention when I signed up to take the job. Workers have been in and out all morning, skim coating the walls and installing cabinets. Evidently I don't get to make decisions about those, I just get to pick out paint and bring in furniture to make this brand-new generic loft look lived in, loved, and stylish. The guy in front of me is installing hardware in the kitchen, where I have been deciding how to make the plain tile floor and light maple cabinets look interesting, which they aren't.

"Weren't you at Resurrection on Sunday night?" he asks, crouched over the sink. That's it. The blond hair, the blue eyes. He was one of the new guys in the back. I noticed him because he reminded me of Matthew McConaughey.

"I was," I say, turning off my digital camera. I like to have pictures of the spaces I work on so I don't have to rely on my shaky memory. He stands up straight and places his screwdriver down on the marble counter. "You were in the back."

"James." He nods, his blue eyes sparkling. I shake his hand. "Do you go there regularly?"

I cringe and put the camera on the counter, nodding. "Was that your first time?" I try to gauge his reaction.

"Yeah. You know Brett?" I nod, thinking about the balding elementary school teacher who comes regularly. "We play basketball together on Saturday mornings, and he invited me." He turns on the spigot and nods as water begins to pour out.

"Luckily for humankind, that guy was just a guest speaker."

"Oh, good," he says, laughing. "Do you often have guest speakers? I hear Mussolini is free if you're looking for someone next week." He leans against the counter, crossing his arms over his chest.

"Does that mean you won't be coming back?"

"Will you be there?" he asks, raising his right eyebrow.

"Unless Mao needs me, probably," I say, smiling.

"Then, I guess the answer is yes." He winks, turns off the tap, and walks past me out of the kitchen, and out the front door.

Ellie

~~~~~~

THE DOORBELL RINGS, AND I GLANCE AT THE CLOCK. Ten AM exactly. I shut my eyes and try to say a prayer for patience, but I seemed to have lost the words. How long has it been since I prayed? Lord knows we could use a little prayer, with the way this house is running.

"Mrs. Routledge?"

I turn around and see Lauren behind me. I gave up trying to get her to call me Ms. Howell-Routledge a long time ago. It was too foreign to Lauren's ears. I see her twitching, trying to figure out how to say that she needs to go now. Sure, she probably didn't want to come over Thanksgiving morning to watch the twins, but I threw an unmentionable amount of money at her and promised that she could leave at ten, when the twins' grandmother arrived.

Originally Mike had said that he would watch them

while I prepared a huge gourmet Thanksgiving for his dear, sweet mother, but then he bailed on me two days ago in a cranky fit. He needed to go into the office for a few hours and suggested I just call his mother and ask her to come over earlier. I insisted that it would be easier for everyone if Lauren could just come over for a few hours, and eventually Mike said he was tired of fighting about it. I just couldn't have Edith Routledge come over earlier than ten. I can bear only a few hours with that woman before I want to hurt somebody.

"I'm sorry, Mrs. Routledge. But I just promised my mom that I'd be home," Lauren says, twining blond hair around her finger.

I wipe my hands on the apron Mike's mother gave me several Christmases ago, the one I wear only when she's coming over, even as the doorbell rings again. I hear the twins running for the door, squealing. This place is pure chaos. How will I manage without Lauren? Still, if I don't let her go now, she'll never come back.

"Thanks so much for coming, Lauren. I could have never gotten Thanksgiving together without that uninterrupted time this morning." I dig in my purse for cash to give her.

I give Lauren the money, and the guilt begins to choke me. What kind of mother pays someone to come and watch her kids on Thanksgiving? Then my more practical side answers my own question. A busy one. A successful one. One who has already cooked nine Thanksgiving dinners for other people and couldn't start her own until this morning.

"Nanna! Nanna!" I hear the twins greet Mike's mother in the other room.

"Happy Thanksgiving, Mrs. R.!" Lauren says, every bit the chipper education major she is.

"You too," I say and begin to walk her to the front door. *Take me with you!* I want to plead to Lauren. And though I'd normally let her slip out the front door by herself, I don't need Edith correcting my manners today.

"Edith." I give her a small hug.

"Ellie," she says. She kisses the air next to my face and returns my hug stiffly.

The twins realize that Lauren is leaving, and they both cling to her legs.

"No," they both wail. "Don't leave us."

I laugh uncomfortably. Is it worth explaining to Edith that they do this for everyone? I look at the old bird, and she has a judgmental eyebrow raised at the twins.

"Now, Seth and Sophie, Lauren has to go home to her own family for Thanksgiving. Please stand up and let her go." I give them my Mommy-is-serious face and they actually obey me . . . for a moment. Sophie begins to bawl, and Lauren scoops her up and hugs her just as I am about to tell Sophie to knock it off. The twins are both already worn out. They've been so excited for Thanksgiving that they got up at five this morning.

"But, Law-wen. We-uh your family," Sophie says into Lauren's shoulder, using the baby talk she reserves for when she's pulling out the crocodile tears.

"Awww," Lauren says in her slight drawl, and pats Sophie on the back. Lauren really does seem to love them, which makes it a lot easier for me to leave them with her.

I glance nervously at Edith. "Can I take your coat,

Edith? I was just relieving the twins' valiant babysitter, Lauren. Have you two met?"

Edith takes off her coat and hands it to me, then greets Lauren warmly. As they exchange pleasantries I feel a twinge of jealousy. She has never been that nice to me. I pry a crying Sophie off Lauren, and Lauren slips out the door. The moment she leaves, the twins recover and begin to obsess over their grandmother.

"Nanna. Lauren made me this beeyootiful bracelet, see?" Sophie says and shows her grandmother a colorful friendship bracelet.

Seth steps in front of his sister. "Daddy said I can have a bike for Christmas."

"Oh, my twins," Edith says and scoops them both up in a big hug. She takes their hands and leads them into the living room, listening to them chatter nonstop about their lives.

"Know what?" Sophie says. "Lauren lives three blocks down, and she's in *college*."

"Her brother is in the army," Seth adds.

Content that everyone seems to be okay, I slip back into the kitchen to check on my Sweet Potato Soufflé. I open the oven and see that the brown sugar pecan crumble top is beginning to crystallize nicely. I shut the door quickly. Now, where did I put that copy of Edith's Green Bean Casserole recipe? I don't like cooking with a bunch of canned foods thrown together in a pot, but I'm trying to bury the hatchet this Thanksgiving, and Edith is very proud of this recipe, so here goes nothing. I look at the can of fried onion strips and shiver. If only the stern chefs at Le Cordon Bleu could see me now.

The hair on my neck begins to rise, and I know she's behind me. Edith has the uncanny ability to sneak around without anyone hearing her, which is really something for someone as robust as she is. I hang a smile on my face and turn around.

"Hi," I say.

She eyes me carefully over her gold-rimmed reading glasses. If I had never seen a picture of Mike's late father, I would have sworn that he was adopted. Though Mike is tall, lean, and the life of the party, his mother is short, stout, and always has a pinched look on her face.

"I was hoping for something to drink. A glass of water, just anything will do. I'm so parched from my trip all the way over here and I'm sure you don't have anything at all in the house and I hate to be a bother to such a busy woman like you, but even just a glass of water would be fine for me. I've just got the simplest taste."

I stare at her a moment, then realize that I'm not smiling and so I force a smile to climb up on my face. "Sure," I say through clenched teeth. This is her way. She likes to correct my behavior through coded messages. Translation: You should always offer your guests something to drink.

"Are you sure you want water?" I ask as I pull open the fridge. "I got that grape juice you like so much." Edith is an old-fashioned Baptist teetotaler and loves grape juice, the closest she's ever gotten to having a drink in her life.

"Oh," she says, clearly surprised at my thoughtfulness. "Well, I'd hate to be any trouble."

Translation: Yes, but don't think we're friends now. I

pour a glass and bring it to her. She takes a tiny sip for someone so parched, and I return to my cooking.

"So you had a lot of traffic on the way over here?" I pause for a moment. Mike really wants me to call Edith "Mom." I shut my eyes and just say it. "Mom?" I turn and watch her as she cringes at the sound of the word.

"Yes, of course I did," she says, as if I'm an utterly stupid child. "It's Thanksgiving Day."

Really? It is? I wouldn't have guessed. I look back at her casserole recipe and try not to think about what this means. Translation: I am an old woman and shouldn't have had to come all the way over here.

But it was Mike's decision to do Thanksgiving here this year. He felt that since she lived fifteen minutes away and was in the pink of health, she should come over to our house. He hates bringing the twins to her place because it's small and full of breakables and they always end up terrorizing her mean Persian cat, Miss Trixie.

"Where is Mike?" she asks.

"Good question," I say, trying to affect a girlfriend-to-girlfriend tone that falls flat. I glance at the clock. Has it been only twenty minutes since she arrived? He'd better get home fast or he's sleeping on the couch. "He had to work a little this morning. That's why I had Lauren come over. I didn't want to trouble you, and I needed a few hours to get Thanksgiving started."

"Tuch," I hear her say.

She makes this short, sucking-in noise with her tongue whenever she is displeased, and it's probably my least favorite thing about her, which is really saying something because I have quite a list. *Tuch*, she goes in my dreams. *Tuch, tuch, tuch.*

"His father was never late for Thanksgiving," she says.

"Hmm," I say and open the can of French-cut green beans. Wouldn't the French laugh at that? I'll just stay focused on this Franken-food recipe and that will keep my mind off Edith.

"Ellie?" she says.

I turn around again and give her my full attention as I hear the soft green beans ease from their can, plop into the bowl, and hit the gelatinous cream of mushroom soup.

"In my day, a wife thought it was important for a family to spend Thanksgiving together. She would have made sure her husband understood this." Edith gives me her most knowing smile.

I feel my face turning red, and force myself to turn back to the recipe. So now it's my fault that her perfect son isn't home for Thanksgiving yet?

"I agree, Mom. He'll be home soon."

I pull the Green Bean Casserole out of the oven and deftly weave my way around scattered toys, then set it down on a trivet in the middle of the table. I stand still for a moment and take it all in. It really is perfect. The twins are dressed up and look adorable in their coordinated outfits. Mike finally made it home and has been doting on Edith, putting her in the best of moods. And every single dish I made turned out. All this cooking I'm doing for Jelly Jar is finally paying off. I'm not as rusty as I used to be.

I sit down next to Mike, and he squeezes my hand under the table. For some reason, the little hairs on my forearms rise. After all these years of marriage, it's still nice to know that he can give me chill bumps. I beam back at him, thankful for this moment. Things have been so rocky lately. I guess I just need a little reassurance that things are okay, that we're okay.

"Seth and Sophie? Do you want to say grace for us?" Edith asks. Even though she's at my house, she is going to be mistress of the table.

Seth crosses his arms over his chest and shakes his head violently no. Lately my twins are really starting to distinguish themselves. Seth is getting quieter, more introspective, like me, while Sophie seems more and more like her father's girl each day. She loves the spotlight, that one.

"I'll do it, Nanna," she says.

"Thanks, Sophie Belle," Mike says.

I do a double-take at Mike. I haven't heard him call her that in a couple of months. Strange I hadn't noticed. Maybe the old Mike has come back to us. He's been so distant ever since I started working at Jelly Jar.

"Please bow your heads," Sophie says and then giggles. She loves the attention. I settle in to hear her adorable rendition of "God is great," thankful that at least we taught the twins that.

"Bless us, O Lord," she begins. I open my eyes. This is new. I glance at Edith, who is staring at her little bowed head. "And these Thy gifts which we are about to receive from Thy bounty through Christ our Lord. Amen."

Sophie looks up and smiles, proud of herself.

Mike has a bemused look on his face. Did he teach her that? "Sophie, honey, where did you learn that pretty grace?" he asks.

"Lauren." She shrugs. "I forgot the other one." She grabs a roll.

"*Tuch, tuch,*" Edith says. I stare at my plate. Has it really been that long since we all sat down together and said grace? I guess Edith isn't going to believe that we're going to a church across town anymore.

Mike tries to change the subject. "What a beautiful meal. Let's dig in." He begins to pass the sweet potatoes when the phone rings.

Mike rolls his eyes. "Salespeople." But I feel a sinking in my stomach.

"I'll just get rid of them," I say and slip out of the room, even as I earn another "*tuch*" from Edith.

I put my hand on the phone and really, truly pray it's not who I think it is, but unfortunately I'm right.

"Ellie? Ellie? Is that you? It's Jo. We have a huge problem. I need you. I'm on my way to your house right now."

I stumble through the front door of the quiet house and set my purse down on the hall table. Crisis averted. While I prepared the seven turkeys for our Thanksgiving delivery service, Cate was in charge of cooking the majority of them this morning since she was just going up to her mom's place in Marietta for dinner and would have the morning free. Daisy was also supposed to cook a couple in her home ovens and bring them over to Jelly Jar, then help deliver them. But managing five turkeys and one vegetarian feast was too much for one person. In retrospect, we should have known that.

After her frantic call, Jo came to pick me up, her own half-cooked Thanksgiving turkey resting precariously in the backseat, on her way to Jelly Jar. One of the Jelly Jar ovens had caught fire, ruining the turkey inside, not to mention the expensive nonstick finish. I had to restuff the bird with my special Sausage Apple Stuffing, which I made on the fly, then cook it, along with the other four turkeys, in the two other working ovens, then deliver the full meal to the waiting Hanlon family.

The whole time, I kept thinking about my twins, eating Thanksgiving dinner without me. That and the glee on Edith's face as I rushed out of the house, deserting my family. She finally had confirmation that I really am a bad mother. But at least, I reminded myself, as I scrubbed out eight roasting pans in the Jelly Jar kitchen, I didn't have to give up my own family's bird.

The front rooms of my house are dark as I walk in, but I see a flickering light coming from the living room. It's past the twins' bedtime, but it sounds like Mike got them to sleep. I walk toward the doorway, then smile as I see Mike curled up in the recliner, a brown crocheted blanket pulled over his shoulders, his eyes closed. *Home Alone* is playing silently on the screen before him. I walk over and sit gingerly on the edge of the recliner and lean into my husband, curling my tired body against his. He wraps his arms around me, and we sit, silently, savoring the quiet moment.

"You know what I'm thankful for?" Mike whispers, nuzzling my cheek with his nose. "I'm thankful for my beautiful wife."

"And I'm thankful for my wonderful husband." I sigh, enjoying the warmth of his body against mine. It's been so long. "And my precious children."

We rock slowly in the recliner, until my eyelids feel so heavy that I know I will just fall asleep right here unless I move. I stand up slowly. I pull Mike to his feet and take his hand, and we walk slowly toward the stairs. I give him a kiss on the nose, then let his hand drop so I can go to the kitchen to get a glass of water to put next to my side of the bed. The stairs creak with the comforting sound of Mike's sleepy footsteps, and I walk into the kitchen, smiling to myself. I flip on the kitchen light and freeze.

The roasting pan, caked with congealed grease, is on top of a stack of dirty dishes that is overflowing the sink. The half-eaten remains of my soufflé sit uncovered on the counter, and the leftover garlic mashed potatoes are turning yellow in their china bowl. There is a biscuit on the floor, and homemade cranberry sauce is smeared on the light blue wall. I peek into the dining room and see that they didn't even bother to clear the table. A stick of butter sits, uncovered, in its little china dish.

I stare at the untouched dishes in disbelief, then burst into tears.

The Grand Foyer of the Freedom Hall is supposed to be awe-inspiring, but Cate has really used the space to its fullest tonight. Part of the King Center, the complex that protects and exhibits Martin Luther King Jr.'s home, church, and papers, the Freedom Hall is decorated with art from both Georgia and Africa. The lights have been turned low, and the room lit with candles. The tables, seats at which sold for hundreds of dollars each, are draped in vibrant African-print tablecloths and topped with rich, dark wooden centerpieces. The symbolism of using this hall—located in what is still one of the poorest neighborhoods in Atlanta—for the Public Housing Alliance event is unmistakable.

I know Mama was doing us a favor by hiring Jelly Jar to cater the Public Housing Alliance dinner. Mama is the chairwoman for the organization that has helped hundreds of needy families find permanent and safe shelter, and every year she organizes this dinner extravaganza to raise money for the nonprofit. The Howell family has been on the board of the PHA since it was founded in 1921, as Mama will tell you. Of all the charities she serves, this is the one that she cares about the most and she does a good job. It's always a swanky evening, and this year, in addition to hiring us to prepare and deliver the food, she has bought Jelly Jar a table, which means that each of us gets to attend the event, with a guest, no less. We hired waiters and bartenders to serve during the event itself. It's been so long since I was on the receiving end of a catered event, I'm not sure I'll remember how to behave, but I'm looking forward to it nonetheless. I need an evening out like nobody's business.

I adjust the black wrap around my shoulders, then grab

Mike's hand and walk through the door. Mike and I haven't exactly been on the best of terms since the fight that erupted Thanksgiving night, but I promised myself I wouldn't think about that tonight. I feel a surge of pride as I see Mama holding court by the head table. Her mahogany skin is radiant in candlelight, her black dress drapes over her slim frame comfortably, and her maroon and green batik headscarf gives her an aura of honor and authority. I walk toward her, but am waylaid by an unexpected side-hug.

I pull back to see my sister Veronica smiling at me. My youngest sister, Delia, is behind her. Veronica is wearing a knee-length black dress with her typical conservative pearls, while Delia, never one to be lost in a crowd, has paired her loud pink dress with a silver sequined clutch purse. Veronica is a lawyer who specializes in public defense cases and she's got her gorgeous baby, Jada, in her arms. Delia, meanwhile, is an artist and is as free-spirited as they come.

They squeal at me and hug Mike respectfully. Mike heads over to Daddy and Jerome to talk about football, I'm sure.

"Where have you been?" Veronica asks. I put a finger on Jada's tummy and she smiles and wriggles.

"You missed my opening," Delia says and arches a brow at me.

"I'm sorry. I'm sorry," I say and make a pleading face at them. "It's just been so hectic with the new company. How was the opening?" I ask Delia.

She begins to tell me about the opening night reception for her most recent exhibit at a local gallery, and a musician she met there. Mama would hate him, so she totally adores him. While she talks, I look around the room and spot Jo standing in a crowd of people. I give her a small wave. She waves back and smiles a bit. That woman just can't relax around me. You'd never guess in a million years that we own a company together. How did she get so far in life being so cold?

"So we have our first date next weekend, but I'm going to have him pick me up at Mama and Daddy's house just so Mama has to, you know, pretend that she likes him. She's the best performance artist I've ever seen," Delia says.

"Delia, don't bait Mama into fighting with you," Veronica says and shakes her head. My sisters continue to bicker for a moment.

"Come here, Jada. Come to Auntie Ellie," I say to interrupt them. Veronica hands me Jada, and I run my fingers through her baby-soft dark curls.

"We're not staying long," Veronica says. "Mama just really wanted all of 'the girls' to make an appearance tonight, but Jada needs to get to bed soon."

I nuzzle Jada, and she coos. I bounce her a little and look around the room, lost in my thoughts, remembering when Seth and Sophie were this age. Should we have another? Mike hasn't touched me in weeks, and that's not exactly the best way to put in an order for a new baby. I look around and see Jo again. This time she's inspecting the food we made. Jo turns around, as if conscious that I'm thinking about her, and sees me. Her face brightens up like she's just heard the most wonderful news, and she rushes over to me.

"Who is this?" Jo says, touching Jada's cheek gently.

"Aren't you so cute? Who's so cute? Is it you, sweetie pie? Is it you?"

I stare at Jo. What in the . . .

"Jo, this is my niece, Jada."

Jo reaches out her hands. "Oh, let me hold her. Please?"

I look at Veronica, who gives me a questioning look, but what can I say? I hand Jada to Jo, expecting Jada to start to fuss. But Jo is a seasoned pro, and Jada is content in her arms.

Veronica is shooting darts at me with her eyes. "Ahem," I say, trying to get Jo's attention. It's like she hasn't even noticed that my two sisters are standing right here. "Jo, these are my sisters, Delia and Veronica."

Jo finally looks up, with Jada's tiny hand wrapped around her pointer finger, and smiles, remembering her manners.

"So nice to meet you both." She goes back to cooing at Jada.

What is wrong with her? I continue to talk, hoping to snap her out of it. "Veronica, Jo is my business partner at Jelly Jar. Jo, Veronica is Jada's *mother*."

Jo's face blushes. "Oh," she says, looking at Jada. "She's just beautiful and such a sweet girl." Then Jo gazes at Jada again and sighs. She passes her to Veronica. "Thanks so much for letting me hold her."

Veronica takes Jada back and studies Jo. I love my sister, but she's not exactly the most trusting individual. "My pleasure. She usually cries with strangers. You're very good with her." Veronica smiles, though I can hear the caution in her voice.

Jo seems to be withdrawing within herself again, faster and faster as each second goes by. "Thanks," she says and smooths her skirt. "I have two little girls at home."

We all nod and an awkwardness hangs in the air, while I try to figure out what this little interaction with Jo is all about.

"Well, then," Jo says and glances around the room. "Just enjoy this time," she says to Veronica. "They grow up so fast." Jo waves at Gerard and excuses herself from our group.

Delia nudges me and says under her breath, "That was a little *Twilight Zone* if you ask me."

"Delia," Veronica and I say in unison.

I spy Cate walking through the door and realize that I'm not fulfilling my duties as a Howell family hostess. I excuse myself from my sisters, but not before making Veronica promise to find me and say good-bye when she leaves.

I hunt down Cate, who is now hovering near the coat check with her date. She looks stunning in a form-fitting, knee-lenth blue chiffon gown. It's been a while since I could pull off a dress like that. I sigh. My body hasn't quite been the same since the twins. Cate's date is tall, and his short dark hair sets off his clear blue eyes, even from a distance. When she sees me coming toward her she breaks into a smile.

"Cate, you look gorgeous." I lean in to give her a hug, then pull back to admire her date. Good cheekbones, smooth unlined skin, straight white teeth. This one's a keeper.

"Thanks," she says quietly, ducking her head. "Ellie,

this is David." She nods at her date, who smiles at me and leans in to give me a kiss on the cheek. A real gentleman, this one. "David, Ellie."

"Thank you for inviting us," David says, taking Cate's hand. A slow blush creeps up over Cate's cheeks, and I can't help but smile. I'm so glad she finally found someone who treats her right.

"Oh, it's my mother who's responsible for all this." I laugh, noticing David stroking Cate's wrist with his thumb. "But I'm so glad you both could make it. Why don't you come on in and get a drink, and I'll introduce you to some people." I notice the governor and his wife stepping through the wide double doors behind us.

David nods, and they begin to walk toward the bar when I see Daisy enter the room, oohing and aahing over the authentic African masks on the walls. Several feet behind her is Tiffany, wearing a long coat and a sour expression. I think it's adorable that Daisy has brought her daughter as her date, but . . . Tiffany looks less than pleased to be here. Actually, I've never seen her look any other way, now that I think about it. I dread the day my own kids hit adolescence.

"Would you look at that picture," Daisy shrieks, pointing to the wooden relief *Freedom and Justice*, which was given to the Center by the president of Zambia. She hands her coat over at the coat check, motioning for Tiffany to do the same. Daisy is wearing a tight pink dress, flirty and flowy, which shows just enough skin, and her long blond hair curls down around her shoulders. Tiffany wears dark tights under a long black skirt, chunky heels, and a white collared shirt. At least her hair looks clean. I usher them into the ballroom, and Daisy envelops me in a Vanilla Mist hug. I lean in to give Tiffany a hug, but she crosses her arms over her chest and leans back. "You look beautiful," I whisper, and her shoulders soften a little. I smile at her and notice that she is wearing a bit of eye shadow and the slightest hint of lip gloss beneath her scowl.

"She's just pouting because the Mathlete team lost an important match today." Daisy punches Tiffany on the arm playfully. Tiff looks down at her shoes. "But they're still doing better than any team in Covenant Christian's history," Daisy says, motherly pride outweighing her confusion over her daughter's extracurricular choices.

Tiffany doesn't acknowledge her mother's praise. Daisy shrugs and plows on. "And then on the way over here, I found out she didn't know who the Coreys are. Can you believe it? What is life without Corey Feldman and Corey Haim?"

I point them to the bar area, where Cate and her hot date are lingering. "Wowsa." Daisy laughs, moving her eyebrows up and down at the sight of David. "Who's that?"

"Cate's date." I shrug. "David? Yes, I think that's it. Some people have all the luck, don't—"

"David?" Daisy repeats. "Oh, no, she didn't."

"Wait," I say, trying to read the expression on Daisy's face. "Is that . . . ?"

"Her ex." Daisy nods. "I'm gonna knock that girl three ways to Sunday."

"I thought she said they were really over," I say, watching him hand Cate a drink.

"That's what she said," Daisy says, her voice high and pinched. "She has a funny way of showin' it, doesn't she?"

She turns on her heel and marches off toward the couple, thrusts her hand in David's face, and glares at Cate. I look at Tiffany and shrug. She looks at me helplessly, her blue eyes wide, so I put my arm around her shoulders and let it rest there. Slowly, almost imperceptibly, she begins to lean in against me.

At last, I find Mike. He's hiding at an empty table in the back of the room, talking to a friend of Daddy's named Ford. We always call him Ford the Bore. Nice man and a generous donor, but I've never seen anyone voluntarily spend time with him. I'd better go help spring Mike from Ford's clutches.

I come up behind Mike and put a hand on his shoulder. He jumps. What is with him? He's been acting like a spooked horse all night.

"Oh. Hi, Ellie," he says.

I sit down next to him. Ford waves at me, but doesn't even pause. He's in the middle of his famous story about meeting Ray Charles in a seedy club in New Orleans before "Ray" was famous. It's one of his longer ones. I'm just going to have to be bold.

"Ford, I'm so sorry to interrupt."

Ford stops for a moment.

"Mike, dear. I'm going to have to pull you away. We need to say good-bye to Jo and Gerard. They're leaving now."

Mike shrugs. "Just tell them I said bye. I want to hear this story." He smiles at Ford, who takes this as his cue to continue.

What is he talking about? He always says how mind-numbing Ford is, and he's heard this Ray Charles story at least three times already. Plus, the Mike I used to know would never be so impolite as to not say good-bye to a guest. He's been such a grump lately. When I first mentioned this party a month ago, he said he was happy to go, but a few nights ago when I was reminding him of the names of all my partners and their husbands he got cranky and said he didn't have time to make it anymore. That's when World War III broke out and eventually he caved in, especially after I explained that it would mean so much to my parents if he were there. But all night he's just been sulking in the corner. I can remember a time when he would have been the life of a party like this.

"I'm sorry," I say again, and Ford stops. I take Mike's hand. "I know you men don't like these sorts of things, but it's up to we women to keep you on track." I physically pull him from his seat and playfully wink at Ford, who laughs.

"Ford, good to see you again," I say over my shoulder, as I escort a glowering Mike away. Mike does not say anything, but I can feel his frustration. Jo and Gerard are at the coat check, retrieving their things and getting ready to go out in the cold night.

I walk up with my arms outstretched and hug Jo.

"Thanks so much for coming," I say and then pull back to smile at her. But she is just staring at Mike, white in the face. I shrug and hug Gerard too, who returns the gesture.

"Everything was just wonderful, Ellie," Gerard says. He shrugs his coat on.

"Thank you." What a nice guy Jo married. He's got

such great social skills. I guess he compensates for Jo. "I had some great help, of course." I nod at Jo.

Jo stares at the floor. Mike is looking over his shoulder, as if he's not really taking part in our conversation.

"Mike, I'll tell you what," Gerard says. "What are we going to do with these two ladies? We don't deserve them, do we?" Gerard chuckles.

Mike makes brief eye contact with Gerard and mumbles something in assent.

"Bye, Ellie," Jo says abruptly, and then marches out into the night. Gerard watches her go with a look of confusion on his face.

"She's worn out," he says quietly. His voice shows a tenderness toward her that makes me happy for Jo.

I press his hand. "I know." Gerard glances at Mike, who is now completely turned around, pretending to study the band. Gerard shrugs and leaves.

"I have to go to the restroom," Mike says, and storms away.

I watch him go, standing alone. I could try to take this up with him later, but another fight is the last thing we need. I'll just let it go. I know that work is really hard on him this time of year. I sigh. A waiter comes over and smiles warmly. He proffers a tray of champagne flutes, and I take one and try to relax.

I look around the room. The food was perfect, and we had such a great turnout. I'm sure we raised a lot of money, which is all that matters. It's nice to think that we contributed, in some small way, to the sustainable low-income housing this benefit will help build.

I smile when I feel what I need most in the world, someone's arms wrapping around me.

I turn around. "Mama."

She leans in to embrace me. "It's wonderful to see you, dear." She sighs, pulling back. Mama is tall, taller than Daddy almost, and thin as a reed. She cuts a commanding figure, but she's all heart, and she's given her life over to making things better for those who don't have it quite so good. "Tell me, how are my grandbabies?"

I fill her in on Sophie's latest playground escapades and Seth's passionate embrace of all things automotive, and she nods, listening intently. Alice Howell is the kind of woman who could make you share your deepest, darkest secrets without even realizing you're doing it.

"Your friends seem delightful," she says, nodding in approval at the mixed-up group of people gathered around the table Mama bought. "That Daisy sure is a riot." She laughs out loud as Daisy demonstrates the Charleston to the bemused mayor's son. "And the food is divine. If this party is any indication, this business is a sure bet."

"I work with some talented ladies." I sigh. I don't want to think about work tonight. I just want to enjoy being here and not think about any of it.

"Eleanor?" Mama says sharply. "What's wrong?"

"Nothing, Mama." I shake my head.

"You can't fool me, young lady." She laughs, reaching out to touch my chin. "Is something wrong with the business?"

I know Mama better than to assume she'll just let this drop now. "It's just . . ." I look over at the table and take a deep breath. I think about how much these women, with their disparate personalities and their unique passions, have come to mean to me in the past few months. "It's just hard sometimes, you know?" She nods. "I love my job. I love doing something I'm good at, and I have this great situation where I can do it on my own terms."

"But . . . ?"

"But sometimes, it just feels like too much," I say flatly. "I'm trying to balance all this with everything at home, and Mike isn't particularly supportive about it . . ." She always does this. She has this way of making me say more than I intend to. It's some weird power my mother has over me. "And sometimes, well, sometimes I just wonder if it's all worth it." I look down at my feet, and kind of wish I could take the words back. Saying the words somehow makes the struggle real.

Mama eyes me up and down, biting the inside of her lip. She nods. "Eleanor?" I look at my mother's face, lined with years of caring about other people's problems. I look around at what she has put together tonight, and I feel a little small. Compared to the real problems in the world, my little traumas seem pretty minute. "I was a mother. That's all I was allowed to be." She takes a deep breath. "In my day, we didn't have the choices you now have. The whole world is open to you." I nod, waiting for the other shoe to drop. She closes her eyes for a second, then opens them and looks at me intently. "We've come a long way. Women have fought for centuries to have the opportunities you have before you."

I nod.

"But we're all in this together," she says. "Whether they work or stay home, every mother wants what's best for her children." I take a sip of champagne and watch her face closely. She clears her throat. "I can't tell you what to do anymore. You're a grown woman, and you need to make the choices that are right for you and your family." She takes a deep breath. "Do the work that makes you glad to be alive, or stay home with your children and enjoy every moment of their lives. It goes so fast. But whatever you decide, remember that you do have the choice, and that's a beautiful thing."

I look around the room, suddenly spinning around me. I think about Jo, and how much she has given up for this business. I see Cate, chatting comfortably with the hunk beside her, and Daisy, who loves her daughter more than life itself. I look back at Mama, who is watching me intently, and I nod.

"Sophie"—I kneel down next to my little girl and look her in the eyes—"have you seen Mommy's pretty ring?"

Sophie frowns and grabs at her overalls with both hands.

"Mommy isn't going to be mad. I just can't find it and I thought you might be able to help me. Did you try on Mommy's ring again?"

Lately Sophie has been trying on my jewelry. While she normally eschews all girly-girl things like dresses and dolls and patent leather Mary Janes, there's something about my jewelry that has captured her imagination. She's like a raccoon. If it's shiny, she's interested.

"No," Sophie says, still looking at the floor.

I sigh. "Have you played dress-up lately? I always put my ring right here on the counter and it's not there today." I gesture toward the crystal ring holder Edith gave me a few Christmases ago. I distinctly remember her words after I got it out of the Tiffany & Co. box: "I've noticed that you hardly ever wear the ring, so I thought it might be nice if you had somewhere fitting to keep it when it's not on your finger."

The ring. Never "your ring." No missing the point with that kind of subtlety.

What am I going to do if I've lost it?

"Okay," I say and stand up and smile at Sophie. "Can you help Mommy look for it?"

Sophie nods. We crawl around on the bedroom floor for a while, running our hands over the thick pile of the carpet. Maybe she'll come clean if I have her help me long enough. I stand up and begin to rifle through my drawers. Maybe it got knocked into one of them. Sophie peeks under the bed.

If she had put it on, what would she have done next? I watch her look in Mike's closet, crawling on her hands and knees, smiling. This is probably the best game she's played all day. I bite my lip. Her favorite game at the moment is Candy Land. Maybe it's in the box?

But the ring is too big for her. It would have just slipped off her finger as she walked down the stairs. I look out the door of our bedroom on the second floor. Suddenly our house feels enormous. I'll never find it. Mike is going to be so upset.

The garage door slams. "Hey, I'm home," Mike yells.

Sophie jumps up and begins to run toward the stairs to greet her father.

I catch her in the nick of time. Let's see, how do I explain this? I put my hands on her shoulders and smile a little. "Sophie, Daddy is going to be very upset that the ring is missing."

She looks down and her eyes water a little.

"So while it's never okay to lie to people, let's just not tell Daddy about it right now. We'll keep looking for it, okay?"

"Okay," she says and sneaks a look at me. I can see in her eyes that she had it. If only I could jog her memory about what happened next. We've got to find that ring.

"Just Mommy and Sophie will know. Don't worry. We'll find it."

She nods and then breaks free to run downstairs.

I should have been wearing it. Sophie never would have put it on if it had been on my finger where it belonged. True, Sophie should know better than to try on Mommy's jewelry, but that's beside the point right now. All that matters is that the ring is gone, and I have to find it before anyone finds out.

What if it's in the trash? It could have gotten thrown away so easily. I'll have to sneak out of bed tonight after Mike is asleep and go through it, piece by piece. As long as it's not in the trash, if I can just rule that out, then it's got to be in the house somewhere. I'll find it.

Daisy

I PULL INTO THE CHURCH PARKING LOT AND touch up my lipstick in the rearview mirror. It's important that I look good tonight. First of all, I hope to make some new friends at my church, and I hope I'll be able to bring some new people to the Lord as well. Pastor Martin preached up a storm this week about the body of Christ and getting involved in the church instead of just sitting in the old wooden pews like a bump on a log. And the Lord convicted me right there on the spot. I paged through my bulletin and looked at my options. There was a knitting circle, but I like shopping way too much to start making my own clothes. I briefly considered working in the church nursery, but, truthfully, I get enough time with young 'uns at work and I know Tiff wouldn't sit in that pew without me. I could join the choir, but they practice Wednesday evenings, and

Tiff's field hockey games are usually on Wednesdays. But then I saw the most perfect calling for me: the Fishing Club. Thankfully, the Fishing Club does not actually go fishing. They are fishers of men, just like Peter and Andrew in the Bible.

I circled the info in the bulletin, went home after church, and called the organizer, Wendy Garten. I love telling people about God. I think it might be just about the most fun anyone can have without chocolate. Plus, I love meeting new people. Wendy was real nice on the phone and said they were going "fishing" this Thursday if I wanted to come along. I told her yes, ma'am.

I get out of my car and straighten my top. I worked real hard on my outfit because you want to strike just the right tone when you're talking to people about the Lord. You don't want to look too rich or too cold or stuck up. You want to look fun and approachable. I finally settled on my dark fitted jeans with knee-high black leather boots and a tight pink shirt over a white tank top. But even then I still looked a little frumpy, so I made sure to wear some glittery makeup. I look ready for a night on the town, so hopefully when we break into groups and start ringing doorbells and talking to people, it will help them relate to me.

I walk into the Fellowship Hall, where Wendy told me to meet the other fishers. There are four men and five women, who are all a little older than me.

"Hey, y'all," I say and start passing out hugs all around. So what if I've never met these people? Mama always said that if you greet with a hug, then you make a friend for life.

The first person I hug is the oldest person in the group. He's got on a brown suit with little elbow patches and has a nicely manicured beard. He's cute. I should tell Lillian about him.

"I'm Daisy Johnson," I say, wrapping my arms around him. "Just started attending church about a year ago."

"I'm Butterscotch," the elderly man says, squeezing me, then pulling back.

"Butterscotch?" I wrinkle my brow.

He reaches in the pocket of his brown tweed pants and pulls out a butterscotch candy and puts it in my hand.

"Real name's Scott. You can call me Brother Scott, or, as the little ones do, Butterscotch."

I pop the candy into my mouth, wink at him, and keep moving down the line. Some of the fishers give me their names. I keep hugging around the circle.

"Whoo boy." I smile as I hug a woman many years older than me. "Were your hearts touched by the sermon that Pastor Martin gave last week or what?" Actually, as I pull back, I notice that her skin is very smooth and clear. I guess she might be close to my age. It's just hard to tell in the long floral print dress she's wearing. "I felt like he was talking straight at me," I say, moving on to the dark-haired man next to her. "So here I am. Joining the body."

The last person I go to hug is a slight woman with a lean, muscular body shoved into a khaki dress, belted at the waist. Her hair is pulled up into a tight bun. She's wearing black, lace-up ankle boots. She looks like she has been clomping around in a muddy field in one of those

Jane Austen movies I like so much. She puts out her hand to me, and I hesitate. I guess she doesn't want a hug.

I smile and stick out my hand, which she shakes perfunctorily. "I'm Wendy Garten," she says, smiling weakly. She pats her hair. "I believe we spoke on the phone?"

I smile. "It's you. Yes, I'm Daisy. Reporting for fishing duty, as promised." I salute her.

I hear a snicker and see Brother Scott laughing at my joke. I smile back at him. This is going to be fun.

"Right. So let's begin," Wendy says. I walk around the circle and link arms with Brother Scott.

"Welcome, all of you, both old members and new." Wendy levels her eyes at me. Her mouth is a thin, straight line. I sure think it might be easier to win people to the Lord with a smile, but I guess everybody has their own style. The Lord's got a place for us all.

I nod to show I'm listening. I learned that from Jo. She's always nodding like a dashboard bobblehead doll when I talk to her.

"We need to break into groups of three."

The men and women begin to scatter and re-form into small groups. I'm still holding Brother Scott's arm, but two elderly women have joined our group and both are eyeing me in an unfriendly way. I pull my arm out of his. I had forgotten how scarce single men are at their age. They must think I'm honing in on their territory. I try to give them a friendly grin, but they continue to glower at me.

"Daisy," Wendy says, looking at our group, "you seem to be the odd man out. Why don't you come over here for a minute." She gestures toward the kitchen, and I walk in that direction. "In the meantime," she says, raising her voice for the group, "here are our updated tracts for the approaching holiday season. Don't forget that this is a great angle to use since many families do attend church this time of year." Wendy hands out the tracts to each group.

She comes back to where I'm waiting, and I try to take a tract too. I need to read it. I'm so behind on all of this. But she holds her stack far out of my reach.

"Daisy, may I have a word with you in private?" She smiles sweetly.

I shrug. "Sure."

We walk a few feet away, then stop. She puts a hand on my shoulder.

"Listen, Daisy," she says, smiling. "I say this as your sister in Christ."

I smile at her. "Shoot."

She takes a deep breath. "Do you have a coat with you tonight?"

"No," I say and shrug. "I'm really hot-natured, and, let's face it, it doesn't really get that cold here. Plus, I've got boots on. That always keeps me warm. Why? Did you need to borrow one?" I could see how Wendy might be the cold-natured type. When you don't have meat on your bones you just about freeze to death most of the year.

"No. I'm afraid you're missing the point here." She purses her thin lips. "What I'm trying to say is, I don't think how you're dressed is appropriate."

Something deep inside my nose stings. I try to swallow. "How I'm dressed?"

"Yes. I know you're new to the Lord, but you need to work on your modesty."

I take a step back and then look down at my outfit. I have big boobs, and keeping them under wraps is like wrestling a greased pig. But tonight, they're pretty much tucked down into my tank top. I have pants and boots on. There's barely a square inch of me showing.

"But I . . . I thought that it might be good to look, you know, fun in order to break the ice . . ."

Wendy shakes her head slowly. "I don't mean to hurt your feelings, of course, but I can't let you go out like that. It's not fitting."

"Oh," I say, crossing my arms over my chest. Maybe I do have a coat in the car. I still really want to go tonight. I can be in Butterscotch's group. He's fun.

"I've seen you parading around church in costumes like this, and frankly, people are beginning to talk," she says, leaning in. Her mouth curls up slightly. "I'm not one to spread idle gossip, but I thought I should just be honest and tell you."

I stare at the ground for a moment. My face feels like it's burning. I didn't mean to, I thought that . . . I look back at the group in their conservative clothes and shake my head. I'm so foolish. Is the whole church talking about me? This is horrible. I can do better. I just thought . . .

"I say all of this in love, of course," she says, putting her arm around my shoulders.

"I know you do," I say, as tears begin to fill my eyes. "I'm glad you said something. That took guts."

I force myself to stop drumming my fingers on the countertop. Ever since I had my fake nails removed, it doesn't make a fun clicking sound anyways, and the Kinko's employee looks like he's going to kill me if I don't stop. I look nervously at the clock. How am I going to convince Tiffany that I'm a whole new me if I'm late like usual?

"They're almost done," the Kinko's man says.

While I was pretty hurt by Wendy's comments the other night, as I drove home it hit me. She's right. I'm a mom. I might only be thirty, but I really can't pull off certain looks anymore. It's just not fitting.

When I came home, I told Tiff I was turning over a new leaf. I didn't mention what happened at church, because that's the last thing she needs to hear, but she seemed really excited to hear that I was going to start dressing and acting like a normal mom.

My mother always seemed so much older than me. She was always mature, in control, and distant, so I tried to be the opposite. I thought I was being the kind of mom any kid would dream of, but the other night it became clear that I just looked silly. Like a circus clown. I mean, look at Dolly Parton. People love her because she's sweet and she's a great singer, but you don't catch many people admiring her fashion choices. How could I have missed that for so long?

And so, here I am, running late to pick Tiff up from field hockey practice again, waiting on her perfectly respectable printed invitations, itching like crazy in my new wool sweater. I'm wearing hose, heels, and even a strand of fake pearls. My old friends would never recognize me, but I feel good. Like a real adult.

The employee comes over with a box of invitations. "Here you are. Want to see how they turned out?" he asks.

I pull one out and smile. These are a surprise for Tiff, part of the new me. She's just going to flip when she sees them. We've never really been into formal parties. For her birthday, we usually just invite a few of her math club friends over, I rent them some movies, and we order a pizza. But she's really becoming a young lady now, and young ladies deserve real parties. Plus, I'm so proud of how well she's doing with field hockey. Sure, at first she just joined the team so that I would buy her that new Sims game, but she's finding that I was right about those genes of hers. She's even started to get some playing time during games, and she's stopped complaining about practice altogether. Her coach told me that she's a diamond in the rough.

"They're beautiful," I say, holding up the stiff, heavy white cardstock, admiring the shiny blue and gold foil lettering. Those girls are going to get a kick out of seeing their school's colors on real invitations.

I pay the man quickly and grab the box of invitations. If I hurry and don't hit any traffic on the way to her school, I just might not be late at all.

———

I wait by the fence with the rest of the moms, making small talk. Usually I miss this part of things because I'm almost always half an hour late, but not today. We wait together for what seems like an eternity, peering through a chain-link fence at the girls. They're in some kind of huddle at the moment. All the moms are talking about their Sausage Egg Casserole recipes for Christmas Day brunch. Finally, the coach stops gabbing at the girls, and they begin to make their way across the field. Tiff walks with another small girl out in front, and most of the team trails behind them.

As she approaches, I wave calmly at her with the box of invitations tucked under one arm. I wish we were celebrating her birthday, but that was two months ago. Hopefully the big game against their rivals across town is a good enough reason to throw a party.

"Hi, Tiffany," I say, using her whole name so that I seem more, I don't know, fancy.

Tiff stops dead still and stares at me. And then, ever so slowly, she smiles. A little. My heart soars.

"Hey." She begins to walk toward our car. "See ya, Beth," she says over her shoulder at the small girl. The girl nods. She has the cutest freckles.

"Oh, honey." I hold my hand out in front of me. "Wait just a moment."

She stops and looks at me, narrowing her eyes suspiciously. I take out the first invitation and hand it to the small girl she walked over with.

"Beth?" I ask.

The shy redhead nods.

"I'm Daisy, um, Ms. Johnson. I'm Ms. Johnson, Tiff's mom."

Tiff walks back over to us and stares at me. I sure hope she's happy about this surprise. I worked so hard on it.

"Tiff and I are throwing a party next week. That's the invitation," I say. "There's going to be food and music and . . ."

I look at Tiff. I'm not exactly sure what she'll want at the party. I think games must be lame by age fourteen.

"What are you talking about?" Tiff asks in her usual blunt way, but her smooth brow shows me she is confused, not angry.

"Surprise," I say, shrugging my shoulders. "I thought it might be nice to have everyone over."

The rest of the team is filing off the field, and I hand out the invitations to them and their moms, making sure that the whole team knows they are invited and that the moms know it will be a chaperoned, all-girl party. Tiff and I are not here to make enemies. We're here to become a part of the tribe.

As the girls study their invitations, I steal a glance at Tiff. Her cheeks are burning red. Oh. I hope I'm doing the right thing.

"Thank you so much, Ms. Johnson. I'd love to come. I'm Angie," a tall blond girl says, shaking my hand.

I nearly melt with relief. Angie seems to be the ringleader. Angie's mother beams at her. What a good kid. So well turned out.

"Well, we'd love to have you. All of you. It's going to be so fun." I smile at them, and a few smile back.

I step toward the car and watch the girls react to the news. Soon, the team is all standing around, talking about the big party, and even Tiff is offering up the occasional comment. I'm so happy, I could die a contented woman. I smile at the other moms. Since the school is associated with our church, I've seen many of their faces, but I've never tried to reach out before. Maybe the JV field hockey team is our chance to make it work.

"Bye, Ms. Johnson," Angie says, walking toward her mom's forest green Escalade. "Bye, Tiffany. Thanks so much for the invite." At her cue, Morgan and Sydney follow, and they all tell Tiff that they'll see her at the party. Tiff smiles at them shyly and waves as they go.

When no one is left, Tiff and I start walking to our red Camry in silence. I don't dare speak first. I fasten my seat belt carefully and turn the engine on. I'll have to wait for her to crack and tell me how she's feeling. I glance at her as I pull the car out of the parking lot, but she won't look at me, so we drive in silence too. The air smells clean and fresh through the open windows as we drive along the highway toward home. It's not until I'm done parking the car in the underground garage and we get into the elevator that she speaks.

"I like your sweater," she says, her eyes fastened on the tile floor.

I shut my eyes and say a little prayer of thanks as the doors slide closed.

It was during the prayer time that I first noticed it. I know you're supposed to keep your eyes closed when you're praying, but I think God hears you no matter what your eyes are doing. And the pastor was going on and on, so I looked around a little bit. So sue me. And while I was peeking, I saw the blond guy looking at Cate. I swear it. I recognized him. He was here last time.

Then I saw him making eyes at her at the coffee hour. Now, I'm not really one to push other people into things they don't want, but I know what those looks mean. And I know Cate needs a distraction from "Mincemeat," or, as she calls him, David. So who can blame me for casually saunter-ing over to him while Cate and Beatriz were dissecting the latest episode of *The Office* over coffee. I just introduced my-self and said I had someone I thought he should meet. Come to find out, they already know each other. The way Cate blushed when she shook James's hand, I knew I was right. The sparks were flying so fast the whole place would have caught on fire if Franny hadn't pulled Cate away to help tear down the music equipment. So I set it up.

But now, as Cate and I drive back to her house for mulled wine and gingerbread cookies, I'm hesitating a bit to tell her all about it. She chats happily about her decorat-ing side project as she steers her car toward East Atlanta. I wait until she takes a break to change the radio station.

"Cate?" I take a deep breath.

She turns to me, her face illuminated by the green glow of the dashboard. She slows for a red light. "Huh?" She looks back at the road.

"What . . . what do you think of that blond guy James?" I watch her reaction carefully, but her expression doesn't change. She shrugs.

"He seems nice." The light turns green, and she presses her foot down on the accelerator. "Actually"—she glances at me and breaks into a smile—"he's about your age. From what I can tell, he seems pretty laid-back. I bet you two would get along just fine." She winks at me, and I finally see what she's getting at.

"N . . . no," I stutter. "I mean, yes, I'm sure we would. But I'm asking, well, not for me." I swallow. "Girl, he's got it for you. I saw that plain as day tonight."

She laughs, then flicks her left blinker on and makes a smooth turn. "No, he doesn't, Dais—"

"And, well," I continue, ignoring her protest, "I talked to him after the service. He said you'd met on your job site, and he seemed really interested in getting to know you. And I just thought . . ." I lose my nerve for a moment.

She glares at the road, unable to glare at me. "Tell me you didn't, Daisy."

"So we're on for Friday night," I say quickly. Whew. Just lay it out on the table.

"What? Who is?" she says loudly, turning onto the highway on-ramp.

Oh, Lord. She's driving faster. "You and me." I smile. "And, James," I say, opening my eyes wide to look as innocent as possible: "And his friend. Um, Bert?" I nod.

"What?!" Cate says, pressing her foot farther down on the pedal.

"It'll be fun." I laugh. "Just four crazy kids out on a Friday night." I punch her on the arm lightly, but she doesn't look at me.

"First of all," she says, taking a deep breath, "his friend's name is Brett." She flicks her eyes at the rearview mirror, then pulls into the left lane. "Secondly, this sounds a lot like a double date."

She is as stubborn as a mule. Can't she see this is for her own good? "Well, that's kind of what it is, I guess."

Cate lets out a long breath. "That's sweet of you. But I'm kind of going out with David again." She mumbles this last part, as if she has marbles in her mouth. "And I don't think he'd be very happy—"

"Dave the Plague?" I roll my eyes. "If he's so great, where is he? Why isn't he at church with us?"

"He had work to catch up on," she says. "Besides, he went this morning—"

This is just ridiculous. I don't even wait for her to finish. It's time for more aggressive maneuvers. Mama used to say that a real Southern lady always gets her way, one way or the other. "But Cate," I say, trying to make my voice sound a bit scolding. "These are our brothers in Christ." I can see she's not buying it. I crank it up a notch. "We'll just have dinner with them. I already arranged it. We can't let our fellow believers down." She is shaking her head. "Come on," I say, reaching for the radio. I press the seek button, trying to distract her. "Don't you think James is cute? He's like a young

Laurence Olivier." She doesn't look up from the road. I stop at a Kelly Clarkson song and turn the volume up. Oh, good. It's "Since U Been Gone." I sing the lyrics, hoping Cate will hear what Kelly's saying. She's making a good point.

"I'm not going on a double date," she says simply.

Oh, dear. Time to bring out the big guns.

"It's been a long time since I've been out with a man I found even remotely attractive," I say, simultaneously praying for my own soul. "But Brett . . . really. . . . seems to get it," I say. She turns her head to look at me, then turns quickly back to the road.

"Cate?" I think she's buying it. Would tears be too much? Probably. I swallow and take a deep breath instead. "Would you do it for me? Please?"

She's caving. Her shoulders are starting to slump, and she's leaning forward toward the wheel. She looks at me, the corners of her lips turning up a bit.

"Fine." She sighs. "I'll do it for you. But you two better fall hopelessly in love."

"I hear them weddin' bells aringin'," I say and smile. I do hear the bells, but they aren't ringing for me. This will all be a funny story someday when Cate and James tie the knot.

I hold out until the waiter takes our order, then I put my plan into action. Cate will not leave here without having a good time. She has been sullen and withdrawn all night, but I will not let her ruin her chance at happiness with a man who really likes her, with a man who would not treat her like that cretin David does.

"So, James, what is it that you do?" I ask sweetly, smiling at the man at Cate's side. His blue eyes sparkle, and his curly blond hair falls over his smooth tan forehead. His gray sweater hugs his chest perfectly. Oh, boy. He's a cutie. If Cate doesn't go for this one, I might have to do it myself. I shove a piece of bread into my mouth to keep my tongue occupied. I learned long ago that the best way to make a guy like you is to get him to talk about himself. I half-listen as he explains the ins and outs of the contracting business, but mostly I watch Cate from across the table.

Her face is in profile, politely turned toward James as he talks, but her eyes are far away. There's something else on her mind, something that begins with a *D* and ends with a . . . well, a *D*.

"And how did you get into the business?" I reach for another piece of bread and smear butter across the surface. James lights up as he talks about taking over his father's business. Cate smiles and rests her chin on her hand, looking just past him.

Brett tops off my wineglass, then pours a bit more for himself. He smiles at me shyly. He's kind of cute, actually. His face is long and narrow, but his light brown hair, well, what's left of it, is cut stylishly short and his striped button-down is pressed. He's a schoolteacher, as it turns out. That's cute. Too bad he's so young, and, well, formal. He sure seems sweet.

"So after the summer with Habitat for Humanity"—

James shrugs—"I knew I not only could manage a building project, but I liked it." He smiles at Cate.

"Cate"—I seize on the moment—"you did some work with them, didn't you?" She shoots me a look, then talks for a few seconds about her Habitat volunteer work. In the silence that follows, James takes a sip of wine and looks down at his plate. I look down at my lap. My new skirt is covering my knees demurely. Tiff would be so proud.

"And how did you end up going into decorating, Cate?" I ask quickly. James looks at me gratefully, and Cate rolls her eyes at me. She talks for a minute about loving decorating shows on TV as a child and always knowing it was what she wanted to do, then the table falls silent again. Brett starts looking around to see if the waiter is coming.

"Well," I say, placing my napkin on the table, "I need to find the little girls' room. Cate, do you want to come with me?"

"I'm fine." She grabs a roll and examines it.

"I could really use your help," I say, shifting my weight to my other foot. These heels may not be as high as the stilettos I used to wear, but the cute shoes never are comfortable, are they? "I think I'm having a wardrobe malfunction," I say and laugh.

She sighs and puts her napkin on the table, standing up slowly.

I weave my way through the crowded dining room, carefully avoiding the sharp corners of the white-covered tables, and push the heavy wooden door open. Cate follows me into the bathroom and watches me. I take a quick peek under the stalls and smile to indicate there are no feet. We're alone.

"What's wrong?" I put a hand on her shoulder.

She shakes her head.

"Did James do something?" I try to read her face, but she looks at her reflection in the mirror and begins to smooth her hair. "Did I do something wrong?" I ask. Our eyes meet in the mirror.

She crosses her arms over her chest. "You don't even like Brett."

"Why, I . . ." I see her nod, and I know it's not worth pretending. She knows why I really brought her here, and she's not happy about it.

"James likes you," I say, but she turns away from the mirror and faces me.

"I told you I was back with David." I turn to look at her. "Why would you try to set me up when I'm not available?"

I take a deep breath. "Honey, this is an intervention. David is no good for you. You said so yourself a few months ago," I say, reaching out to touch her arm. She pulls it away. "I know you love him, but you've got to get yourself away from him." I've got to convince her I'm right. "After the way he treated you, he doesn't deserve you."

"David is a good man," she says.

"But you said yourself that he never called when he said he would, and he forgot your birthday. Cate, he made you wait all those years, and then he left. Remember? Trust me on this one, honey. If he treated you badly before, he'll do it again. The leopard don't change his spots."

"I shouldn't have said all those things. It wasn't fair to David. And it's not fair of you to bring them up now."

"I . . ." I stumble for words. Wait. Isn't it fair? She was the one who taught me to hate him. "I want you to be happy more than anything. That's why I want you to stay away from him."

She purses her lips. "I love David. And this feels so right. He thinks so. I think so. God told him so. So whether you like him or not, we're together now." She leans in to the mirror and squints at her reflection.

And then I've had it. I guess it's just the mom in me, but I just can't stand here and let her give up on herself. "You have to stop loving him, Cate. He's bad news."

"I can't," she says, throwing her hands up in the air. "So let it go. I love him. I can't stop. Can't you see, Daisy? I'm the deer."

"What?" I study her face.

"I'm the deer. I hate change. I stay where I'm comfortable and when I do try something new I get hit by a car. I'm the deer. I'm going back to David. He makes me happy most of the time. That's enough for me."

My heart breaks. How do you help someone who doesn't want help? Happy most of the time just isn't enough. "Cate—"

"And I'm quitting Jelly Jar. I decided last night."

My head snaps up at her. "What?!"

"I—" She looks down at her feet. "This whole adventure was all wrong."

"You can't quit. We need you. You're one of us," I say, but I can see that she is serious.

"I'm sorry, Daisy," she says. "I've already made up my mind. And please, don't tell anyone yet. I want to do it myself. I'm going to call Jo this week and schedule a time to chat."

"But . . ." I say and then my voice fails. This can't be happening.

Cate looks at me and frowns. She turns and slowly walks out of the bathroom. I watch the door shut, and I am alone again.

We spent all day cleaning, and the apartment is spick-and-span. I laid out bowls of chips and dip and buckets of soda all over the ground floor. The kids can just wander around, and anywhere they go, there'll be snacks at their fingertips. I lit the special lavender candles that Tiff likes so much, and she helped me pick out some chick flicks in case the girls just want to chill. I look around and smile. It's all ready and with five minutes to spare. I just have to sit back and enjoy the party. It feels nice not to have to do a lot of work setting up for once. I sit on one of the kitchen stools and pour myself a Diet Coke.

I look up when I hear footsteps on the stairs. Tiff is holding on to the handrail carefully as she walks down in my red heels. Can you believe the kid wears the same size shoes I do at fourteen? But, then, her dad was tall. She finally stomps onto the ground floor, and I start to clap. She looks darling. She's wearing a new pair of jeans, low-slung and form-fitting, and a red knit shirt she picked out herself in Macy's.

"You look great," I squeal and wave her over to me. She blushes, but obediently stands near me. I can see she's wearing mascara and a hint of blush. I pull her into a hug and rest my chin on her shoulder. She's growing up so fast. My little baby is turning into a woman. Her first high school party.

The doorbell rings. "Seven on the dot." I laugh. Her shoulders tense up, but I nod at her. "Go get your first guest," I say, scrunching up my shoulders. She takes a deep breath, bobs her head, then walks slowly to the door.

I hear squealing, and a few minutes later she ushers cute little red-haired Beth into the kitchen.

"Hey, honey," I say, getting up. I wrap Beth in a big hug, then let go and hand her the bowl of pretzels.

"Thank you," she says quietly. Such good manners. I knew field hockey would be a good place to meet friends. That's why I insisted on Covenant in the first place. I wanted Tiff to be around good Christian girls and make good Christian friends.

"Would you like a Coke?" Tiff asks, gesturing toward the ice-filled bin on the table. I melt with motherly pride. My daughter has good manners too!

Tiff gets Beth a glass and fills it with ice, and the two

chat comfortably about their big game next week. Beth played field hockey in junior high, so she knows some of the girls on the opposing team, and she gives Tiff the rundown of the players. Tiff listens closely, but I can't help but notice that she keeps looking toward the door.

There's a lull in the conversation. "So what subjects are you taking, Beth?" I ask quickly. The other girls will be here any minute. I bet there's traffic tonight. With the holidays so soon, everyone is on their way to Christmas parties and out visiting family. Beth begins to talk about her biology class, where they will soon have to dissect a frog. Tiff listens carefully, but her fingers toy with the phone. She tosses a few chips into her mouth and munches on them. I smile at her.

The doorbell rings. I let out a long breath as she jumps up from her chair to answer the door. Finally. I should have known they would be fashionably late. Girls these days are smarter about this kind of stuff than I ever was. I listen for squealing, but all I can hear is some low mumbling. Beth and I look at each other and wait. A few minutes later, Tiff comes back into the kitchen carrying five pizza boxes, stacked on top of one another.

"He said the total is $42.97," she says quietly. I nod, then walk to the door, hand the delivery guy a fifty, and close the door quietly. I peer out the front window. There are cars coming and going on the street down below, but, then, there are a lot of people who live in this complex. It's only 7:35. I walk back to the kitchen, where the girls sit silently.

"Well, now," I say loudly, smiling. "Let's not let the pizza get cold. Grab a plate." I gesture to the red plastic plates on the table. "We have two pepperoni, one sausage, one plain, and one combo. Dig in while it's hot." Tiff watches me. "There'll be plenty left for the other girls," I say. They nod, then fill up their plates.

We chat about school some more, then I grill Beth on her favorite movies, and we laugh. I help myself to seconds on the combo, and try to keep the conversation going. Beth chats easily, but as the conversation wears on, I notice Tiff getting quieter. Where are those girls? They all said they would come.

"Do you want to pet my rat?" Tiff asks, sitting up straight.

"Uh . . ." Beth looks from Tiff's excited face to mine, and I smile encouragingly at her, then try to catch Tiff's eye. Her math friends don't seem to mind Archimedes, but I should have warned her that not everyone loves vermin. "Not really." She shakes her head, her face a little sad. Tiff looks confused, but thankfully the phone rings, and Tiff grabs it.

"Hello?" she says excitedly. Watching her face fall, I think my heart just might break. "It's for you," she whispers. "It's Jo."

I take the phone and sigh, then walk into the living room to talk. Jo wants to discuss the cake options for the upcoming wedding we're catering, but I tell her I'll have to call her back. I get rid of her as quickly as I can, and I walk back into the kitchen. The girls are silently eating the now-cold pizza.

"Hon, maybe you two could watch a movie?" I say brightly. Tiff looks at me and nods, trying to smile.

"Actually, Mrs. Johnson," Beth says quietly. It still cracks me up that kids always call grown-up women "Mrs.," married or not. "My mom is coming to pick me up at nine." I look at the clock. It's 8:45. "We have church in the morning."

"Oh. Okay." I try to smile, but I can't quite bring myself to do it. "Then we'd better get started on the cake while we can." She smiles at me, and follows me into the kitchen. Tiff doesn't come after us, but I suspect she wants a few moments alone. I take the full sheet cake out of the fridge and place it on the counter carefully. It says "Go Trojans!" and has a picture of their school mascot on it. I made it with chocolate cream filling, Tiff's favorite. It's enough to feed a hundred people. I cut three slices and hand one to Beth, who reaches for it.

The doorbell rings. My heart stops. They're finally here! Tiff seems to want to stay in the living room, so I walk to the door to great her guests.

"Hey, y'all," I say as I pull the door open. Beth's mother smiles and laughs good-naturedly.

"I'm here to tear Beth away from the fun," she says. She looks a bit confused as she steps into the hall and takes in the quiet apartment, but she smiles anyway. I turn to see Beth walking toward her mother.

"I said good-bye to Tiffany," she says, looking at me apologetically.

"Okay." I glue a smile to my face. "Thanks so much for coming. We'll see you on Monday."

I smile as they walk out the door, and I close it behind them.

I lean my back against the door as a tear begins to leak out of my eye. How could those ungrateful little girls say they were coming and then not appear? They could have at least made an excuse so that we weren't expecting them. I take a deep breath. I need to pull myself together for Tiff. I wipe the tear away and wave some cool air at my face. Once I feel composed, I go to find her.

When I walk into the living room, I find Tiff lying facedown on the couch, crying quietly. I sit on the edge of the cushion, but she doesn't move. I rub her hair for a few minutes, but she won't even acknowledge me. I turn on Animal Planet, hoping to cheer her up. Richard Simmons jumps up onto the couch to nuzzle her, and we stay there, silently.

We're still lying in my bed when Lillian comes to get us for church the next morning. We haven't showered, and our hair is greasy. The kitchen still has five boxes of pizza sitting out and bowls of snack food are scattered all over the apartment.

"Yoo-hoo," she sings, wandering through the apartment looking for us.

"We're up here," I yell weakly. She follows the sound up the stairs.

"Hey, sleepyheads," she says, the bird on her turquoise hat bobbing. "You're going to be late for church."

I push myself up on my arms, and Tiff pulls the blanket over her head. I see makeup smears on her pillowcase and my heart sinks, thinking back to last night.

"Oh, honey," I say, biting my lip. "You go on without us today. We had a little—" I hesitate for a moment, worrying about upsetting Tiff further. "We had one of Tiff's friends over last night and, well, as you can see, we stayed up pretty late. We'll go next week."

Lillian looks around the apartment nervously and then curls up the corners of her mouth. "I'm so glad you two are kicking up your heels a little."

I nod, wearily. I really don't know what I'll tell this sweet lady next week. She's great, but the rest of that church is shallow and mean-spirited.

"Okay, well, there's no rule you have to go every week. You two girls have a wonderful relaxing morning."

"Have fun."

Lillian nods. "I'll just let myself out. See you next Sunday, if not before."

"Okay," I say. "See you then." But even as the words come out, I'm already making plans to be out of town next weekend. We're not going back there.

Jo

~~~~~~

MY HEART SINKS WHEN I SEE THAT ALL THE good greenery at Michael's has already been taken. I should have gotten here weeks ago. I've been living in Atlanta long enough to know that the only Michael's in the metropolitan area will be picked clean by the week before Christmas. I pick up an emaciated sprig of faux pine and sigh.

This morning when Gerard suggested that maybe this year I didn't have to make my own wreaths for Christmas, I gave him a withering look. At the rate I'm going, I'm going to drive my husband away, while losing my business *and* letting my family go to rot. I shut my eyes tight and try to center myself. No more destructive thoughts. No more destructive thoughts. Lately, I feel so close to going over the edge, to really, actually, and finally losing it, that it's frightening.

After a moment or two, I open my eyes and look at the piece of greenery in my hand. It doesn't look so pathetic anymore. I can make this work. I'm practically a wizard with wreaths. And this morning I read an article in the *Atlanta Journal-Constitution* that said that those struggling with depression heal much faster if they force themselves to put a smile on their face as much as possible, whether they feel like smiling or not. I grimace and slowly but surely force a smile out of my poor, bedraggled body.

I begin to peruse the giant wall of craft materials with a big, slaphappy grin on my face, trying to come up with a vision. Last year I worked little silver picture frames with shots of our immediate and extended family into the wreaths, and they looked gorgeous. I need some kind of inspiration this year. I spy some nice silk oak leaves and grab them off the wall before someone else does. Oh, and I need to remember to get some metallic gold and silver spray paint. I'm out of those at the moment.

As I continue to walk down the wall, though, my thoughts go back to Gerard. He meant well by saying I should skip making the wreaths. He knows how stressed I am about the business. He's such a light sleeper that he hears me slip from our bed and go downstairs to read until dawn. I haven't had a good night's rest in weeks and weeks. And this is exactly why he wants me to take it easy this year for the holidays. I understand that. But what he doesn't see is that this is exactly why I have to do every- thing the way I always have. I need to make the wreaths, I need to pretend that I am still together, I need to distract myself from the fact that my business is failing. My fake

smile fades when my mind feeds me the word *failing*. I
never fail. I've had setbacks, sure. I was practically jilted at
the altar, for crying out loud, but this is different. This was
my responsibility, and I failed those women. I failed my
friends. How will I tell them? And what about me? I simply can't lose this.

I spy the most gorgeous little red berries that might be
just the thing, but there's only one cluster left. I reach for
them quickly, but as I do I see another hand going for
them and stop.

Startled out of my thoughts, I turn to the left to size
the person up.

"Oh!" Cate says.

"Cate. My goodness!"

We both stare at each other for a moment, then put
our hands down and laugh. I try not to sound too forced.
I worry that my fears about the company are written all
over my face. Cate is the last person I want to see today.

"Just buying materials to make wreaths for the house,"
I say, gesturing at my shopping cart. "Better late than
never, I say." I paste a smile on my face and try to play this
off as some kind of great joke, but Cate's an interior decorator. I'm sure her place has been decorated for Christmas
since December 1.

"Impressive," Cate says and then moves to stand in
front of her cart. "Sounds like you need the berries more
than I do, so why don't you take them." She pulls them
down and hands them to me.

I wave my hands in front of my body. "Oh, no. I
couldn't. You must need them for . . ." I trail off and try to

peer into her cart behind her body. If I didn't know any better, I'd swear that she was trying to hide the contents of her cart. But what could she possibly buy at Michael's that would be embarrassing?

She coughs for a moment and stares at the berries. "No," she says and bites her lip. "I'm just doing a little project for an old friend. Some . . . staging. I don't really need them. It's not important."

I cock my head at her. "Staging?" I didn't know Cate was into drama.

"It's the latest thing," she says and rolls her eyes. "I do it for my ex-employer. Basically, they've found that empty apartments don't sell well. It's my job to 'stage' a potential home so that the people can imagine how it will look once they move all their stuff inside."

I smooth the wrinkles out of my wool slacks.

"It's so stupid, of course." Cate laughs. "I mean, unless they hire a professional decorator to help them, it will never look that good once they move in. It's all about the dream, I guess."

I laugh a little, going along with what she's saying. "Oh," I say. My mind is blank.

Cate seems to sense my awkwardness and coughs. "I'm only doing it right now, of course . . . when things are a little slow at Jelly Jar."

"Right," I say and nod, smiling, but my heart sinks to hear her say what we all know. We are a little slow right now, and it's the prime party season. I blink back tears of frustration. "Well, good for you. I'm glad to hear it."

Cate looks at the floor. "I've actually been meaning

to"—she tosses the berries into my shopping cart—"call you. I was wondering if we could talk sometime."

I look up at her and try to read her face, but she's still looking at the ground like Martha does when she's trying to tell me she did something wrong.

"We certainly could," I say and then clear my throat. "Just say wh—"

"Let's just talk at the meeting," she says, all of a sudden, and smiles up at me again. "It's no big deal, really."

"Are you sure?"

"Absolutely," she says, and then makes a big production of looking at her watch. "Oh, gosh. I'm running so late. Would you forgive me," she says, turning around, "if I dashed off?" she finishes over her shoulder.

She's already halfway down the aisle when I say, "I'd forgive you."

"Jo?"

I jump. I've been slaving over the accounting spreadsheets on the computer at Jelly Jar for two hours now, and I had forgotten that other people existed. I turn and see Ellie coming through the door, with Seth and Sophie trailing behind her. She flips on a light and points to a corner of the room, where the twins obediently sit down and flip open a portable DVD player. What a brilliant invention. I hear the first strains of "When You Wish upon a Star" and know they're set for the next two hours. Lauren called in sick today so I took my girls to Mother's.

"Do you always work in the dark?"

"No." I look back at the screen. There's no time to explain that when I came in at four o'clock light was still streaming in through the windows and that I was so busy I didn't even notice the sun had set. I need to keep working. The Jelly Jar meeting starts in fifteen minutes, and I've got to think of a way to tell them the horrible news.

"I'm sorry, Ellie. I'm almost done over here. I'm just hurrying to finish before the meeting begins. I've got a new packet for everyone with the latest reports."

Ellie nods, then starts to put on a pot of coffee. "I got a call from Cate," she says, filling the basket with coffee grounds. "She's sick, so she won't be in today."

"Sick?" I turn away from the computer and stare at Ellie. "But I saw her this morning. She seemed fine."

"I don't know." Ellie shrugs. "That's what she said. Maybe she has what Lauren's got? Something's going around." She pours water into the back of the coffeepot and shakes her head. "Cate wouldn't say that if it weren't true. You want to give her a call?" She picks up the handset to the company phone and holds it out to me.

"No," I say, shaking my head. "You're right. She wouldn't just make it up. She's serious about this," I say, as if saying the words will make them true. "She probably came down with something this afternoon."

"I'm sure that's what it is." Ellie nods. We both look up as the front door opens and Daisy . . . well, I think it's Daisy . . . walks in.

"Hey y'all," Daisy says, waving as she closes the door

behind her. I do a double take. She looks totally bizarre. She's wearing a crisp white collared shirt, an argyle sweater vest, and conservative brown slacks. Her hair is pulled up in a bun.

"Daisy?" I ask, warily. Did she hit her head or something?

"What?"

"Is that you?"

She turns around very slowly so that we can feast our eyes on her ensemble. I always thought I'd be excited to see my colleague wear conservative attire, but seeing Daisy like this makes me feel uncomfortable. She looks like . . . just anybody now.

"Whadaya think?" she asks.

I shrug and mumble. Ellie watches silently.

"I went shopping at the Loft. There's one right near my apartment in the little shopping center. Nice, huh?"

I frown. "But why? I never minded your clothes before." But even as I say it, I know I'm lying a little. The truth is, though, I've become used to her attire and even fond of it in a way. It made Daisy unique. We've got enough people in the world who shop at the Loft.

Daisy cocks a brow at me. "C'mon, Jo. You know you did, just a little."

I shrug. "Maybe. But this just doesn't look like you."

Daisy looks at Ellie.

"I agree." Ellie scrunches up her nose as an apology. "You're still young, girl."

Daisy bites her lip, and her eyes water a little. I leave

the computer, and we all sit down at the table. The Jelly Jar meeting is now in progress.

Daisy sniffles quietly for a moment and then finally says through tears, "My church doesn't like me."

I take her hand and pat it. I don't doubt this is true, actually. I know her church well. There are some amazing people there, but it's also the kind of place where you have to keep up with the Joneses. It's not exactly the most welcoming place for someone like Daisy. "Well, so what?"

Daisy steals a look at Ellie, and then looks at the table again. "Where's Cate?" she asks quietly.

"Sick." I want to ask if Daisy knows anything about Cate's sudden illness, but I bite my tongue. Now is not the time.

Daisy shakes her head.

"Any church that doesn't love you the way you are," Ellie says, handing Daisy a tissue, "isn't worth bothering with."

I look at Ellie. Do they go to church? Mike used to be very earnest in his faith, and I suppose I've wondered where he was now with God.

I smile at Daisy. "I just want you to know that at least at Jelly Jar, you should wear whatever makes you comfortable. I left the corporate world to get away from all those suits and heels."

Ellie snorts a little and tries to stifle a laugh. I look at her, confused. Daisy chuckles a little.

"What? What's so funny?"

"Jo," Ellie says, "you love suits. Look at what you're wearing today."

"This is not a suit," I say. "It's just a blazer and some . . ." I look down at my khakis. "Just some old chinos that I wear around the house."

Daisy cocks her head at me. "You wear chinos around the house?"

"Well, what do you wear?" I raise an eyebrow at her.

"Sweatpants," she says, and Ellie gives her a high five. I shudder. I don't own a single pair of sweatpants. I feel my face growing hot. I know they're just teasing me, but it still stings a bit.

"Okay, fine. I like to dress up." I shrug. "But that doesn't mean Daisy should have to."

Ellie nudges me. "I think that means all the more coming from Jo." I look up at Ellie and smile.

Ellie holds a finger in the air and proclaims, "Daisy, there is no such thing as 'a work-appropriate outfit' at Jelly Jar." She laughs. "God gave us hips, butts, and bags under our eyes. Whatever you need to do to work it, go for it."

"You're right," Daisy says, pumping her fist in the air. "You're so right. Since when do I care what people think of how I dress? Dolly would never give in like that. I don't know how I lost my way there for a while." She bounces up from her chair and starts taking off her sweater vest. "I guess when you're getting a message from your church, it's easy to assume it's from the Lord." She undoes a few buttons at the bottom of her conservative, collared shirt and ties the little tails into a knot at her stomach. Then she pulls the hair-tie off her bun, and her wild curls come tumbling down. "Man, that feels good."

I dig in my purse and find a tube of lipstick that Mother gave me. It's a horrid fire-engine-red color that I would never wear, but it's perfect for Daisy. "And now for the final touch," I say and hand it to her.

Daisy slicks it on her lips and looks like her old self again.

"Glad to have you back. Now, just five more minutes to finish up some stuff, and I'll be with you guys."

They nod and begin to discuss the menu for a couple of upcoming gigs. I slip away from the table while they talk. From the beginning, Ellie and I agreed that I would handle the business side of things and she would handle the cooking side of things. She's held up her end of the deal, but I haven't. I've failed them, and today I have to come clean.

I sit down at the computer. Overhauling the building cost more than I had budgeted, but that's a sunk cost. That doesn't explain why each month I'm dipping further and further into the money Ellie and I invested to pay everyone's salaries and the bills. I knew it would be tough the first year to make ends meet, but I thought our initial capital, plus the loan I took out, would have lasted longer to help us stay afloat until we got the formula just right. Charge too much, and no one will use you. Charge too little, and you don't make any profit. And now our prices are competitive with other caterers around town, maybe even a little higher, but we're still not making any money. I just don't get it. I've been through the spreadsheets hundreds of times, and I don't see where I could be wrong. We're just going to have to face it. We've started a business that is fun, woman-friendly, and provides a great service, but doesn't make money. It doesn't even break even.

I look over my memo to my colleagues, explaining that we have only three months left at Jelly Jar and then we'll have to shut our doors forever and liquidate what we can. I take full responsibility. I'm supposed to be the expert on this kind of thing. All those years at the bank helping small businesspeople get loans, I got so good at spotting the holes in their business plans, I began to believe that if I opened a company, it would be different. It'd be a breeze. How arrogant I was.

I listen to Daisy and Ellie hammering out the menu for a wedding we have scheduled. They've become so important to me now. How can I tell Ellie that we lost all that money she invested, money she could have put aside for the twins? What about Daisy? This job meant that she could see her daughter more. Now she'll have to go back to long hours at a restaurant, working nights and weekends. And Cate? I feel her pulling away, but somehow I feel like she needs us as much as we need her.

With my finger poised on the print button, I bite my lip. Maybe I can get Gerard to look at the books. Maybe his fresh eyes will spot the problem. I just can't tell them today. They're too happy. Besides, I can't do this without Cate. It isn't fair. I'll just figure something out. I've come through worse scrapes than this. I can do it.

I close the document hastily and open up some inconsequential files I have been working on. New restaurant and catering statutes from the state of Georgia. An updated list of our clients and some potential new marketing ideas. The cost breakdown of advertising in the different local papers. And, finally, a typed copy of "The Rules." I add a new rule at the bottom and begin printing the papers. Then I staple each packet and walk back to join the others.

Ellie flips through the packet quickly, but it's Daisy who notices what I've done. "Love the new rule." She winks.

Ellie flips to the last page and laughs as she reads, "There is no such thing as a 'work-appropriate' outfit. God gave us hips, butts, and bags under our eyes. Whatever you need to do to work it, go for it."

"I love this place," Daisy says.

As I park the car, I steel myself for this little adventure. Santa arrived at the Lenox Square Mall via parachute this year, and the girls won't let me forget that I promised we could go and watch him land but then had to cancel thanks to a clogged sink at Jelly Jar. The plumber had to come take a look at it. Again. So, like it or not, we are going to fight the crowds today, a Saturday afternoon of all things, and go see Santa. It's going to be a madhouse in there.

"Santa, Santa, Santa, Santoob, Santu, Wabu," Agnes sings. Lately she likes to say words over and over again, trying out different sounds and permutations.

Martha shushes her sister.

"Santa is a stinky bear," Agnes says, undaunted.

Okay, I understand where she got the word *stinky*. She learned it from Martha. It's one of the few negative words that Gerard and I allow, but I don't understand the "stinky bear" part. She's been saying it for weeks. Three is such a funny age. Not a kid yet. Not a baby anymore.

"Mommy," Martha asks, "how can Santa be in the mall? Shouldn't he be working on the toys in the North Pole?" Now that Martha's five she's so aware of the world around her that it's almost frightening. Whenever she sees a commercial she says, "Oh, Mommy, we should buy that!" It's made us be more careful about what we say in front of her. She's such a little sponge.

"Um." I hesitate and look at Mother in the passenger seat. I confess, I'm bad at this part of motherhood. I'm just not the creative type. My impulse is to just tell her the truth about Santa right here and now.

"Well, what do you think he's got all those elves for?" Mother asks Martha.

Martha puzzles over this for a moment.

When Mother first asked to come today, I told her no. I mean, what kind of mother can't handle taking her kids to see Santa alone? But Mother kept nagging, harping on my need to do everything. Finally, I relented to get her to shut up. Maybe she's right. Apparently I can't do it all. I'm a mommy failure.

Mother hops out of the passenger side of the van and opens the sliding door on Martha's side. "The elves are working on the toys while Santa travels around the world, finding out what everyone wants." I open Agnes's door and smile at Mother, thankful for her save.

"Ooooh," Martha says, grasping the infrastructure of Santa's little world.

I'll bet Santa doesn't even pay those little elves over-time, I think, as I unclip Agnes from her car seat and Mother helps Martha down. Martha insists on unhooking the straps of her own booster seat now.

"Mommy," Agnes says, tugging on my hand, "Santa is a stinky bear."

"Hmmm," I say. I know I should be thankful that she's trying out complete sentences, but how does one respond to that? "I see."

"Mommy?" I pray this question is an easy one. "Is Mrs. Santa Claus going to be there?"

We begin strolling across the parking lot, making our way to the mall, while I explain that Santa Claus is a very independent sort of guy who sometimes travels with his wife and sometimes doesn't, just like their daddy. The truth is, I didn't read the flyer from the mall very closely. I have no idea if Mrs. Claus will be there.

As we reach the doors and push them open, I see that the crowds are even thicker than I had imagined, and my heart sinks. We'll be here for hours.

"Does Mrs. Claus help Santa Claus?" Martha asks.

I glance at Mother for help, and she just shrugs.

"Oh, yes," I say. "Mrs. Claus is an integral part of the whole Christmas process. She's a working mom, like

Mommy," I say, proud of myself for single-handedly up-dating the gender politics in the North Pole.

Martha nods, but I know she will have more questions. "Who are their babies? The elves?"

I grab my forehead. Whoops. I don't think Santa is supposed to have children.

"Mommy, I have to go bafroom," Agnes says.

"Okay, honey."

"Now," she says and begins to paw her pretty dress. Getting these two into matching red velvet dresses with fancy, lacy petticoats was quite a feat. We can't have an accident now.

"Martha, do you need to go to the . . ." Her kinder-garten teacher has asked us to try to call it the restroom now instead of the potty. "To the restroom too?"

Martha shakes her head violently.

"We'll meet you over by Santa's Workshop," Mother says.

"Thank you," I say, relieved that she came with me after all.

"I'll even explain who Santa's children are," she says and winks at me.

"Nothing too bizarre," I say to her back, but she just waves and disappears into the crowd with Martha. Great. She's probably going to tell Martha that Santa's children are the Easter Bunny, a leprechaun, and the Tooth Fairy.

"Now, Mommy. Pwease!" Agnes says, dancing around.

I scoop her into my arms and make a mad dash to my

favorite restroom in the mall. When you become a mom, you learn where the best ones are right away. Macy's, here we come. I pray there won't be a line.

By the time we join Mother and Martha in line, they've made some progress, but the line is moving very slowly.

"There you are," Mother says. She snaps a few pictures of me holding Agnes, and we mug for the camera. Now that the crisis is over and we're in the line, I'm beginning to relax. This is supposed to be one of the fun parts of being a mom. It's a rite of passage, and before I know it both of my girls are going to be too old for Santa Claus. Already, Martha's line of questioning shows that she smells a rat.

"Mommy, Santa's children is all the children of the world," Martha says. I set a fidgeting Agnes down, and she takes her sister's hand. Martha lets her, though I suspect soon she won't tolerate this much longer. Martha is definitely my kid. She's about as independent as they come.

"Oh," I say and smile at Mother. "You're right, Martha. Santa loves everyone."

Martha finally seems content with her working image of how things happen in the North Pole.

"Can I have my list, please?" Martha asks her grandmother.

Mother helped both the girls make Christmas lists while I was at the Jelly Jar meeting. I haven't been allowed to see the lists, as they are a big surprise.

"I'm going to read mine to Santa," Martha says.

"No peeking," Mother says with a mischievous smile as she hands it to Martha.

"Yeah, no peeking," Martha says and goes to "read" it behind Mother's back. I can't help but laugh. She only knows how to read the words *cat* and *go*.

"Here, Agnes," Mother says to her. "Here's your list too."

Agnes's eyes light up, and she opens a piece of construction paper that has swirls of crayon marks on it.

"Feel free to read that one," Mother says to me.

"You're too much."

We wait in line for an hour, and, much to my surprise, the girls are pretty good. Last year, Martha was still fairly afraid of Santa and Agnes was hysterical from start to finish. But now that Martha goes to big-girl school, she has heard enough about Santa from her friends and teachers that she better understands who he is. Now she is a woman on a mission. She tells me that she has a very special Christmas wish, and I make a mental note to listen when she reads her list to Santa. I'm pretty sure that what she means by special is the Baby Alive doll she's been asking for, but I'd better make sure she hasn't changed her mind.

At last we are next in line. Mother and I break out our cameras like a couple of tourists in Hawaii. I brought the digital camera so we can easily e-mail the pictures to everyone, and Mother brought film for archival purposes. I look at my little soldiers, and they seem calm and collected. Martha takes Agnes's hand, and they wait patiently. Now that we are close to the front, I can see that only Santa will be in the picture. Mrs. Claus is the photographer, and there are several elves assisting in the process.

A female elf bounces over to our little group, radiating joy and light. "Now, who do we have here?" she asks.

"I'm Martha Vann and this is my sister, Agnes," Martha says, puffing her little chest out. Mother and I begin snapping away. I see through the viewfinder that the elf is very tickled by Martha's response. I'll have to remember to tell her about it someday when she's older. Such a driven little girl.

The elf takes Martha's hand. "Okey-dokey, Martha and Agnes, it's your turn to see Santa!" She leads them up to Santa, but as Agnes gets closer to the man in red, she begins to wail.

I run up to try to help, and Mother continues to snap pictures. While I calm Agnes down and wipe the tears away, Santa hoists Martha up to his lap and she straightens her skirt like a little lady.

"Well, little girl," the kindly older gentleman with a real white beard says, "what can I get you for Christmas?"

Martha opens her list and pretends to read. "Dear Santa," she begins.

I swing Agnes up on Santa's lap and try to hide behind his knee so that I can keep a hand on her back. Hopefully it won't be visible in the picture.

"I am Martha Vann."

It's working! Agnes sits still and faces forward. She's probably not smiling, but they're both sitting on his lap and no one is crying. Mother snaps pictures like crazy.

"This Christmas I want a baby brother," she says loud and clear.

My head shoots up. "What?!"

"Brudder!" Agnes screams and puts her arms in the air.

"Smile!" Mrs. Claus says and I try to duck down, but the flash catches me.

"Ho, ho, ho," Santa says, with a little bit of awkwardness in his voice. "We'll see. Aren't there any toys you want?"

"No," Martha says, hopping down from his lap. "Just a baby brother. That's what I most want in the whole world!"

"Brudder," Agnes parrots again. The elf helps them down to the waiting arms of their grandmother.

I stand up slowly, my head spinning, and totter behind Santa's Workshop. I sit down on some tattered carpeted stairs, away from all of the hullabaloo, and collect myself. Where did Martha learn that? At school? My eyes begin to well up. I know it's harmless. Probably all kids her age ask for a baby brother or sister, but for some reason I feel like I can't breathe. My breaths come fast and gasping, and I'm thankful for all of the noise in the mall so that no one can hear me.

And then it hits me. I'm having a panic attack. As the realization comes, my breaths get more shallow and frantic. My head feels woozy, and my vision is blurred. My palms are slick with sweat, and I feel ice-cold.

I pray again and again and try to focus on calming down, on breathing deeply, and slowly—very, very slowly—it starts to work. Soon I can inhale a long breath, even though it catches some as it goes in. I stay another few minutes, dabbing at my eyes with a tissue and fanning myself with the brochure from Santa's photography company. Finally, I hear a noise behind me.

"Ma'am," the cheery elf says, "is everything all right?"

I purse my lips and push myself up with my arms. "Yes. Just catching my breath."

The service ran fifteen minutes over. I blame the pastor's infernal puppets. The kids love sitting in the front of the church and listening to those puppets so much that Pastor Weller just went on and on, answering the kids' questions about the manger, the shepherds, and frankincense through the mouths of his ventriloquism puppets as if no one had anywhere else to be. I guess that's what you get for attending the family-friendly Christmas Eve service. I miss the lovely candlelight service we used to attend in our prechildren days, but the girls had a good time, and I suppose making sure they know what we're really celebrating is worth a few minutes of panic. Still, Mother will be at our house in forty-five minutes, and the potatoes need at least an hour in the oven.

As the final notes of "Silent Night" reverberate through the church, I grab Agnes with one arm and take Martha's hand in the other and move into the aisle.

"Jo?" I turn to Gerard, who looks at me expectantly.

"I'm sorry, honey." I sigh, stepping back into the pew. I

lean in to give him a kiss. "Merry Christmas. I'll see you in about an hour?"

He winks. "Don't forget, it's 97.4," he says, leaning over to kiss Agnes's curls. "Six-thirty on the dot."

"We'll be listening." I turn toward the aisle again. I smile at a few people as I fly up the aisle, dismissing them with an "I'm very very busy at the moment but can't wait to catch up later" nod.

"Mommy, why isn't Daddy coming home with us?" Martha asks as we step out into the cool night air.

"Daddy has a few things to do, but he'll be home shortly." I push the door-unlock button on the keychain. The headlights flash in response, and we walk quickly across the parking lot. I suppose I should have come up with a more exciting answer for them, like he's directing reindeer traffic or something, but I've been so busy baking fruitcakes for Jelly Jar's special Christmas Eve deliveries that all my thoughts involve nuts and raisins these days. Plus, it just feels wrong to lie to your kids on Christmas Eve.

The truth is, Gerard has a friend who runs a local public-access radio station, and he's on his way over there to deliver a special Christmas message to the girls, but I certainly can't tell them that.

"Will Gigi be there when we get home?" Martha asks as she pulls open the car door and climbs into her booster seat. I strap Agnes into her seat while Martha buckles herself in.

"Grandma will be there soon," I say. Mother is staying

in our guest room tonight to "help out" with Christmas. I know she just wants to be there to watch when the girls wake up and see what Santa has left, and I am not altogether annoyed about it. The panic attack at the mall really got my attention. Mother has started picking up Martha from school every day. It makes me a little sad to be missing out on that ritual, but I have to admit that it has helped me to calm down some.

The girls sing "Joy to the World" over and over as I drive through the quiet streets, getting at least some of the lyrics right. The houses are all lit up with colored lights, and the moon is big and full, casting a peaceful glow over the neighborhood. I glance back at the girls in the rearview mirror, and my breath catches. They're holding hands, their dirty-blond curls falling over their red velvet dresses, singing their little hearts out. They're beautiful. And they're mine.

"Mother, could you turn it up?" I yell as I slide the potatoes au gratin into the oven. Coated with cheese and garlic and thyme, they smell delectable already. I shut the oven door, then walk into the living room, where my mother and the girls are hanging ornaments on the Christmas tree. Martha is carefully placing all of her handmade ornaments front and center, and Mother is lifting Agnes up to reach the top branches. I strain to hear the radio, then make out the sound of bells. I run to the tuner and turn the volume up quickly.

"Do you girls hear that?"

Both heads turn toward me, and Martha breaks into a huge smile and runs toward the speaker. Agnes starts to squeal and squirm in my mother's arms. Mother puts her down, and she runs to join Martha in front of the speaker.

"Ho, ho, ho," Gerard says over the airwaves. He has practiced his Santa voice for weeks, and, I have to admit, I wouldn't recognize him if I didn't know who it was. "This is Saint Nick, live from the skies."

"It's Santa!" Agnes screams, jumping up and down. I look at Mother, who is stifling a laugh. Agnes grabs Martha's Fluffy Makeup from the couch and hops across the floor back toward her sister.

"Shh!" Martha hisses, leaning in closer to the speaker, grabbing her bear. Agnes has her own Build-A-Bear, but he doesn't compare to her sister's, of course.

Gerard's golf buddy Pete does a weekly show on the little-heard public station. Several weeks ago, he was talking about canceling his Christmas Eve broadcast, since it traditionally has the lowest ratings of any night of the year, but Gerard had a brainstorm and asked him if Santa could make a special appearance on the airwaves instead. We may be the only people listening tonight, but Pete and Gerard have just made these girls' Christmas.

"I'm just passing over England now. Ooh, I think I see Peter Pan!" Gerard says. I stifle a laugh. *Peter Pan* is Martha's favorite movie right now. "I'm on my way to a very special place," Gerard says. "The reindeer are going strong, and we should be in Atlanta soon." He rings the bells again.

"'Lanta!" Agnes yells, stomping her feet. She begins to wiggle her bottom and raise her arms.

"That's where *we* live!" Martha says, turning to me, her eyes wide. I nod and smile at her, and she turns back to the radio.

"Atlanta is one of my favorite places," Gerard says, laughing. "And do you know why?"

"Santa!" Agnes yells.

"There are some very special boys and girls in Atlanta that I can't wait to visit tonight." He laughs. "And there are two little girls in particular who have been very good this year. I can't wait to pay a visit to Martha and Agnes Vann." Both girls start clapping and squealing. "Martha and Agnes, if you're listening, Santa loves you very much."

Tears fill my eyes as Agnes throws her arms around Martha. Gerard rings the bells again.

"Thanks so much for calling in, Santa," Pete breaks in. "Folks, we're going to take a short break, then we'll be right back with some more Christmas carols for you."

As Pete's voice fades into a car commercial, Agnes and Martha turn and look at us, their eyes wide.

"He's really coming," Martha says quietly, pulling her sister closer to her.

"Wasn't that nice of Santa to say hello?" Mother asks, holding out another ornament for Martha to hang on the tree. They nod, then slowly walk toward the tree again. They're still in shock, poor things. I guess when Santa speaks directly to you from his flying sleigh over the Atlantic Ocean, it can be a bit overwhelming.

"How far away is the radio station?" Mother asks under her breath.

"He should be home in fifteen minutes." I check my

watch. That should be just perfect. He'll arrive just in time to help set the table.

"We're back here at the station," Pete's voice booms from the speaker. The girls turn to listen. "And our circuits are overloaded! We've been flooded with phone calls for Santa. Santa, are you still there?"

Gerard rings his sleigh bells again and laughs. "I hear you loud and clear. It's a beautiful night for flying."

"Santa, it looks like we have several boys and girls who would like to speak to you. Can you hang on the line for a little while to say hello to them?"

"Of course, of course." Gerard laughs.

"What? No, he can't," I say, looking at my watch again.

"Mommy, shh!" Agnes hisses, sitting in front of the speaker again.

"Santa?" The little boy's vice is shaky and uncertain. "Are you really there?"

"Hello there, little boy. What's your name?" Gerard asks.

The boy gasps. "Ethan," he says with wonder.

"What would you like for Christmas, Ethan?"

"A bicycle!" The awe in the kid's voice is cute. Gerard chats with Ethan for a few minutes, then Pete patches another call through. This one is from a girl named Ada who would like a playhouse and a puppy for Christmas. Gerard speaks with a few more kids who heard him on the radio, then Pete breaks in to announce that Santa will be back on the line after a short commercial break.

"He will?" I croak. The ham will be dried out if I don't take it out of the oven soon.

"Stinky Santa," Agnes says, getting up and spinning around in a circle. "Stinky Santa, stinky Santa. Yay, yay, yay!"

The phone in the kitchen begins to ring, and I know what Gerard is going to tell me even before I pick it up.

"I'm so sorry, honey," he says quickly, "I had no idea this many people were listening, but the lines here just lit up. We've got dozens of kids waiting to talk to Santa."

"But Gerard, what about the girls?"

"I'll be home to my girls as soon as I can."

"But dinner will be ready soon." I know I sound amazingly selfish.

"Jo, I'm sorry. I didn't know I would get stuck here doing this," Gerard says patiently. "I want nothing more than to be there with you all. But how can I disappoint all of these kids on Christmas Eve?"

I look toward Martha and Agnes, waiting by the speaker for Santa to come back on the radio. It won't be long before they stop believing that anything really is possible.

"Just get home as soon as you can." I sigh. "We'll be here listening."

The house has been dark for hours, and even Mother is asleep. I've cleaned the kitchen from top to bottom and prepared the pastry for tomorrow's breakfast, and I'm trying to relax with my second cup of cider when I hear Gerard's key turn in the lock. I turn toward the door and see him tiptoe in, his face sheepish. He pulls a cheap, gas-station-issue, plastic-wrapped red rose from behind his back and smiles at me. "I'm sorry," he whispers, and I stand up and wrap my arms around my husband.

"Welcome home, Santa." We walk into the kitchen, where I put the rose in a bud vase, and Gerard heats up a plate of leftover ham.

"Did they miss me?" he asks, nodding toward the stairs. The girls are asleep in their rooms, though it took a bit of coaxing to get them to settle down enough to fall asleep.

"Once Santa came on the radio, they forgot all about you."

"Gee, thanks." Gerard grimaces. He lifts a bit of ham to his mouth. "Did you have a nice dinner?"

"It would have been nicer if you'd been here." I pour him a glass of water from the pitcher in the fridge. "But you did a good thing tonight."

"It was so fun." He smiles, shaking his head. "These kids, they just . . . they were so funny. And so . . . I don't know, Jo. Do you remember what it felt like to believe in Santa? How exciting it all was?"

I don't deserve him.

Gerard shoves a few pieces of ham into his mouth, then wipes his hands on his nice gray church pants. I try not to wince.

"Okay," he says, smiling. "Let's get some presents going." We walk to the living room, where the white lights on the Christmas tree cast the dark room in a soft glow. He opens the door to the hall closet, which has been locked since October, and begins to unload. Gerard grabs the gifts from the shelves, and I place them carefully under the Christmas tree. Gerard whistles quietly, and I smile, enjoying the relaxing task, imagining the girls' faces in the morning. I recognize the box of the Baby Alive I bought for Martha, and run my hand over the red paper.

"Gerard," I say, then falter. I shouldn't bring this up now.

"Yeah?" he says, smiling. He holds out another box, and I put the Baby Alive down. "What's up, honey?"

"Do you . . ." I bite my lip.

"What is it, Jo?" He stops unloading and looks at me, his face etched with concern.

"Gerard, do you ever wish we had another child?" I say before I talk myself out of it. "A little boy?"

He looks at me, eyebrow cocked. He considers the question as if it's never occurred to him before. "I don't know. I guess so." He nods, thinking about it. "Sure. Why?" His eyes get wide, then light up. "Jo, are you . . ."

"No." I look down at the packages around me to steady myself.

"Oh." His face falls.

Nice, Jo. Raise his hopes, then crush them. Merry Christmas, Gerard.

"But I would like to be."

Gerard looks at me, nods, then wraps his arms around me and pulls me in close.

"I'd like that too," he says, burying his head in my shoulder. "If you want." He begins to rock, side to side, and we sway gently in the dim light. "Only if you want."

I nod. "I do."

"But Jo," he says, pulling back suddenly, "what about the business?" I lean back and try to read the expression on his face.

He knows I'm concerned about the finances, but I haven't exactly let on how dire the situation is. I've decided to tell him after Christmas. I don't want to spoil the holiday.

"What about the business?"

"Is it the best time to take on more?" he asks, gently.

I sigh. Maybe he's right. What made me think I could do this anyway? I'll just shutter the silly project and get back to my life. I'm a woman. I have kids. I love them more than life itself. I'm satisfied with that. I bite my lip and look down, trying to smile.

"Jo?" I look up to see Gerard smiling at me. "It's okay to want both."

He pulls me back into his arms, and I lean against my husband, and suddenly I'm crying. All the frustration, all the aggravation I've been harboring for months, comes out now.

"Of course you want children." He rubs his hand up and down my back. "They're the best thing God ever invented. But you're too smart and too driven to be content changing diapers all day. I wouldn't want to change diapers all day," he says, shrugging. "Jo, your life would be easier if you were satisfied with one or the other, but that's not who God made you. And that's okay." I hide my face in his shirt, feeling the wet cotton against my cheek. "You'll struggle, and sometimes you'll fail, but refusing to use the gifts God has given you is failure too."

I lift my head up and look at him. He's watching me tenderly. "But see," I say, gulping for air. My voice shakes. "That's just the problem. I'm a failure either way, right?"

"Josephine." Gerard brushes hair back from my forehead, then strokes it for a moment while I try to compose myself. He points to a photo of the girls on the mantel. "Look at those gorgeous girls. Does that look like failure to you?"

I shake my head, letting the tears pour unchecked down my cheeks.

"I would be thrilled if we had more children," he says, pulling me close again. "And I would be perfectly content if we don't. I love our little family," he says. "I love you, Jo."

I look at Gerard. In the soft light of this holy night, he's smiling at me.

It's times like this that I can understand why God would want to come to earth to take part in it all for a while. Despite all the chaos and the hurt, sometimes life gives you startling moments of grace.

I'll admit it: I was nervous. When Ellie invited me to have lunch, I said yes mainly because I couldn't think of any graceful way to decline. She said she needed some time away from her family so she didn't hurt anyone, and I agreed that I could use a little time away too. Three days of sugar highs and tired meltdowns have worn me out, and Gerard is already back at work again, leaving me to fight off the advances of two Christmas-weary little girls. I'm still finding crumpled wrapping paper stuffed into odd corners of the living room. Thankfully, I could get away today because grandmas never get sick of babysitting. But if I'm honest, I know it's more than child woes that brought me here today. I seem to have drifted away from my Junior League friends since the business started, and I'm not too proud to admit I could use a like-minded friend. Ellie extended the olive branch, so I'm here. It will be fine.

She asked me to meet at a French café, and its warm walls and effortlessly elegant decorations make it feel welcoming and homey on this cool, gray day. Nothing beats a steaming-hot bowl of cheesy French onion soup and a café au lait when it's raining outside. This feels good. Gal pals. I can do this.

I look at Ellie, who is relating a story about her twins' adventure with a battery-powered stove on Christmas morning. "Sophie just told Seth to get right in there and start cooking. And he did. I just about died." She laughs. "He was all right with it, because that's what Mommy does." She laughs again. "I have never been prouder."

"That's hilarious," I say, taking a sip of water. "Martha has been very into baking recently. She turned up her nose at the Easy-Bake oven my mother gave her and insisted on using the 'mommy stove.'" Ellie chuckles, and we fall into a comfortable silence. I use my spoon to poke at the layer of cheese on top of my soup.

"Jo." Ellie takes a sip of her Americano and smiles. "Thanks for meeting me. I needed this." She sighs and leans back in her chair. "I feel like you are one of the few people who can understand." She grimaces.

I nod and blow on a spoonful of my soup. The steam rises off the brown liquid in a smooth, wispy plume. In a strange way, I agree. We really are alike in so many ways, and it's nice that we're finally starting to be friends.

"Sometimes I think we were crazy to do this," she says, sitting up and leaning into me conspiratorially.

Oh, Lord. I have to tell her about the business. Okay. I can do this. I open my mouth to mention that we're almost bankrupt, but she rushes on.

"But that's just part of it," she says, rolling her eyes. "Mike has been so moody. He definitely does not love my working." She takes a bite of quiche. "And do you want to know the worst part?" I nod absently, trying to think about how to break it to her. She would want the direct approach, I think. "I've lost my engagement ring," she says, lifting up her shoulders helplessly.

My stomach sinks. The ring.

"That horrible ring. Do you remember it? It had the big ugly garnet, and the gaudy pearls?" I nod mutely. I feel lightheaded. He hasn't told her. He's never going to tell her. "Well, it's gone. And I can't find it anywhere. And when Mike finds out, he's going to flip. It was an heirloom. And with him acting so weird about this job thing recently, I just don't know . . ." She shakes her head. "It's going to be ugly, and—" She looks at me sharply. "Jo. Are you okay?"

I'm not okay. How can she not know about Mike and me? Things are starting to go well between us, but this is not fair to her. If we're ever going to really be friends, she has to know. I nod and make a decision. I don't care what Mike thinks anymore.

"Ellie." I take a sip of coffee to buy a few seconds. She watches me, her eyes narrowed in concern. I swallow, then clear my throat. "Mike isn't really upset about the ring. Or the job." I lay my hands neatly on the table in front of me, trying to line the tips of my fingers up evenly. "He's upset about me. I mean, you and me working together. Mike and I . . ." I watch her expression change as confusion washes over her. "We were engaged once."

"You were . . . what?" she stammers. She shakes her head, and the color drains from her face.

"We were engaged, Ellie. A long time ago. Before he met you." I take a deep breath. "I'm sorry."

Ellie's face crumples, and her eyes fill with tears. Abruptly, she stands up and grabs for her purse. She reaches in, pulls out a twenty-dollar bill, and places it carefully on the table.

"I have to go," she says and bolts out the door.

Cate

THOUGH I WAS SOBBING HYSTERICALLY, DAVID somehow figured out what I was saying. I just couldn't tell them. It was our first company meeting of the new year, and I was going to tell them to start the year off right. David and I had even practiced what I was going to say. But then Ellie wasn't there, and it didn't feel right to do it without her, and Daisy wouldn't even look me in the eye because things are so weird between us, so I just couldn't bring myself to do it. Nothing about it felt right, which sent me into a hormonal downward spiral. So David came right over with a bag of groceries, vowing to fix everything with his Famous Dr Pepper Chili.

"Here," he says, putting an onion in my hand. "Let's give you something to really cry about." He smirks at me. Bless him. This is just what I need.

I put the onion on the cutting board and make a small incision in the papery skin to peel it back. David is boiling down two cans of Dr Pepper, smiling and pretending he's preparing some gourmet treat. His thin blue T-shirt stretches over his shoulders nicely.

"Are you sure this stuff is safe to eat?" I ask as the Dr Pepper bubbles. I don't want to be ungrateful here, but he is cooking with soda and it's not even Coke. As an Atlanta native, I might forgive Coke. But Dr Pepper? Apparently this is one of the great divides between Southern food and Texas cuisine.

"This is a Texas delicacy, young lady. I promise you will love it." Does he know that cooking a ridiculous recipe is just so right? He must. It's how David works. So perfect. Being here in my kitchen with him feels so right. "And you shouldn't look a gift horse in the mouth, missy." He pauses and swirls the thick brown cola in the saucepan. "Ain't that right, John the Baptist?"

I laugh and get back to cutting the onion on the wooden chopping block. My eyes, predictably, fill with tears. I hope David assumes they're from the onion. Why couldn't I just tell the Jelly Jar girls that I quit?

David's phone rings. "Oops. It's your mom," I say, glancing at the screen. I nudge it toward him with my elbow, since my hands are covered in onion juice.

He rolls his eyes and doesn't move to answer it.

"David," I say, stretching it out in long, coaxing syllables. "Just get it. I don't care."

He looks at me and smiles his dashing smile. "No way. I told her I was hanging out with you tonight. She can wait."

I bite my lip as the phone rings again, and he looks at his handwritten recipe. "Please, get it," I say, picturing his mother assuming I told him not to answer it.

"Fine." He shakes his head and flips his phone open. "What, Mom?" he says with more than a little annoyance in his voice.

I walk over to the recipe to see if the onion is supposed to be sliced, chopped, diced, minced, or what. Chopped. Okay, done with that. What can I do next?

David sighs loudly. "Mom," he whines, which isn't very flattering, but I guess we've all been there. "I *told* you that we'd talk about it later. Jeez. I'm cooking dinner for Catie right now."

I hear a muffled voice on the other end.

David turns to me. "Mom says hi."

"Hi," I yell back, hoping she can hear that I'm happy she called.

"Okay, I'm hanging up now." He opens and closes his hand rapidly to show me that she's still yapping. I stifle a laugh. She *can* be kind of meddlesome and chatty. "Okay, bye," he says and hangs up, but I could swear that she was still talking.

I stare at him for a moment, feeling uncomfortable. But it's not really my business. Every family is different. I'll just stay out of it.

"So, you're done with the onion? Perfect. Can you chop up this now?" He puts a green bell pepper in my hand.

"Got it, chef." I walk back to my post at the counter.

He takes the reduced Dr Pepper off the heat and then begins to fry some bacon in my skillet.

The phone rings again, and he turns around and scowls at it. "She is so insane." He walks over and answers it.

They chat for a moment while he mumbles and grunts and then he finally gets off. "You should be thankful your family isn't crazy," he says.

I look up from my stack of little green cubes. "What's going on? Anything?"

"No," he says. "It's nothing. Just some trip they're planning for my dad's retirement."

"Your dad is finally retiring? Wow. That's a huge deal."

"Yeah. So I guess we're all going to Hawaii. It's his dream." He looks over at me. "That's why she keeps calling. She's trying to schedule it. But I keep telling her, I can go whenever. Just let me know when."

I nod. "I'm so excited for your dad. And the trip sounds cool."

"Whatever," he says. "I'm happy for my dad, but he's only going to putter around the house even more and drive my mom nuts and that week in Hawaii is probably going to be a nightmare. I can't spend a whole week with them."

I frown at him. I hate it when he's like this. It's his dad's retirement present and a free trip to Hawaii to boot. Why can't he be a bit more grateful?

"Anyways," he says. "It's not important. Tonight is about you."

"Then can we leave the Dr Pepper out of the chili?"

"No. Any other requests?"

"Tell me what to do with my life," I say as I carefully slice the green pepper into thin strips. "My head hurts just thinking about it. Should I quit? Should I tough it out at Jelly Jar? You've known me at both jobs. Do I seem happier now or then?"

David begins to brown the ground beef. "I thought we had this all settled. You told me you wanted to go back to working with Mollie. And you said Mollie was ecstatic to hear it. So all you need to do is tell the women that you quit Jelly Jar."

I nod. It all sounds so simple when he puts it like that. "Yeah, that's what we decided last time."

The meat sizzles, and the savory scent begins to fill the kitchen. "So why do you think you didn't tell them you were quitting?" he says.

I put my knife down and look at him. Why couldn't I tell them? "I'm afraid. I guess that's why."

He looks at me, his dark eyebrows raised.

"Oh, right. I mean, I'm afraid of change, which is why I should have never taken the job in the first place and can't wait to get back to my old life, but I also am afraid of hurting them." I look down at the green pepper.

David shrugs at me. "It's just a business, Cate. I doubt they'll be hurt by your quitting."

He goes over to look at the recipe again, and his words ring in my ears.

I know what he meant to say. He wanted to give me

confidence to do what I need to do, but for some reason, the idea that my new friends wouldn't really care if I left the company is more painful than the idea of hurting them. They're my friends now, right?

Or maybe David's right. It's just a job. I've probably built it all up in my head about how important I am to them when they couldn't really care less. In fact, I'll bet they all know I'm quitting. Maybe Daisy already told them. It's not like she's a vault or anything.

"I think I just choked," I say, tossing the chopped bell pepper into the saucepan. "I'll just send them an e-mail about it later tonight. That way they'll all find out about it at once, well, aside from Daisy, who already knows, and I can take some time to say exactly what I want to say."

"That's a good idea," he says. He comes over behind me and wraps his arms around me. I lean my head back and nuzzle my face into his.

"Mmm," he says as he rubs his cheek on mine. "Didn't I say we'd get everything all worked out for you?"

I smile. I do feel better already. That's a good solution. Just send them an e-mail. They aren't going to care that I quit. It's no big deal, really. People do it every day.

David's phone rings across the kitchen, and I feel his body slump behind me.

"Okay, that's it," he mumbles to himself. He walks across the room and shuts his phone off.

I open my mouth to protest. What if his mom really needs him? But I shut it again. Everything is going so well between us. I don't need a fight with David on top of everything else I'm dealing with. Besides, he's just having a little spat with his mom. It happens.

Then he turns back to me and smiles. "Now we're finally alone. Let's hurry up and cook this chili so that I can convince you that I am the only man in the world for you."

When I step inside the Intercontinental Hotel, it becomes achingly apparent that the twenty bucks I have stashed in my cute black clutch is not going to be enough. I follow the signs through the gorgeous marble lobby and quickly find my way to XO Bar, where I'm meeting Beatriz. When I peek into the glittering hotel lounge, complete with a piano player in a tuxedo and a wall of cognac bottles behind the bar, I wonder if I'm going to blow my entire savings on just one little drink. Why did I let Bea talk me into this?

The soft tinkle of piano keys gives the bar a quiet, serene feel. I spy the back of her head and walk across the smooth marble floor, trying not to wobble on my heels too much or attract any attention to myself. This is the hotel for celebrities, and it's Saturday night. It's very possible there are somebodies here. And I don't want those somebodies to see me. Just Cate.

I come up to Bea's sleek black leather banquette and she stands up to give me a hug. She's wearing a black turtleneck under a short jumper dress. Her hair is in a loose sexy knot on her head. In short, she looks like somebody. I do not. I am wearing a pair of dark denim jeans from Banana Republic and a flimsy top from Forever 21, which I thought seemed like just the thing, but now seems rather cheap and tacky.

"Hey," she says, kissing my cheeks. I sit down quickly, because in the relative quiet of the immaculate bar I can't shake the feeling that people are staring at me.

"Isn't this place amazing?" Bea asks. If Franny is on a mission to try every greasy spoon in Atlanta, Bea is on an unspoken countermission to get us out to all the best and brightest hot spots. I play ping-pong between them. I don't care where we go, as long as I don't have to decide.

But this place really is beautiful, with high ceilings, lavish paintings, and a sleek cherry bar. I start to relax. A sexy, glammed-up night on the town might be just the thing I need. "It's really cool."

Soon the waiter comes over, and we both get settled with cognac cocktails served in cool, sparkling martini glasses. XO's specialty is cognac, and they have the largest selection in the country.

"So," Bea says and holds up a glass. "I haven't told you yet, but we're here tonight to celebrate."

I hold my glass up too. "Oh?"

She clinks hers on mine. "I met someone." She takes a happy gulp of her drink and raises it in the air again.

I put mine back down on the table. "What?! That's so exciting. Who? Where?"

She laughs. "He's a substitute teacher at my school. New to the area. When I saw him, I knew that he was going to be snapped up fast, so I gave myself a little pep talk and went over there and asked him to coffee."

"You did?" I take a sip of my cocktail. It's warm and spicy, a little sweet. Yum. So this is why cognac is so expensive. "I'm so impressed with you."

Bea talks for the next forty-five minutes straight about William, whom she already calls "Wills." I can't decide if that's annoying or endearing. It's certainly walking the fine line between the two. The more she talks about him, the more wonderful he sounds.

"I can't wait to meet him," I say. "Have you told Franny yet?"

"Yeah, I told her this afternoon, when she said she couldn't make it tonight."

I take a drink. "I hope she's doing okay. What with me with David again and you with Will now, she's the odd man out," I say.

"She seemed fine," Bea says, batting a hand at me. "You know Franny. She never takes anything too seriously. Plus, Daisy is still single. Hey, where's she been lately, anyways?"

I shrug and look down.

"You invited her, right?" Bea takes a sip of her drink and looks at me over the edge of her glass.

"Um . . ." I take another sip. "It's a little complicated right now with me and Daisy, so I didn't exactly . . . I mean, she called, but I didn't call her back so I guess she wasn't invited."

Bea looks at me. She has this annoying habit of making eye contact for much too long. It must be some kind of

Brazilian thing. It makes you feel like you have something on your face.

"Cate?" she says, her voice lilting.

I blot my face with my napkin self-consciously. "Beatriz?" I sing back.

"What's going on?"

I could deny that something is wrong, but it's really no use. Bea always gets her confession, so I might as well be out with it now.

"It's all very complicated and Daisy is involved, and so until it's resolved I thought I might just . . . not hang out with her. Just a temporary break."

"What on earth are you talking about?"

I roll my eyes, wondering if I can explain this all over again. "Buy me another drink?"

Bea winks at the waiter across the room and he practically trips over himself to get to our table. She gets us another round, and I begin to tell her everything about Jelly Jar and Daisy.

"And so I was supposed to send them an e-mail last night saying I quit, but I didn't."

She narrows her eyes at me. "And this is after you didn't resign in person, which was after you didn't tell Jo at the craft store, and after you didn't call Jo up?"

I think back. "Yep. That's pretty much the time line of inactivity there."

"You really need your head checked, you know that?"

Thanks, Bea. I dip into my second drink. Some friend. "Yeah, I know. The problem is, I'm the deer."

"What?"

"I'm the deer. Deer stay where they're safe because they don't like risks. And when they do take risks they, um, get squashed in the road."

"What?" She shakes her head, and a dark curl tumbles out of her bun.

"I don't know," I say, my shoulders sagging nearly into my drink. "It's just something someone told me."

I can see the long hard stare she gives me, even in the dim light. "Did Franny tell you this? It sounds like one of her wacky ideas."

I press my palms into my face and squeeze. "No. If you want to know, it was Shawn who told me this. That horrible blind date that you set me up on? Remember?"

Bea gives a big belly laugh and I sort of want to punch her. Some time to laugh. "I'm sorry about that. I had never met him. He came highly recommended."

I cross my arms.

"And you yourself said he was crazy. So why are you taking weird advice from him about the laws of the animal kingdom and how that proves that you're, I don't know, unable to cross the proverbial road of life?"

"But he said . . . well, you know I'm very averse to change. Everyone thinks so. David too." I chew on my lip.

"What's this really about, Cate? What are you trying to tell me? Try again, but no deer this time."

I stare at her, and she stares back, unafraid. I feel a big helping of tough love coming on. "I don't know what to do. I'm horrible at making decisions and I just want to be happy again. Which is why I have to quit Jelly Jar. I used to be happy, didn't I?"

Bea looks stunned and shakes her head. "Look, Cate." I fumble with my martini glass, my face flushing. "You know what to do."

"Really," I say, unable to keep the sarcasm out of my voice. "What is that exactly? I'd love to know."

"When did you stop listening to your instincts? I've never seen someone so blindly trying to ignore them in my life. You're not the deer or whatever. You're just Cate. And it's just life. You need to get over yourself."

My face flushes. I need to get over myself? I clear my throat. Well, Beatriz is usually right about these kinds of things. Maybe I am making too big a deal of all of this. Remember who's in control.

"So you're saying that I don't want to quit Jelly Jar."

"Well, praise the Lord, the blind man can see," Bea says, smiling at me.

I nod. "But if this was the right thing for me to be doing with my life, wouldn't it be easier? Aren't things supposed to fall into place when you're following the path God means for you to take?"

"What Bible have you been reading?" Bea leans back against the soft black leather. "Mine seems positively littered with hard knocks and tortured journeys."

I nod, thinking back to these past months. When did I start to doubt myself?

"Cate, change is hard. New careers, new friends, new experiences, they're always hard." Bea leans forward and focuses her dark eyes on me. I can't bring myself to look away. "It's just life. You've got to grow up, stand tall, and face them head-on."

"Really?" I squeak. I don't know. It sounds so easy when Bea says it.

"You can do it," she says, shrugging.

"Maybe you're right." I've been looking for a way out, wanting to go back to my comfort zone, but maybe the only way to grow is to press on forward, rocky though it may be.

I take another sip of my drink, then start to snicker. I don't know if I'm just so relieved from all the agonizing back-and-forth or if the humor of the situation is finally sinking in.

"So I'm not the deer."

"Please stop saying that. It's really bizarre."

We both laugh, and I even pretend to be a deer looking into the headlights of a car, setting off another peal of laughter from Bea.

"Thanks," I say to her. "For being honest."

She shrugs. "Now, when are you and David free for a double date?"

It's almost midnight by the time I get back to East Atlanta, but I don't feel like going inside my dark, empty house yet, so I decide to take a walk. I wrap my scarf around my neck and button up my coat, then slam my car door shut and head up Gresham toward Glenwood. The houses on my street are dark and quiet, and I take a deep breath of clean, cold January air. I pass the Cantina, where I learned about Daisy's tattoo, and chuckle. The place is still hopping, but I'm not in the mood for chips, and I walk on by.

My head is muddled, but it feels good to have made a decision about Jelly Jar. I'll tell Mollie tomorrow. Things with David are less solid, though.

He's been so sweet recently. We belong together. I know him better than anybody. I turn right onto Glenwood, the main drag in East Atlanta, and sigh.

Maybe that's the problem. I know him a bit too well. The way he acted with his mom the other night brought back so many memories. The thing about David is, when you're the one he wants, there's nothing better in the world. He makes you feel like no one else matters. But the truth is, when you're the one he wants, no one else *does* matter. And sometimes, unfortunately, I was the one who got left out in the cold.

The wind whips my hair around as I look up the street. There are a lot of people out for a cold January night, huddled around the entrances to bars and hurrying to their cars. Down the road a few blocks, on my left, there's a brightly lit marquee for the East Atlanta Theater, a historic theater that in its heyday was the center of this neighborhood, but now shows mostly indie films to empty auditoriums. Every weekend night they have a midnight showing of a classic movie. I squint to read the sign to see what this week's selection is . . . *Sunset Boulevard*.

Huh. How appropriately depressing. I cross the street to take a look at the poster, but even before I get there, I know I'm going to buy a ticket. I'm not the kind of person who goes to midnight movies alone. I'm not the kind of person who goes to movies alone at all, actually. But hey, new year, new Cate.

I buy a ticket from a bored teenager at the glass box office and make my way inside the plush red lobby. When they restored this theater, they did their best to make it look like it might have when it first opened, and the art deco accents on the walls and on the ceiling make it feel like I've stepped into a whole different world. I try to imagine the lobby filled with men with cravats and ladies in flapper dresses, but the neon signs at the snack bar area make it nearly impossible. I walk toward the theater, but stop when the smell of buttered popcorn wafts my way.

I'm not the kind of person who buys snacks at theaters, but tonight is full of new experiences. I order a large, and ask for a medium Coke to go with it, then stroll into the already darkened theater. I settle into a seat in the back row—David always wants to sit near the front because he doesn't like to wear his glasses—and start crunching on my popcorn. A few other lonely souls file in, but the theater is mostly empty tonight, and I lose myself in the story of Norma Desmond, the silent film star who can't accept that the film world has moved on without her. It's funny and tragic at the same time. How can she not see that she's just living in the past? The world has changed. She's yesterday's news. Nothing is ever going to be how it was.

An hour into the movie, I realize I am going to break up with David.

It's almost three AM when I finally stumble into my house. I'm worn out, and my eyes are red and puffy. I've been crying for the last hour and a half. But it feels good. I feel clean and blissfully empty. I turn on a few lights, toss some food into John the Baptist's bowl, and walk into my still-never-used office. I have to do this before I change my mind again. I turn the computer on and give it a few minutes to boot up, looking around uncertainly. Maybe I'll repaint in here. The walls are a soft blue, but I think I'm in the mood for something brighter. Maybe a hot pink or a turquoise. Something that stands out and says this is my room and I'm proud of it.

When the computer screen lights up, I turn and sit down in front of it. I open up Gmail and type in the Jelly Jar e-mail addresses. In the subject line, I write the words "New Rule." And then I type out my simple message:

There's no "I" in quit.

I hit send.

"Thanks for coming," I say as I stand up and lean in to give David a hug. I hold him close, breathing in his scent. He smells clean, like soap. I try to stop myself from enjoying it. The ambient noise of Café Red is soothing, and the smooth white walls and the plain wood floor feel simple and uncomplicated. Like my life will soon be.

I spent all day today painting the walls of my last show condo, and it was nice to do physical labor, which somehow helped keep my mind off what I'm going to do here tonight. I asked him to meet me after work for a quick

drink after my realization last night, because I figured
these things are supposed to go better in public, where
there can be no messy fights or big blowups. Now,
though, I'm not so sure.

"It was no problem," he says, pulling a chair out and
taking a seat. He runs his hands through his hair, then
clears his throat and looks at me. "I wanted to talk to you
anyway." I watch him. He's fidgeting. Something's weird.
He looks down quickly.

"Do you want to get a drink?" I gesture toward the
full menu of coffee and tea beverages. He shakes his
head.

"I can't stay long," he says, tapping his fingers on the
table. "Look, Cate. I . . . I don't know how to say this." He
clears his throat, his clear blue eyes trapping me in their
gaze. He takes my hand. "But I've been praying about . . .
this. All of this. You and me. And . . . I really feel like God
is . . ." He coughs. "I feel like God is telling me not to date
you again. This isn't what God wants."

"What?" I stammer. My mind is swirling. How can he
do this? Out of nowhere? Everything was going so well.
Sure, I wanted to end it, but he was supposed to be heart-
broken. How can he want out too? How dare he? How
dare he dump me again? Especially before I dump him?

But what can I say? I know that God does direct our
paths when we ask him to. And I know that he speaks to
all of us differently. And maybe it's providence that we
both came to the same conclusion at the same time. Still,
though . . . God seems to be changing his mind a lot.
Maybe David has gotten the message wrong. How are any

of us supposed to know God's will for us? It's not like he gives us neon signs.

And suddenly, I'm angry. I'm angry because David knows I can't say anything. I'm angry because David has pulled out an ironclad excuse, again. I can't argue with God. And yet, it's amazing how what God wants seems to correlate so precisely to what David wants. It's uncanny, really.

"David," I say, raising my eyebrows. He rubs his fingers along my hand, as if to convince me that this is hurting him as much as it's hurting me. "Why are you really breaking up with me?"

"Catie, I . . ." he says, faltering. "I love you. You can't understand how much I don't want to do this. But I really just feel like God—"

"Stop it," I say, cutting him off. He looks at me, his eyes wide. "Three weeks ago you said you knew this was what God wanted. And now—"

"I don't know what to say." He shrugs. "I'm sorry. This isn't what I want. But I have to do what God wants."

"God?" I laugh as I stand up and pick up my purse. I pull my wool coat on and look him straight in the eye. "It seems like God is a bit wishy-washy." I watch as his face registers shock, then turn on my heel and walk out.

I call Franny as soon as I get home, but she doesn't pick up. I flop down on the couch and call Bea, but she's on the other line with Wills and asks if she can call me back. I know Daisy would be willing to talk, but I'm not ready to call her yet. I can't face how awful I was to her.

The funny thing is, I'm not even that upset that David dumped me. I hate how he did it, but I'm not really that sad that it's truly over. I'm angry, sure, but somehow my anger is tinged with the distinct feeling that I'm finally, really, free.

I get up off the couch and walk through the house aimlessly. I guess I could do some laundry . . . aha! I spy the computer and sit down at the keyboard. I'll check my e-mail. I've been away from my computer all day, and there's sure to be a backlog of messages now.

The first thing I see when I open Gmail is two replies to last night's Jelly Jar e-mail. The first is from Daisy, sent at four AM. It says, simply:

> What? Umm . . . The third letter?
> —Daisy
> *There's no "I" in quit.*
> *—C*

Oh, Daisy. God, I miss Daisy. Maybe I will call her.

Oh, good, the other one is from Ellie. I click on it and hold my breath. I'm pretty sure she'll get the joke, but I guess you never know. And as I read her message, I shake my head and smile:

> More like, there's no Cate in quit.
> —EHR
> *What? Umm . . . The third letter?*
> *—Daisy*
> *There's no "I" in quit.*
> *—C*

I stare at the screen for a few minutes. Thank God for Ellie. Maybe, just maybe, they do care after all.

I click on a few more e-mails, replying to most of them. I try Franny again, but she's not answering her phone. I check my bank balance. I check out a few blogs I read. I Google my own name. And then I know I can't put it off any longer. I have to e-mail James. It's the first step on the way to my new life.

Dear James,

What am I supposed to say? How do you apologize to someone for acting like a jerk on a date that you didn't even realize was a date until it was too late? How do you tell someone that you are interested in him, even though you need to take a break from the dating scene for a while?

It's Cate. Daisy gave me your e-mail a long time ago, and I've been meaning to write.

I frown at the blank screen. Is there any kind transition that would work here? Just plunge in? What if he thinks I'm a stalker? Daisy says he likes me . . . but who's to say?

I thought I should apologize about that night we all hung out together. I'm not sure if you could tell (you probably could), but things were a bit tense between Daisy and me.

Hmmm . . . things were tense between Daisy and me, but that was more the symptom than the problem. The real issue was that I was on a date with someone I was a little interested in while dating someone I was addicted to. Daisy was trying to force me to move forward, and it was freaking me out. But if I hadn't been attracted to James, it wouldn't have mattered.

> *The truth is I was dating someone else at the time. Daisy was trying to . . . well, when you get to know her better I'll try to explain. She's the best kind of friend a girl like me could have. So I'm sorry for being so . . . intentionally disinterested in you.*

My brain offers me a quick flash of James's face, and I smile in reflex. He's really very handsome. How could I have blown it with him so badly? It's not like good men are just hanging from the trees, ripe for picking. But then I reread my e-mail, and my face flushes. It's so bold, so un-Cate. Can I really send this? I read it again and resolve to just finish it. I don't have to send it, but at least I can put my thoughts into writing.

> *I'm not. That is . . . I'm not disinterested. In fact, I'm very interested, and I've finally purged that toxic guy from my life.*

My pinkie finger frantically reaches for the delete key on my computer, begging to take it back. But I have to do this. If I'm serious about growing up and getting over myself, then I need to learn to take risks.

> *But (there's always one, isn't there?) as you might suspect, I need some time. I've got to get my head together, and I don't*

know how long it will take. I could really use a friend, but I
don't expect you to wait for me.

The date was weeks ago. Will he even know who this
e-mail is from? Will this create an awkward rift between
us? Maybe he'll start attending another church? But then I
think about Daisy. She said that he liked me, and she's
someone who listens to her instincts, who knows stuff
about people, even when they're lying to themselves. She
knew I found him attractive, though I was trying to will
myself not to. I think back to that night when James was
telling me all about his work. Even though I was trying to
ignore him, it would have been hard to miss the light in
his eyes, the animation in his voice. We have a connection. I'm sure of it. I just need to trust in that.

So shoot me an e-mail if you'd like to catch a movie and find
a new friend. I can't make any promises, but who can, right?
Cate

I chew my lip. Am I really going to do this? I take a deep
breath, slide the cursor over to the send button, shut my
eyes and say a quick prayer for strength, and press the button on the mouse.

For a moment, I stay perfectly still with my eyes shut,
listening to the silence of my house. But nothing seems
to have happened. The world has not ended. The earth
did not move. There are no sounds of bombs going off as
my stable life is reduced to shambles. I peek open at my
e-mail screen and see "Your message has been sent," and

I feel relieved. I did it. I was vulnerable, and I told the truth. I put myself out there. I exhale and sit back in my chair, smiling a little. I really did it. And it feels pretty good.

I go to close out my e-mail, but a new message catches my eye. It's Jo's reply to my last message. Finally. That Jo is usually quicker on the e-mail. I hope she's not mad. Maybe that wasn't a good use of the e-mail list? I click on her message, holding my breath.

We need to talk.
—Josephine Vann
More like, there's no Cate in quit.
—EHR
What? Umm . . . The third letter?
—Daisy
There's no "I" in quit.
—C

Ellie

MY PURSE STRAP IS LOOPED UNDER MY CHIN, and my arms are full of dry cleaning and Tupperware. I swing my hip (in all its post-twins-childbirthing glory) at the door of the station wagon and it slams closed. Seth and Sophie stand by the door in their blue soccer uniforms, waiting for me to come and let them into the house. I shuffle over to them slowly, careful to keep my weight balanced just so because my right arm is carrying two weeks' worth of Brooks Brothers shirts for Mike, while my left arm is clutching three slippery, empty plastic tubs that once contained cupcakes for Seth and Sophie's soccer team. I'm horribly unbalanced. Story of my life.

I get to the door and knock with my high heel. *Please, please, please,* I say to myself again and again. Mike should be home by now, and I could use some immediate help and a warm welcome. It's almost eight-thirty, and we're all starved and tired. The poor little House of Pancakes Hornets lost their soccer game because of the mercy rule again. What are they feeding the kindergartners across town? They made Seth and Sophie's team look puny.

I kick the door again, a little too hard this time, and feel my big toe throbbing.

"Grrrr . . ." I start to juggle the stuff in my arms, trying to work a hand free. "Where is your father?" I say under my breath, even though my chin is pinned to my chest.

Sophie looks up at me, reaches out both hands, and takes hold of my purse. My neck muscles relax and I let it go. Bless the little angel.

"Thank you, sweetie," I say. "Can you pull out my keys?"

Sophie puts my Louis Vuitton bucket purse (a remnant from a long-ago life) on the garage floor, and she and Seth dig for my giant ring of keys. Really, there's no way to miss it, but they're five, so it takes a while. As I watch them, I play the role of the patient, doting mother, but all I can think about is how my eyes itch with exhaustion and my feet are covered in blisters. I suppose that's what I get for forgetting until the last moment that Seth and Sophie had a soccer game. I deserved to watch it in heels. But at least *I* remembered.

Finally, Seth produces the keys, and I hand Sophie the Tupperware. I unlock the door left-handed—a true feat—stumble inside, and lay the dry cleaning across the break-fast bar. The twins run in behind me and drop the Tupperware and my purse onto the floor, chattering about the game. And that's when I notice it. Seth and Sophie notice it too, and they run into the living room.

The house isn't dark. In fact, the TV in the other room is on, blaring some dull history program. The blood drains from my face, and I bite my lip. My first impulse is to walk into the living room and ask why on earth Mike didn't help us at the door (when I'm carrying his dry cleaning, no less), but I decide for the twins' sake to stay in the kitchen for a moment and cool down. I can hear the kids telling their father all about the big game, completely oblivious to the fact that he forgot to come.

I slide my shoes off and retrieve my purse and the Tupperware off the floor. I place the Tupperware in the sink, where it joins a rather large stack of dishes that neither Mike nor I have seen fit to put in the dishwasher, then slip my hand in my purse and pull out my phone. My heart is slamming in my chest.

When I saw that it was Jo calling at the soccer game, I turned it off. We haven't spoken since her confession. She keeps calling and calling. At first she didn't leave messages, but now she does. I've been erasing them for days. She wants to "talk about it." I roll my eyes. Talk about what?

I turn the phone on and watch the screen as it boots up. I've tried getting the truth out of Mike, but when I bring up Jo and "the old days" he always laughs and dismisses it. It really doesn't seem to mean much to him, so I have started to think that maybe they dated in high school and that was it. Sure, maybe there was some kind of silly "promise ring," and I'm sure dear old Edith was probably throwing Jo at Mike, hoping he'd marry her someday, but I doubt they were really engaged. That's just the problem with Jo. She's so uptight and serious about everything. I'll bet teenaged Mike said something like, "Someday we'll get married," and she took it too literally.

I dial into my voice mail and type in the password. Jo's message plays.

"Ellie, it's me again. I know you're avoiding me and I just want you to know that's okay. But I've called to tell you that you have to see me. Well, you have to see all of us. We have to have a Jelly Jar meeting. The company is in trouble, Ellie. I wanted to tell you first since you're my partner, but you're not taking my calls. Either way, the situation is so dire now that I have to tell everyone this week. The meeting is Wednesday at noon. I hope you'll be there. It's your company too. If you want to talk, about this . . . about anything, call me."

I snap my phone shut. The company is in trouble? Just wonderful. I grab my forehead and massage my temples with my fingers. I can't deal with this.

I take a deep, cleansing breath. There, that's a bit better. I'll bet the company isn't really in trouble. Maybe a little trouble, but nothing we can't fix. This is just another great example of how Jo can be. So dramatic. Okay, no sense in worrying about this now. I'll call her tomorrow and find out what she's carrying on about. I can't do anything about that right now. But I can do something about this mess.

I pick up an empty cupcake container and start rinsing

it. Hopefully the moms didn't notice that the cupcakes were store-bought, since I did swing by Jelly Jar and grab the Tupperware to put them in. Quick save. I place the sticky container in the dishwasher.

"Mom?" Seth calls from the other room. "What's for dinner?"

I frown. It dawned on me a few days ago that I have made dinner every single night for this family ever since Seth and Sophie started eating solids. Mike hasn't made dinner for the family once. When we were dating in Paris, he would always insist on cooking for me. He'd tease me and say that his meals weren't good enough for my refined palate. I don't know when things changed, or when I changed to just accept that this is the way things are. At first when he was working and I was a SAHM, I didn't mind. I love to cook, and it was a nice way to do something to help him. But now we both work. And it still seems like I'm always the one who has to get the cleaning, plan and execute the meals, and attend the games. I know he's busy but—

"Ellie?" I stop rinsing dishes and turn around to see Mike and the twins in the kitchen. "Did you bring home dinner? I'm starved. I thought you guys would never get home." He musses Seth's kinky brown hair.

I turn back around and visualize screaming at the top of my lungs, but I keep quiet. Give him a chance, Ellie. Give him a chance before you bite his head off.

I swallow back my anger. "I . . ." I cough. "I don't have anything planned for dinner. Do you?" There. I got the question out without screaming.

"Me?" Mike laughs. "Why me?".

I turn the water off and whirl around, wringing my hands on a mildewed kitchen towel. "Well, why *me*, Mike?" I roll my lips in and take a deep breath.

"Because that's usually how things work."

"In case you haven't heard," I say calmly, marching over to the pantry—maybe we at least have some Easy Mac?—"I was at the Hornets game tonight." I give him a meaningful look. "And before that I was at work. What did you do all day that made *you* so busy?"

"Ellie," Mike says, his nostrils flaring. "Don't make this about me. You know I'd do anything for this family. If you would have told me to pick up dinner I would have."

"I also got *your* dry cleaning." I point to it on the counter. "And I got the cupcakes for the game. It turns out that today was my turn, pardon me, *our* turn, to bring the snacks for the end of game."

"Look," Mike says, reaching for the phone book. "We'll just order Chinese, okay? It's no big deal."

"But I hate Chinese food," Sophie says quietly. She looks at the floor.

"Pizza," Mike says, flipping to a different section of the Yellow Pages. "We'll get pizza."

Seth and Sophie smile at each other.

"We are not having pizza." The kids look at me, confusion etched on their faces. The children are practically in danger of turning into pizzas, but that's not the real problem. It's him. It's us. I hate how we're living. "We just had pizza." I peek in the pantry again and spot a horrid box of Tuna Helper that Edith left here when she babysat the kids one afternoon. "We'll have this," I say, pulling the blue box out of the cabinet.

Seth and Sophie love prepackaged food like this, but Mike hates it. I hate it too, but that's not the point.

"Okay, we'll have that, if it will make you happy. Whatever," Mike says and stalks out of the room. He's not even going to offer to help make the Tuna Helper?

"Happy?" I scream at his back. He turns around to face me. "Do you really care about my happiness?"

"What do you think?" he screams back at me. "Tell me. What do you really think, Ellie?"

"No!" I say. "I think—"

But I'm interrupted by the faintest of noises, a sniffle. I look down and see that Seth has tears running down his face. When Sophie sees him crying, she bursts into tears too.

My face flushes, and I can barely breathe, thinking about what awful parents we have turned out to be. How could we do this to our kids? How have we turned into the kind of people who scream at each other in front of their children? I shake my head, watching Mike walk toward the refrigerator out of the corner of my eye. How could we have known when we said "I do" that it would end up like this?

I scoop both of my children up in a hug while they cry harder and harder. For a while I can feel Mike hovering over us awkwardly. But eventually the shadow of his frame disappears.

I arrive ten minutes late to the meeting. I almost smile when I see Daisy, Cate, and even Tiff, who is doing her homework at the high bar in the Jelly Jar kitchen. I've really missed them. I think back to the Madden birthday party when Daisy and I took on the Momzillas and the way Cate and I can exchange commentary on Jo with just a quick look. But then I lay eyes on Jo, and I just want to get this whole thing over with.

"Sorry I'm late," I mumble, not really taking pains to sound sorry. Jo knows that I'm late on purpose. I never called her back.

"That's okay, Ellie," Jo says, the consummate professional. She's wearing a blue power suit, her hair in a bun. She looks like she's about to preside over an important board meeting. "I made a handout for everyone," Jo says, passing out an impressive packet of papers with pages and pages of graphs and numbers. Oh, great. Here we go. "Hopefully it will make what I'm about to say easier," she says and then scratches her eyebrow. "Well, not easier, probably, but clearer."

"What's wrong?" Daisy asks. "You're killing me here, Jo."

"Yeah, just tell us," Cate says, studying Jo's face.

Jo nods for a moment and then takes a deep breath. "It is with a very heavy heart that I must tell you that Jelly Jar is seriously in the red. Our business is, in fact, a money pit and must cease operations next month. At that time it would be wise for us to—"

What is she saying? I'm trying to process what Jo has just said as if it were just some ordinary piece of news like "the sink is clogged again."

"What?" Cate bursts out. She begins to laugh bitterly, spitting out each chuckle. "You're kidding us, right?"

Daisy looks at her lap, and I slip a hand over and give her hand a squeeze. I reflexively look at Tiff. Should a child really be hearing this? Tiff studies us through her smudged glasses, and I try to give her a reassuring look.

"No, Cate," Jo says, shaking her head sadly. "I've been putting off telling you because I'm so upset, and I kept thinking there must be a way to turn things around, but nothing has changed."

And then, slowly but surely, a feeling washes over me. In a way the feeling is so foreign that I don't recognize it at first, but eventually I know its name: relief.

Cate laughs sardonically. "Beautiful, just beautiful." She claps her hands. "I only just decided that Jelly Jar was what I was meant to do with my life."

Jo looks Cate in the eyes. "I blame myself one hundred percent. This packet is a full accounting of every single penny that we have earned at Jelly Jar."

Daisy glances over at Tiff, who has gone back to staring at her graphing calculator. I peer around Daisy's shoulder, trying to read her face. I've never known her to be this quiet. I watch her, biting her lip, and realize she has the most to lose out of all of us. She doesn't have the option of staying home with Tiff. She'll have to go back to working in a restaurant, slaving away nights and weekends, not being home to watch Tiff grow up. I cringe, thinking of how blessed I am and of all the ways I've taken it for granted these past few months.

"Well, this is just rich," Cate says. She looks up at the ceiling tiles she personally installed. "Really, God?" She puts her hands out. "Really?! I don't have much left in my life to give, you know. You got the boy. You want this too?"

Jo frowns at Cate. "I know you're upset, Cate. I'm simply beside myself too. I wish there was a way that we could fix it, but once you go through the packet, I think you'll see that liquidating everything is our only chance to escape this adventure without filing bankruptcy."

"Unbelievable," Cate says, shaking her head.

Jo locks eyes with me. "I'm sorry, Ellie. I wanted to tell you but . . ."

I don't let go of Daisy's hand. "I know," I say. I dare not breathe another word because if I did, they'd hear it. They'd hear the relief I feel. This is what Mike has been so upset about, and while I loved working at Jelly Jar, it isn't worth sacrificing my marriage for. Nothing is.

"I hear your business is folding." Edith smiles at me pleasantly, as if this is the best news she's heard all day. I turn to look at Mike, but he won't meet my eye. Wonderful. My downfall is my mother-in-law's delight.

I clear my throat and turn to help Sophie cut her pot roast. We always have to have steak when Edith comes over. She only likes red meat. The redder the better.

"We're going through a bit of a rough patch." I exhale slowly.

"Oh, that's not what Mike told me," she says, her eyes crinkling with excitement.

I glare at Mike, but he's suddenly very interested in the label on the milk jug. I got my first *"tuch"* of the evening out of Edith when I plunked the plastic gallon container down on the table without pouring it into a proper serving pitcher, but since she's not the one doing the dishes, I can't bring myself to care.

"It's so much better this way, don't you think?" She cuts her meat into neat little squares. "It obviously wasn't working, and this way you don't have to quit. You don't have to tell the other women you couldn't handle it after all." She shrugs. "You can leave with your pride intact." She places a bite-sized piece of meat into her mouth and chews carefully, rolling it around.

How do I respond to this? Should I defend the business, demand that women with families be allowed to have a fulfilling career too if they want one? Do I explain how liquidating the assets may get us out of this mess? Can I tell her to take her masticated cow and get out of my house? What else can I do? I certainly can't tell her that she's right, even if it is the truth.

"Seth, honey, would you please pass the potatoes?" I say, nodding at him. He's busy carving a sculpture out of the pile of mashed potatoes on his plate, but he looks up and passes the potatoes. I stare at the bowl and will myself not to say anything I'll regret. I use the silver spoon—garishly detailed, part of the sterling collection Edith gave us for our wedding, dug out from the closet whenever she comes over—to drop a lump of potatoes onto my plate, then take a bite. Surely she wouldn't expect me to answer her while I have food in my mouth. How déclassé. I'll just keep shoveling it in.

"I guess now that you won't be working, you'll be able to wear your ring more often," Edith says, looking at my left hand pointedly. *"Tuch."*

Oh, no. She knows. I don't know how she knows, but she knows. Is it possible to be a superpious churchgoing Baptist *and* an all-seeing witch? I glance at Mike, who is looking at my finger with interest. Apparently this is the first time he's noticed.

"Hey, where is—" Mike starts, but I cut him off.

"Probably," I say coolly, nodding. I look from Mike's confused face to Edith's triumphant one.

"Aah!" Sophie screams as her glass of milk topples and spills all over the table. I could kiss her. Mike springs up to grab paper towels, and I reach for Sophie's plate, rescuing it from the flood and placing it on the counter. Sophie begins to cry, and I reach for my daughter, pulling her onto my lap. Her beautiful caramel skin is warm and soft, and I hold her tight, letting her cry against my shoulder. Mike is valiantly trying to clean up the milky mess while Seth watches quietly. Edith sits calmly in her chair, carefully cutting precise little squares of meat as if nothing has happened. *"Tuch."*

A few minutes later, Sophie has calmed down, Mike has sopped up most of the milk, and everyone seems to have forgotten about the missing ring. I am pouring a new glass of milk for Sophie when Edith speaks again.

"I called you on Wednesday, Michael." She spears a green bean and examines it carefully before placing it into her mouth. "And you didn't call me back." I think back to the message Edith left on our voice mail last week, and remember how excited I was when he blew it off. I wouldn't want to call the Dragon Lady either.

"Didn't I?" Mike asks, shifting in his chair. "I thought I did. I left a message."

Edith shakes her head. "There were no messages."

"Then maybe I didn't leave a message. But I definitely called you back, and you didn't pick up." Mike nods. "What did you want to talk about?"

"The phone said no missed calls," Edith says, cutting a green bean. "Why didn't you call me back?"

"Was there something you needed to ask me?" Mike says. I feel a little bad for him, but it feels so nice not to be the one under scrutiny that I can't quite bring myself to jump in. It's not like he helped me out earlier.

"You're avoiding my question, Michael," Edith says, cocking an eyebrow at him. Mike looks at his mother's face, then quickly glances away from her eagle-eye gaze, back down at his plate.

"Fine," he says, sighing. I watch with interest as Mike crumbles. "I forgot to call you back. I'm sorry, Mother."

"*Tuch*," she says. "I was just calling to see if you'd like me to take the kids to the Ice Capades when they're in town next month."

And that's when it hits me. I've been trying to get Mike to tell me about Jo for weeks, and Edith somehow got Mike to confess in two minutes flat. I look at her severe face, her white hair pulled back neatly in a bun, and feel a touch of admiration. She may be annoying, but the old bird ain't stupid.

"I was just thinking it might be nice for them to get out once in a while," she says, looking at me pointedly, as if I keep my children locked in cages. "And I would like to spend some time with my grandchildren before I die."

I watch their exchange just across the table, but it feels like I'm far away, observing through a thick piece of glass.

Mike was avoiding Edith's questions because he didn't want to admit the truth. And Mike won't answer my questions about Jo because . . . well, the answer is obvious to me now. These past weeks, since Jo confessed, I've tried to convince myself that the problem with our marriage was my job. In fact, I almost laugh to myself, I *wanted* to believe that was the problem, as sick as that is. I wanted it to be the job because that's something outside of us, that's something we can fix. But the truth is actually much more frightening. Jo was right. It's her. He won't talk about it because it's true. In fact, he may even still love her. I feel my stomach drop.

I'm not sure whether to hug Lauren or punch her when the kids throw themselves into her arms.

"Hey there, guys." She wraps them both in one big hug. "We are going to have so much fun today." She lets them go, holds up a paper bag and shakes it, and Seth and Sophie jump and clap at the prospect of a surprise.

"Have a good afternoon," I say, waving at them, but Seth and Sophie don't even look up. They're too busy jumping for the bag, which Lauren is holding just out of their reach. "The numbers are on the fridge," I say, mostly to make myself feel better, since I know Lauren knows where the emergency numbers are. She spends as much time in my house as I do.

"Have a good time," she says, waving us out the door. I sigh as Mike hits the garage door opener. There are very few things less fun than our annual trip to our accountant. A root canal. Giving birth. Wiping out the self-cleaning oven. That's about it. I can see Mike feels the same way, since we both climb into his Saab silently. I don't know when it became a habit that he always drives when we leave together, but somewhere along the line I stopped offering. Mike backs the car down the driveway, and I flip through the radio presets on the dash. Every channel is news. How is that even possible? I lean back and stare out the window as the bare tree branches rush by.

There has to be a way to save Jelly Jar. The relief I felt when Jo announced that Jelly Jar was closing has faded. Suddenly, I want this more than I've ever wanted anything in my life. Jelly Jar has to make it. There has to be a way. I can't fail at this too. I know Jo said she went over the numbers dozens of time, but maybe if I go over them I'll find something. Or I could get Mike to take a look. He's so good with money. Maybe he'll be able to see where we're going wrong. With the loan we've already taken out, no bank will give us another, but maybe there's some way to . . . maybe, I think, looking at my silent husband's handsome profile, he'll let me use some more of our savings. But I dismiss the thought as quickly as it comes. I have a little income from the fund Daddy set up when I was born, but that money should go to the twins. Still, the money has to come from somewhere.

I'm so lost in my thoughts that I don't notice, at first, when the car starts shaking. But when I hear Mike curse under his breath, I realize that the car is trembling violently.

"Mike, what's—" I start to ask, but stop when the car stops shaking and the engine cuts off totally. Mike turns the wheel sharply, and the car begins to roll toward the side of the road. He steers the car to the shoulder, then brakes. He looks straight ahead, out the windshield, at the smooth gray asphalt in front of us. The engine is dead, but, eerily, the radio is still going, the nasally voice talking on and on about stock prices. Mike shuts it off with a quick flip of his wrist.

"Mike, what's wrong?" I ask quietly. He won't look at me. The bright noonday sun reflects off the asphalt of Ponce De Leon Drive, blinding in its intensity.

"How long has it been since you took the cars in for a tune-up?" Mike asks, taking a deep breath.

"I don't know. I'm not sure. Why?"

"You used to take the cars in every year, right on schedule, Ellie."

"What's wrong with the car?"

"The engine died. Did you notice that the engine light

was on?" A truck is passing to our left on the crowded road, and I wait until it passes before answering.

"Why would I have noticed that the engine light was on in *your* car? You're the one who drives it. Did you notice?"

"I noticed that the oil light was on," he says slowly. He grips the steering wheel, his knuckles white. "But I figured you would take the car in soon, like you always do, so I didn't worry about it. And I didn't notice today, but the engine light must have been on. Because the car is dead, Ellie. That was what it feels like when your engine goes. That's why you take the car to get a tune-up every year."

I can't believe what I'm hearing. He's actually blaming me for not noticing the engine light was on. He has eyes too.

"I used to take the cars in regularly," I say, my voice shaking. "But maybe you didn't notice that I have a job now."

"Oh, I've noticed," Mike says, rolling his eyes. "Trust me. Things used to work like they were supposed to, and ever since you started working, our household has gone straight to hell."

"You're an adult. You know when your car needs a mechanic. You are responsible for taking your car in." A tear rolls down my cheek.

"Thank God this silly job thing will be over soon." He rests his forehead against the steering wheel.

I snap my head around to look at him.

"What did you say? Did you just say you're thankful my company is going under?"

He doesn't answer me. He just knocks his head gently against the leather.

"Is that what you're saying, Mike?"

"I thought we had a deal," he says quietly.

"What?" I ask. His lips are tight, and his face is pale.

"When we got married, you never mentioned you wanted to work. The deal was that you would stay home and take care of the household, and I would work."

I think my mouth is actually hanging open. I've never heard anything so ridiculous.

"What are you talking about, Mike? We never made a deal like that. I never said I wouldn't want to work someday."

"Of course we didn't lay out the details in ink, Ellie," he says, pulling his head up and looking at me. "But I went into this marriage thinking we were on the same page. It's not fair to change the rules like this now."

I am so shocked I don't even know what to say. My husband is treating me like his neighbor's daughter, whom he bartered forty head of cattle for. This is the man who promised to love and cherish me forever. I heard it, and I have witnesses.

"You listen to me, Mike." I bite my lip to keep myself from crying. "This isn't ancient Babylon. And I am not your servant. I am an educated woman who wants to do more than make trips to the mechanic during the kids' naptime. It's been an adjustment for all of us, but I want to keep working. I need this. If not Jelly Jar, then something else."

He doesn't turn his eyes away from the road.

"Mike?"

He looks out the front windshield, toward a yellow pickup truck coming our way.

This is how it goes lately. He'll talk about this stuff with me, but only to a point, then he shuts down. I roll my eyes. I guess we'll just get back to this later. But then I remember Edith's take-no-prisoners approach and decide that at least this once I'm going to take a cue from her.

"But that isn't it, is it, Mike? That's not what's really bothering you, is it? I know it's not what's really bothering *me.*"

Mike looks at me and fear washes over his face.

"Were you engaged to Jo?" I lock my eyes with his.

"Ellie, this is ridiculous. The problem is—"

"Were you engaged to Josephine Vann?" I say, enunciating every single syllable.

"That's not what matters now. What matters now is our family and our future."

My nostrils flare. I cross my arms over my chest. "Were you," I say, narrowing my eyes at him, "engaged to Jo before you met me?"

He hangs his head and sighs. "Yes, okay. I was. What does it matter?"

"If you had told me years ago, I would have said it didn't matter at all. But the fact that you've been hiding it from me, that you've been acting so weird, makes me realize that it *does* matter."

"Ellie, I didn't want to tell you, but I promise it's nothing to me. That's not the problem."

"Do you still have feelings for her?" I ask, barely able to get it out. He'd better not make me ask this three times.

"No," he says, as if horrified. "Absolutely not. We were children, Ellie. Even then we knew it wasn't, that there was—"

"Then what on earth is wrong with you? I've been an absolute mess for months, worried sick about your behavior. I feel like I don't even know who you are anymore. You won't talk to me. Then I find out you were engaged to someone else, and you all but deny it. Mike, you're tearing us apart with this behavior, and it's killing me."

Mike frowns and looks at his lap. He leans back in his seat and grabs his hair in big handfuls. "Okay, I'm sorry. All right?"

I shoot a look at no one out the window. Some apology.

"I'm sorry about the Jo thing, for letting you worry about it. We were engaged once, but it was years ago. I have zero feelings for her. I didn't want to tell you. She wants to be your friend, and I thought it was just ancient history. But I should have told you, so I'm sorry."

I take a deep breath and feel a little better. I study his profile. If he's not in love with Jo, if that isn't it, then we'll make it. We'll be fine. We can start again.

"But I'm not sorry about how I've been acting. You didn't ask me what I thought about your going back to work. You didn't give me a vote in that, and frankly I hate it. It's making our lives a wreck."

Whatever hope I had melts away. I cross my arms over

my chest again and purse my lips. I stare out the window a moment, collecting my thoughts and my calm.

"Mike, I need this," I say again. "Do you know what it's like now that the twins are in school? I'll go crazy if I have to stay home with an empty house."

I turn and look at him. He's staring at the ceiling.

"I should have consulted you when I took the job. It was my money, but we're a family. I'm sorry about that. You're right. But I need you now. I need you to see that this is what I need."

He turns to me and locks his eyes with mine. He's not angry anymore. He's just looking at me, studying me. I almost blush. It's the first time in months that he's done that. Maybe I'm getting through?

"And I need more than that. I need you to start pitching in. They're your children, and it's your house too. We're both going to be working, and we're both going to be sharing the household responsibilities."

His face falls, and he turns back to the front. Mike closes his eyes and grips the steering wheel.

"Are you listening? Will you please acknowledge that I need you to start helping out?"

Mike keeps his eyes closed, but begins to rub his hands over the steering wheel slowly.

"Mike?"

"I don't know if I can," he says, then pulls the car door open and steps out onto the shoulder of the road. He shuts the door, pulls his phone out of his pocket, and dials the number for AAA. I watch, silently, trying to make myself move. But somehow I can't make myself do anything but sit in a stranded car, thinking about the fact that my marriage is over.

Thank God the lights are off. I don't think I could deal with running into anyone else here right now. I certainly couldn't deal with Mike right now, which is why I escaped as soon as the kids were in bed. I'm not rattling around that house with him all evening in silence.

I slip my key into the lock and push the Jelly Jar door open. At nine o'clock on a Sunday night, it's not too likely anyone else would be around anyway, but you never know, I guess. Daisy and Cate could have dance parties in here every night for all I know. Oh, to be single and care-free again.

I flip on the lights and walk into the room. It's so peaceful in here when no one is around. I take a deep breath and walk toward the office, where I'll boot up the computer and take a look at the financial files. But as I get closer, I glance toward the kitchen and head there instead. I look around the beautiful tile floor, the high-end equipment, and the crayon marks on the walls. It really was something, what we were trying to do. I spot a copy of the rules, typed neatly and tacked onto the bulletin board, and I shake my head. We almost had something really special here.

I walk to the pantry and open the door, inhaling the sweet aroma of mixed spices. Why do all pantries smell the same? I flip on the light and walk into the small room, noticing that we have enough food stocked in here to feed us all for weeks. I look around at the large bags of flour and the rows of canned tomatoes. I see rows of colorful little jars, and I smile at the industrial-sized bags of chocolate chips. I reach for one, and know what I am going to do.

I'm combining the wet and the dry ingredients in the pistachio-colored mixer when I hear the front door jingle. Uh-oh. At this time of night, it can't be any of the other women. What if it's a thief? Or an ax murderer. I reach for the big meat cleaver on the knife magnet. I quickly jump back away from the doorway. I wait, and sure enough, the door opens. I tighten my grip on the cleaver and prepare to jump out at the intruder.

"Hello?" the intruder calls. I sigh. It's Jo. I think I would have preferred the ax murderer. I put the meat cleaver back on the wall magnet.

"Hi," I say weakly, turning the mixer off.

"Ellie." Jo's voice falters a bit. She peels off her coat. "What are you doing here?"

"Just making some chocolate chip cookies," I say, looking down at my feet. Well, this is awkward. "You?"

Jo sighs. "I thought I'd take another look at the books. Try to make them work one last time." She shrugs. "I won't bother you. I'll just go into the office . . ." She coughs. "Don't mind me."

"Thanks." I try to smile at her, but she doesn't move.

"Ellie?" She looks at me with concern, and I suddenly imagine how I must look. I am wearing the jeans I've had on all day, grease-stained from our trip to the mechanic, and my face is puffy from crying. And I haven't fixed my makeup since this morning. "Are you okay?"

I look down at my wrinkled button-down shirt and my scuffed shoes. I can feel her watching me. I don't know what to say. I don't need her pity, or her duplicitous offers of friendship. But I can't tell her that. Even in my wretched state, I know there is only one thing I can say to her.

"I'm sorry, Jo."

"What?" She looks at me, confusion written across her face.

"I'm sorry I doubted you," I say quickly, before I can change my mind. "I'm sorry I've been horrible to you."

She waves my words away with her hand. "I'm sorry about how you found out," she says quietly. She walks toward me, and I stand still, watching her. She smiles shyly, then leans in to give me a hug. I stiffen, but Jo always has been pushy, and she won't let go. "Do you want to talk about it?"

She looks directly at me. I can't meet her eye, so I turn toward the mixer and begin to dump in a fourth of an industrial-sized bag of chocolate chips. The beater stirs the stiff batter frantically. I shake my head, but before I can stop them, tears are running down my cheeks. And suddenly, I'm telling Jo the whole story. About how Mike wouldn't tell me the truth, and how he blamed me for the car, and how he doesn't want me to work at all, and how suddenly I want Jelly Jar to work more than ever.

"This place is a sinking ship, Ellie," she says, shaking her head. "So maybe it's not worth risking everything for this."

"I'm not throwing it all away for this." I look up at her. "It's for me. I have to do this. I need it for me."

Jo looks around. She runs her hand over the counter-top. "I know. Me too." She frowns. "I'm just not a stay-at-home mom. Sometimes I have a lot of guilt about it . . . but I guess guilt is just how we make ourselves feel better about doing what we want to do anyway, isn't it? I admire women who can do it, but I'm no more like them than a dog is like a cat."

I smile at her, listening to her put into words my very own feelings. We really do have so much in common. I nudge her. "You can tell me not to chase my own tail and howl at the moon, but that doesn't mean I can stop."

"Exactly," she says.

I let the mixer run for a moment, but when I turn it off the silence swells up around us. I look at the bowl and have an overwhelming desire to eat some, just like when I was a kid. I walk over to the drawer where we keep our silverware and take out two spoons. I hand one to Jo, then dig a spoon into the batter. It tastes so much better than I ever remembered. How long has it been since I did this?

"The problem is, though, that Mike is never going to accept my working. He feels like I've pulled the bait-and-switch on him. He thought he married a stay-at-home mom."

Jo stares at the bowl of batter. "Ellie, you just have to give him time. I've known him my whole life. I know he can do this. He's stubborn and old-fashioned, but he can do it."

I suck on the spoon in my mouth, trying to think of what I can say to break the awkwardness.

Jo puts a hand on my shoulder. "Ellie, we were just teenagers. It was all so silly."

I glare at her.

"Okay, not silly. I was devastated, but in time I realized it was for the best. At first I resented you when his engagement was announced, but it wasn't until you marched right back into my life that I realized that you had never even heard of me."

I swallow back a lump in my throat, thinking about how awful Jo must have felt when Mike broke off the engagement. It's the South. People don't take broken engagements lightly. She must have thought she'd be an old maid forever.

"But then I met Gerard, and he swept me off my feet and, well, everything turned out so perfectly."

I take another bite of cookie batter and look at her. Perfectly? Maybe for her.

"For everyone," she says, as if answering my unspoken thoughts.

I shake my head. "Why on earth did you take my money? You must have wanted to kill me when you saw me." I chuckle, thinking back to our first meeting. I thought she seemed a bit odd, but I would have never guessed the truth.

Jo finally dips a spoon into the batter and pulls out the tiniest bite of dough. "Would you hate me forever if I said I really needed the money?"

I laugh. "Of course not."

Jo tastes the small smudge of cookie dough, and her face lights up. "That *is* really good." She dips her spoon in to get a bigger glob. "And truthfully, I felt like I was supposed to take the money. I'm one of those people who thinks everything happens for a reason. So even though I knew it would be hard for me, there didn't feel like there was any other way. And I wanted Jelly Jar so much," she says and spoons the cookie dough into her mouth.

I sigh. "Me too. And at least Jelly Jar showed me that I have to work. It doesn't matter what Mike thinks. I have to. Maybe I can just do it without his support. We could hire someone to help out with all the stuff he doesn't want to do." My head starts reeling. What a great idea. This way, everyone wins. People hire full-time assistants all the time. Lauren is about to graduate from college. She might even want the job.

"We'll just hire a wife," I say, dusting my hands off. I laugh a little, but Jo suddenly looks serious again.

"This is your husband, Ellie. That's a big deal."

"I don't need him to support me in this." I realize I sound a bit like Sophie when she claims she's not tired, rubbing her eyes all the way to bed, but I don't care. "I can do this on my own." Jo cocks an eyebrow at me. "I have to do this on my own."

"Ellie?" Jo looks at me. "You can't do this on your own." She leans back against the counter and crosses her arms over her chest. "None of us can." She takes a deep breath. "The whole idea was to create a company that puts families first, right?" I nod dubiously, refusing to think about what she's getting at. "Having a family doesn't have to mean we can't run a business," she says. "But without the support of our families, this won't work."

"But you and I are the same. We both need this, and Mike's not like Gerard. He doesn't want to help out. You can't be saying that I have to give this up. You know how I feel. Put yourself in my shoes."

"I'm not saying I want you to leave, Ellie. I'm just saying we need them. I know sometimes we don't want to admit it, but we need them. If they're not behind us, we might as well close up shop tonight. Without the support of our families, we are nothing."

Daisy

THERE'S A LOUD KNOCKING AT THE DOOR. TIFF AND I both sit up and look at each other, bleary-eyed. She's on the couch, and I'm sprawled out on the living room floor.

"Are we in trouble with the Mafia?" I muster through my dry mouth.

Tiff pulls a Cheeto out of my hair and tosses it on the coffee table. We hear the loud knocking again. We both look at the door. I rub my eyes.

"Sounds like the police or something," Tiff says and slumps back down on the couch.

"All right," I yell at the door. "I'm coming, but it's nine in the morning, I'll have you know." I stumble into my bedroom, looking for my robe.

It was my turn to come up with the theme for our latest tradition, Movie Marathon Saturday Nights, and I chose "I

Can't Believe I Gave My Panties to a Geek: A Loving Tribute to Molly Ringwald." We started watching in reverse order so that we wouldn't wimp out and fall asleep before we got to see *Sixteen Candles*. After finishing *Pretty in Pink*, we both felt great. This was going to be a snap. But after watching *The Breakfast Club*, Tiff began to make some rumbling about skipping the last movie. That's when I brought out the can of frosting, the Cheetos, and the Coke, and she agreed that we could make it to our goal. Needless to say, I think we were both asleep by three in the morning, and we saw only a few minutes of *Sixteen Candles*.

The banging continues as I slip into my robe and run to the front door. What on earth could it be? I throw the door open.

"Lillian," I say with relief. "I thought the building was on fire."

"Did you?" Lillian says with a huge dollop of sass in her voice. She marches through the door. She's wearing a red suit and a red hat that has black netting that falls just over her eyes. I follow on her heels.

"Have you been working out?" How can such an old lady knock that loudly?

Lillian walks into the living room and finds Tiff curled up on the couch and Richard Simmons licking the icing out of the can. She shoos Richard Simmons off, moves a bag of pretzels from the couch, and sits down. "Well, I never."

What has gotten into her? I plop down next to Tiff. "Tiff, say hi, will you? Lillian's here."

Tiff lifts her heavy head and mumbles something in

tired teenager-speak. Lillian smiles sweetly and then turns her viper eyes on me.

"Whoa, there. What'd I do?" I ask, raising my hands in surrender.

"I suppose you're not going to church with me again today?"

I pick up a pillow off the floor and cuddle it. "Oh, goodness. I think we'll just have to take another rain check. We were up all night watching Molly Ringwald movies. You know who that is?" I yawn.

"No," Lillian says, glaring at me.

"She's this eighties star with bee-stung lips and—"

"Daisy! I don't care who she is."

I raise an eyebrow at her. What's gotten her support hose all in a wad? "Okay." I shrug. I sit up a little and feel all the knots in my back from sleeping on the floor.

"Daisy, Tiffany," Lillian begins, forcing Tiff to sit up a little and make eye contact, "I have always prided myself on being the kind of woman who doesn't beat around the bush, so I will simply say what I have come here to say."

I shrug. "Okay, shoot."

"I think what's going on over here is very disheartening."

I look around the apartment. Maybe she's right. It really is a mess. And Lillian is from another generation, the kind that no doubt disapproves of keeping a teenager up all night to watch bad eighties movies. But how can I help her see that this is very necessary bonding for Tiff and me? That this is the sort of thing that's going to hold us together through her difficult high school years?

"Lillian, I know Tiff was up late, but these movies are a lot of fun for us and—"

"This isn't about those movies. It's about church. Why have you stopped going to church?"

"We haven't," I say, lying a little. The truth is, we haven't been in months. "We've been busy, but we'll get back there. Next Sunday. We'll go next Sunday."

"Fiddlesticks," Lillian says. "That's just a pile of horse manure. You will not. That's what you tell me every week to put me off. I'll tell you ladies something right here and now. I thought we were a family. And I might be old, but I'm not dumb."

I watch her, her left eye twitching. And I begin to realize that she's not only right, she's also hurt.

"Oh, Lillian, I'm so sorry. It must seem like we don't want to spend time with you." I get up and go sit next to her. I put my arm around her. "Honey, I'm sorry for being so insensitive. It wasn't about you. We've really missed *you*." I look at Tiff, who nods vehemently. We have missed Lillian. "You are our family."

"Daisy," Lillian says and wriggles away from me. "This *is* about family, but it isn't about you and me and Tiff. It's about the family of God. They're your family too, and they miss you."

I cock my head at her. Some family they were. "Look, I've been meaning to tell you." I nod, trying to work up my courage. "I think when you hear what happened, you'll totally understand why Tiff and I think we just can't go to your church anymore."

Lillian holds up a black-gloved hand at me. "I already know."

"You do? About how they ran me off from the Fishing Club?" I accidentally scoot away from her. She should have told me she knew.

"Idle gossip has a way of getting around," Lillian says, carefully pulling off her gloves. "And I've heard how those girls didn't show up like they said they would at Tiff's party. That was mean. But that's certainly no reason to disown an otherwise perfectly good church family. There are bad apples in every bunch."

"But that woman said—"

"I don't care what she said, Daisy. It's still no excuse. The body of God is your family. No one ever said they were perfect. And just like a real family, sometimes you're going to get into rows with one another. It can't be helped. But that doesn't mean that at the first sign of trouble you hightail it out of there. You're a family, and you're stuck together through thick and thin."

I look at the modern wood floors of our apartment and frown. Well, when you look at it that way, it's kind of another matter, isn't it? "Did Pastor Martin send you over here?"

"No," she says, and then softens her mouth a little. "But Butterscotch did."

I look up at her and smile. Brother Scott. He was so fun.

"He's a dreadfully handsome man, don't you think?" Lillian asks.

I smirk at her. "Dreadfully," I say. I look over at Tiff, who is lying horizontally on the couch again. At first I think she's dozing, but I spy her open eyes. I'm glad she has heard what Lillian said.

The truth of it is, she might be right.

Lillian stands up and dusts off the back of her skirt as if it might have gotten dirty on our couch. I laugh. She's still the same old grand lady she always was. "But you know, dear," she says, pursing her lips for a moment, "it wouldn't hurt you to see a little more of your other family too."

I smile at her. "What about we institute a Family Dinner Night every week? Tiff and I miss you."

"Yeah," Tiff says sitting up. "That'd be fun."

"I don't know," Lillian says. "I wouldn't want to be any bother."

"Bother? Gracious, no. It'd be a help to me. Tiff needs to see you more and I just hadn't thought how to ask you to spare that time. I know you're busy."

"Well"—Lillian looks at Tiff—"I suppose I can manage it if you think it's what's best for Tiffany. Family is important."

The buzzer goes off in the kitchen and I run in to take the roast duck out of the oven, passing Tiff at the computer on my way. She squints at the screen and sucks on the end of her ponytail. I pull the duck out, and the savory scent fills the air.

"What's that?" Tiff turns to me.

"Duck." I grab the baster out of a drawer, draw the juice up, and shower it onto the piping-hot bird.

"Whoa," she says.

I smile. "And I also made a mesclun salad with oranges, avocados, and a honey ginger lime dressing. Oh, and a rice pilaf."

Tiff stares at me in shock. "Lillian's too good for Frito pie?" she asks wryly.

Tonight is our first family dinner with Lillian, but Lillian isn't why I cooked duck.

"I thought *you* liked duck." Two weeks ago, the math-lete team beat a magnet high school from Decatur and qualified for the state championship. I insisted we celebrate by going to dinner at a restaurant of Tiff's choosing, and, much to my shock, she chose Dish, a high-end restaurant in the Highlands, where she ordered the duck. I didn't say anything at the time, but as I watched her happily eat duck, quinoa, and even kale, I couldn't believe my eyes. When I look at her I still see the little girl who wouldn't even eat jelly on her peanut butter sandwich.

So tonight when I was planning our first family dinner, I decided to make duck for Tiff. It was a splurge for us, but we won't have many times like this together in the coming months.

"Smells good," she says and turns back to the computer, mumbling at the screen.

I turn the oven on warm and slide the duck back in. I glance at the kitchen clock just as my cell phone rings.

"Oh, good," I say to no one. "Janice? Hey!" Tiff looks up, then looks back at the computer. Janice is my old manager at Seeger's, and though we never hung out socially, she was a great boss. It was very hard to leave her when I accepted the job with Jelly Jar.

"Daisy!" she says, loudly. I know she's excited to hear from me, but she's also talking over the roar from the kitchen. "I can't believe we haven't talked once since you left."

"I know. How's everything? Mickey still a pain in the neck?" Janice married the head chef, Mickey, a few years ago. They are very good together, but only because Mickey knows better than to cross her at work. She's the boss.

"Oh, you know Mickey. I couldn't live without him, so now I have to live with him. But listen, I got your message."

"Oh?" I say. I open the fridge and pull out the bowl of greens. I should probably go ahead and dress the salad now. Lillian will be here any moment.

"Yes. And the good news is that I do think we have something opening up here that might be right for you."

"Really?" I slice the avocado down the middle and pull the halves apart. "You know, I really miss Seeger's. Jelly Jar's been great, but we all had such fun working at Seeger's together." I try to sound like I mean it. I almost do.

"I'm so sorry it didn't work out with your company. I thought that was really brave of you to try to do your own thing."

"That's okay," I say, trying to keep my tone upbeat. I really can't talk about Jelly Jar closing just yet.

"So why don't you just come by tomorrow night when I'm on, and we'll talk about different options for you?" she asks. I hear the line cooks yelling in the background.

"Sure," I say, wiping my hands on a paper towel. "That sounds great. And thanks so much for getting right back to me. You know Tiff and me. We can't go too long without a job. We have shoe habits to support," I say, hoping my joke works. Janice knows my financial situation well, and I want to thank her for helping me out. But I don't want to worry Tiff.

"Of course," Janice says. "We'd be very lucky to get you back. The macarons haven't been the same ever since you left."

We hang up, and I say a little prayer of thanks that this might work out. I don't want to start working restaurant hours again, but I also don't want our home to be taken from us. I'll just work at Seeger's while I look for something else. I'll have to be honest with Janice about that. But I'm sure I can make her understand my reasons. She'll get it. I need to spend every single moment I can with Tiff. She'll be in college before I know it, eating duck with her new brainiac friends, forgetting all about me.

As the line rings, I have to concentrate really hard to keep from laughing. I can't look at Bea or Franny. They'll only distract me. Franny is rolling on the hand-woven rug in silent hysterics, and Bea is staring at me wide-eyed. Maybe they don't prank-call people in Brazil?

"Hello?" a deep voice says. I freak out silently, pointing at the phone and making faces at Franny and Bea. It was Franny's idea to call David and see if he was actually home tonight. We all agreed that he'd better be since it's Valentine's Day, and so I volunteered to make the call while Cate went to the bathroom. The way I figure it, it was her fault for leaving her phone lying around. Unfortunately, we didn't exactly plan what we'd say once he got on the line.

"Hello? Hello?" he says. Franny and Bea press to either side of me to listen in. I hold the phone in front of us. "Catie? Is that you?"

We stare at one another, uncertain how to respond. Should I just hang up?

Ooh, I have a better idea. I put the phone back to my ear.

"You'd better recognize," I say, and Franny loses it completely and begins to guffaw out loud. "You'd better recognize, fool," I say and snap the phone shut, proud of myself, only to turn and see Cate standing in the doorway to her study. Busted.

"Guys," Cate says, putting her hands on her hips. "What was that?"

"Oh, nothing," I say. I throw her phone back on the table nonchalantly. With any luck, she'll forget about call history.

"Daisy was just, um, calling an old friend," Franny says, trying to wipe the smile off her face. Cate levels her eyes at Franny. "I mean, she was just prank-calling an old flame. Yeah, that's what it was."

"Please," Bea says, rolling her eyes. "Look, Cate. We called David to make sure he was home tonight."

Cate frowns at us. "And?"

"You'll be happy to know that he was," says Beatriz.

Cate continues to glower.

"Oh, come on," I say, rolling my eyes. "Didn't you want to know if he was home tonight?"

"What was that I heard you saying as I walked in?" Cate asks, her lips tight.

"Oh, we were just having a bit of a chat," I say.

Cate crosses her arms on her chest. "Daisy, did you call David a fool?"

I bite my lip. Tonight is the first time I've hung out with Cate, Bea, and Franny since Cate and I had our big falling out. And even though we went out for coffee and I apologized profusely, it's taken a while to earn her trust back. Maybe I should have shown a little more restraint. Why do I always do these stupid things and get myself in trouble? I need to seek professional help for my impulsive personality. "Um, well, I might have."

Cate stares at me for a moment, then breaks into a huge grin. "Good work," she says. "I think our First Annual Bitter Bash is off to a perfect start."

I smile and give Cate a high five.

Bea stands up. "No, not quite yet. In Brazil, it's not a party until there's a toast." She holds up a giant thermos.

"Ladies," Cate says. "Let's reconvene in the kitchen. Bring your food and drink contributions."

When Cate called and invited me to the First Annual Bitter Bash, I had no idea what she was talking about. A bitter bash, it turns out, is kind of like an unbirthday, except it's an un–Valentine's Day party. Cate explained that everyone wears black and eats thematic food, and we spend the evening celebrating our singleness. It sounded like fun to me, especially since Tiff and her new friend Beth had decided to go to the sock hop at school and then spend the night at Beth's house, leaving me utterly alone. My little girl at a school dance. Who'da thunk it?

Cate gets four martini glasses down from her cabinet while Bea unscrews the lid to her thermos. Bea pours the first drink, and it's as black as coal.

"What on earth is that?" I ask. Franny nearly brought the house down with little conversation-heart cookies inscribed with sayings like "Later, Boy" and "Single and Loving It," but I don't know what to think of these black cocktails. They better not be licorice. I hate licorice.

Bea pours some into the next glass. "These are Godiva chocolate martinis, ladies." Cate hands one to me and one to Franny. "I figured that if you don't have a boyfriend, the next best thing is a chocolate martini."

"I'll drink to that," I say. "And they'll go perfectly with my Better Than Sex Cake." I pop off the Tupperware lid to reveal my dense chocolate masterpiece.

Beatriz slaps her hand over her mouth, "Daisy Johnson!"

Cate turns bright red. "I can't believe . . . what's this called again?"

I put my hand on my hip. "Good gravy, you two. It's just a Better Than Sex Cake. I got the recipe from my great-aunt Mildred, who was a confirmed spinster. It's just a superdense chocolate cake. It's amazing."

Franny sticks a finger in the whipped cream and caramel topping and has a taste. Her face lights up. We all dissolve into fits of hysterics.

"Hey, Bea, what's your boyfriend doing tonight?" I begin to cut pieces of the cake and put them on the little serving plates that Cate hands me.

Beatriz makes a funny little pout. "He is *not* my boyfriend. I told you that."

I shoot the other girls a look and hand her a piece of cake. "Okay . . . what's Will doing tonight?"

Bea blushes. "He's at home watching film noir movies."

"It's so nice he understood that you wanted to spend Valentine's Day with us," Franny says.

"We would have totally understood if you couldn't have," Cate says.

Beatriz shrugs. "I've never celebrated Valentine's Day before, and I'm not starting now. You crazy Americans and your weird holidays. No one has ever been able to explain to me why this day involves a naked baby who shoots people with arrows. That is deeply sick, just so you know."

We all laugh and raise our glasses. "To the Bitter Bash," I say.

"To a new year of love," Franny says.

"To naked babies with weapons," Bea cheers.

"To us," Cate says. "The luckiest so-and-sos that ever walked the earth. Who needs men when you've got friends like this?"

We all clink glasses and laugh. I take a sip of my martini, and it tastes like the liquid form of my cake. I'm definitely going to have to pace myself with these.

"But wait," Franny says, reaching for one of her heart cookies. "Cate, did you make any thematic food tonight?"

"Why, of course." Cate laughs. "Did you really doubt me?" She walks over to her fridge and pulls out a cookie sheet. "Ta-da! I made us all boyfriends," she says. On the sheet are four gingerbread men with incredible icing details. Only Cate. She always could take things to the next level.

"Daisy," she says and hands me my little man, who is

wearing boots and a cowboy hat. He has a Bible in his left hand and a big red heart on his chest. I smile at him. He's perfect, actually.

"Bea, yours was easy," Cate says and hands her a cookie that is the spitting image of Will.

"Franny, yours gave me some trouble at first, but finally I had an epiphany." When Franny sees hers she bursts out laughing, but Bea and I don't quite get it. This gingerbread man has a stick in his hand. It looks like a little wooden skewer. And he has a funny outfit on.

"He's playing shuffleboard!" Frances squeals, and then Cate explains the significance to us.

"And finally, this one is mine," she says, holding up a cookie that just says "Not David" across his chest and has a big question mark over his face.

I smirk at her. "Shouldn't that cookie say 'James' on it?" Franny and Beatriz dissolve into laughter, and Cate puts her hands on her hips.

"You guys. We only got coffee," Cate says.

We can't stop laughing.

"Once. We only got coffee once," she says again, but we can barely hear her over our laughter.

Once is enough, if you ask me.

I'm singing along to Dolly when I first notice Tiff and her friend Beth in an earnest conversation in the backseat. I've recently adopted "Travelin' Through" as my new theme song, and I've been playing it on endless repeat as I shuttle the girls to and from practice. Though I'm interested in

what the girls are saying, I'm not about to let them interrupt my big solo.

"*God made me for a reason and nothing is in vain*," I belt out in
my best church choir voice. Tiff doesn't even look up.
Hm. Weird. This usually gets a rise out of her. I keep
singing, watching for a reaction, but I go on when she ignores me again. That Dolly sure knows what she's talking
about. I try to remember not to close my eyes as I get into
the song more and more, and finally I hit a nice vibrato on
the last note.

"Hey, Mom, can you turn it down?" Tiff yells, shaking
her head.

I shrug and comply. Kids these days. They wouldn't
know good music if a saxophone hit them over the head.
"You're welcome."

Tiff mumbles something under her breath, then turns
back to Beth.

"What are you two plotting back there?" I ask.

"The youth group lock-in at my church, Mrs.
Johnson," Beth says, her freckled cheeks turning pink.
Even though Beth goes to Tiff's school, her family doesn't
attend Peachtree Hills Presbyterian Church. They go to a
nondenominational church over on Monroe. "There's
going to be games and snacks, and oh, I don't know, lots
of stuff. It will be fun. Can Tiffany come?"

"I don't know. Will there be boys there?" I ask, trying
to sound stern, but when Tiff and Beth dissolve into giggles, I can't keep a straight face. I guess we've hit the "boys
are hilarious" phase, which is a good sign. I was starting to
get worried for a while there that we would never move

past the "boys are icky" phase. "Sounds awesome. Can I come?"

Tiff looks at me, her eyes wide with horror, but Beth just laughs.

I let them go back to their plotting, thanking the Lord that Tiff seems to have found one Christian friend who seems seminormal. At least one thing in my life is going right. Those girls at church . . . I get steamed just thinking about them, but I know I need to get over it. Lillian is right. They're family too. Maybe they're like the weird cousin who always smells a little funny and cheats at Monopoly, but they're still family.

"Now arriving at Chez Malone," I say, pulling up in front of Beth's impeccable two-story home. She hops out and slams the car door, then waves as she runs up to her front door. Beth's mom comes to the door and waves at us, and I start to drive away.

"I have time to take you home before the meeting," I say, glancing at the clock on the dashboard.

"That's okay," Tiff says, looking out the window at Beth's perfectly manicured street.

"It's probably going to be a long meeting." One of Beth's neighbors has this adorable picket fence around the front lawn. Very charming. "We're deciding how to liquidate our assets, so it will be kind of boring."

"It's okay."

"Okey-dokey." I shrug and turn Dolly back up. That kid gets stranger every day. When I was her age, you couldn't have paid me to hang out with my mom. Although, actually, a few months ago, you couldn't have paid Tiff either. I look back at her in the rearview mirror, and she's looking out the window and moving her head to the music. Maybe some good has come out of this whole thing after all.

"I guess we all know why we're here, so we might as well get started," Jo says brusquely. A few months ago I would have thought her words cold, but now I can see that she's trying to appear businesslike to hide what's really going on inside. And if you look at her face, it's clear: this is tearing her apart. None of us is happy that our little company is going under, but I think Jo is taking it the hardest. It was all her idea, after all, and, well . . . the business failing is one thing. Jo failing is another thing entirely.

I glance at Tiff through the doorway to the kitchen, working on her homework, and thank God for the time we've had together while Jelly Jar held on. It was worth it, if only for that.

"I've put together these charts showing our net assets," Jo says, handing around packets stapled neatly in the corner.

I look down at the colorful papers. These columns of numbers are useless to me. Squiggles on the paper can't convey all the hard work and sacrifice that they represent.

"I made this packet last week, but frankly it's meaningless to me now," Jo says. We all look up at her. I can see in Ellie's and Cate's faces that they are just as lost as I am. "I look at the numbers," she says, rifling through her handout, "and they make sense to me in theory, but when I look at all of you, I just can't wrap my mind around the fact that this is all over. It's not. It can't be."

I nod. "Yeah, me too."

Jo snatches my handout from me and then takes back Ellie's and Cate's. She walks over to the trash, lifts the lid, and throws them away.

"Jo? Are you okay?" Cate asks. "That wasn't even the recycling bin."

Jo flushes for a moment, returns to the trash can, retrieves the handouts, and puts them in the recycling bin. I chuckle. Even in her darkest moments, Jo likes to follow the rules.

"Ladies," Jo says, returning to our table. She looks at us and softens. "Friends," she says in a hoarse whisper. "Last night as I was begging God to tell me how to fix our business the answer came to me as clear as day."

I sit up. I love a good story about when the Lord speaks. He's no chatterbox so you'd better pay attention if you ever hear him.

"And so I have an announcement." We all lean in a little closer. "I know how we can save the business."

For a moment no one breathes.

"I'm giving up my salary," she says, in the same way that someone might say, "I've decided to wash my hair tonight."

"Excuse me?" How's she going to live, feed her kids, pay her mortgage?

"I don't know why I didn't think of it sooner," Jo says. "It only makes sense. I don't need the money in the present, and it would free up some cash flow in the short-term so that we could get back on our feet."

"And so will I," Ellie says. Jo looks at Ellie with surprise, then tears start to glisten in her eyes. "We were living just fine on Mike's salary. I'll give up mine too until Jelly Jar is saved."

I stare at Ellie. I feel heat creeping into my cheeks. I swallow a lump in my throat. I'd do anything for this company, I really would, but I can't do that. Tiff and I need that salary. "Listen, I—"

"Don't speak." Jo holds her hand up in the air to me. "I don't even want to hear you say it. Your salary and Cate's salary will remain the same."

I look at Cate. She's looking at the floor. I groan internally. I hate money. It always makes you feel poor and silly.

Ellie touches my arm. "Jo's right. This is the only way to save Jelly Jar."

"Why don't I just resign?" I ask.

"What?!" Jo says abruptly.

"It would save more on salary. Less costs. I'll get another job in the meantime, and when things are in the black again, I'll come back," I say.

"Yeah," Cate says. "Daisy's right. Then there would be no salaries."

Ellie glares at me and then at Cate. "Absolutely not. I'm not sparing either of you for even a moment." She points a finger at me. "Daisy, do you think my profiteroles hold a candle to yours? Because they don't."

"Yeah," Jo says. "And it would be a fiasco if you let me come up with the themes, Cate. I only know how to implement a Victorian theme."

I snicker.

Jo looks at Ellie. "Ellie and I own this business, and we

can pay people as we like. And from here on out, the two of us will be getting no pay until Jelly Jar is a success."

Cate bites her lip. "Are you sure? I feel bad drawing a salary when—"

"Absolutely," Ellie says. "Are you both still in if we give this crazy thing one more try?"

I look at Cate. She shrugs and glances nervously at me. "I've got little to lose. It's just me and my goldfish."

"Daisy"—Jo speaks slowly—"if we decide we can really get this going again, are you in? I know you have something else lined up at Seeger's, and I know that you have Tiff to think about, and so . . ." She falters, looking at me. "So I guess that plays into the decision. If it's not right for all of us, it's probably not right."

A pause hangs in the air. I say a quick prayer for courage. Can I do this again? How can I take a risk like this with Tiff so close to college?

But as I look around, I see three women who are willing to give up everything for a dream. It's crazy, but it's also kind of beautiful.

Maybe we really can make this work. Dolly says, "You'll never do a whole lot unless you're brave enough to try."

"I'm in," I say, finally.

"You'd give Jelly Jar a second chance?" Jo asks, looking at me with unmasked hope in her eyes.

"Honey, I've been given enough second chances in my life, I don't see how I could do anything else." I wave my hand and wink. "That's something I learned at church this week. Jesus was all about second chances."

Jo smiles. "I suppose he was."

"Good," Ellie says, relief spreading over her face.

"I feel better than I have in months," Jo says. "I was just so worried that you guys were going to be silly and proud about this when it's really the best solution." She stands and crosses the room to the computer.

"Last night, after I decided what we had to do to keep afloat, I looked at the books again." Jo leans over to the computer and clicks on something. The printer begins to whir, and starts spitting out sheets. "And it's like the scales fell from my eyes. All of a sudden, I saw a couple of ways to help the numbers. They'd been there all along."

Jo grabs the stack of printed pages and passes them out to us. "We'll need to do more than just give up our salaries. The goal is not just to turn Jelly Jar around but to make it profitable, to make a great source of revenue for our families."

I look at the new handout.

"First off, our suppliers are ripping us off," Jo says, handing me a list of food items we've purchased since Jelly Jar started. Next to each item are two numbers. "This first column is what we're currently paying. The second is what we could be paying if we went with another supplier."

"Where am I going to get Scharffen Berger chocolate for thirty dollars a case?" I shake my head.

"That's my second point," she rushes on. "We don't need Scharffen Berger. We should be buying Nestlé. That's what our competitors are doing."

Ellie looks at the paper in her hands. "Are you saying we could have saved over ten thousand dollars if we'd bought less expensive supplies?"

"I'm afraid so," Jo says.

"I've spent almost fifteen thousand dollars on flowers?" Cate shrieks. Jo nods. Cate looks a little pale.

"We could do so much more," Ellie says. I can see the wheels in her brain turning. "Do you know that Mike told me that we could apply for a grant from the government for being a female-owned business?"

Jo smiles at her. "We should have a meeting and brainstorm all the ways each of us can cut costs individually and then come up with a new budget and business plan."

"Yeah," Cate says. "We could make the Web site more dynamic. Maybe use some flash or something. And we could post some flyers at church and stuff," she says.

"I could use Nestlé."

"I could make do with a smaller budget," Cate says. "Use cheaper flowers and stuff."

"And I could—" Ellie coughs. "I could maybe ask Mike about marketing techniques. I know his business just did some extensive research on new Internet strategies. Maybe he could help."

"Exactly," Jo says. "And I'm beginning to see what the real problem was all along."

"Look, I said I would use Nestlé," I say. I get a laugh out of Cate. Even Jo smiles at me.

"No, Daisy. It wasn't you. It was me. I should have told you guys what was going on, but I was afraid of looking like a failure."

Cate shrugs. "We're not owners. You didn't have to tell us."

Jo looks at Ellie and smiles. "I didn't have to tell you, but I should have."

Ellie leans over and gives Jo a hug. "Jo, you didn't fail us. *We* failed us. We were fractured and working independently. But going forward, things will be different. Things will be better."

After a silent car ride home, Tiff went up to her room and has been hiding out there ever since. It's okay. I know that times of uncertainty are hard for her, and she's probably not too excited about the prospect of me keeping my job at Jelly Jar. I lay out cold cuts and cheese and crackers for her to eat when she's ready, then fix myself a plateful and take a seat on the couch. Richard Simmons jumps up on my lap, and I stroke his mangy gray fur absently. Images flash across the television screen, but I'm miles away.

The sitcoms have turned to news by the time she finally comes downstairs and sits quietly beside me. I don't say anything. I just put my arm around her and pull her close.

"I have to tell you something," Tiff says. She stares at the television as she speaks.

"I'm all ears." Richard Simmons, tired of being jostled, jumps off my lap.

"You're going to hate me." She looks down at the cat, licking his paw imperiously on the floor in front of us.

"There is nothing in the world you could do that would make me hate you," I say, stroking her shoulder. "I sure hope you know that. You are the best thing that ever happened to me."

"I let Archimedes out on purpose."

"What?" I sit up straight, turning to look at her.

"That time when the inspector came? I brought him along and set him loose in the kitchen on purpose." She bites her lip.

"Tiff, what are you saying?" I look at her in confusion.

"I wanted you to fail," she says, her voice rising to a high pitch. "I thought everything would go back to being how it was before."

"You did that on purpose?" I know I'm a little behind here, but I can't seem to understand what she's saying.

"But now, I don't want you to fail anymore. I want it to work," she says, nodding. "I . . ." She sniffs as tears begin to roll down her cheek. "I like having you around."

I watch Tiff as she wipes her nose on my blanket. I know it wasn't easy for her to tell me the truth. She looks at me, then looks away.

I want to kill her, but I'm also kind of . . . proud, I guess.

How could that amazing girl have come out of me? I've always known Tiff was smarter than I could ever hope to be, and I've always known she's beautiful and will someday come to realize it, and I've always known she's creative and thoughtful in ways that I could never approach, but I've still never been prouder of her than I am at this moment.

I don't have any idea how to respond, so I just pull her close and say the first thing that comes into my mind. "I love you." I pull her in closer to plant a kiss on her fore-head, then wrap my arms around her and let her cry against my chest.

"I'm awful," she says under her breath.

"You're not awful," I say, stroking her hair. "You're a teenager." She doesn't laugh. I hold her, listening to the sound of her breathing.

"You know, you're one of those girls I always wanted to be in high school."

"You don't mean that," she says, her face pressed against me. "You were popular. I'm . . ." She lets her sen-tence trail off, unwilling to put into words what we both know is true.

"I was loud, and I goofed off and got lots of attention," I say, stroking her hair. "Because I wasn't smart like you."

She shakes her head.

"But I was always jealous of the girls who were. They were special in a way I could never be."

She doesn't respond, just lies against my chest.

"I'm so proud of you, Tiff. Do you believe me about that?"

"Yeah," she says quietly.

I don't really have any reason to be at Jelly Jar today, but since I had to drop Tiff off at Beth's youth group, I fig-ured I could find something to keep me occupied. Maybe I'll whip up a batch of chocolate tarts or something. I

need to experiment with the cheaper ingredients anyway.

I'm not too surprised when I see Jo's car in the parking
lot, since she has been working overtime on the overhaul
of Jelly Jar. Jo's not in the office, though, when I walk in,
and I'm a bit relieved to see the light on in the bathroom.
Apparently she is human. I walk into the kitchen, then
start when the bathroom door opens suddenly. It's Jo. And
in her hand is a . . . I know what that is.

No. She can't be.

Jo looks up and tosses the pink box into the bathroom
trash can quickly when she sees me. "Hi, Daisy," she says,
her voice so cheerful I know she's hiding something.

"Hey, Jo," I say coolly, eyeing the box in the trash can
behind her. She sighs. She knows I know.

"I'm not pregnant, Daisy," she says, her voice low and
sad. "Don't worry."

"I'm sorry, Jo, I . . ." I look at her crestfallen face, and I
wince. "It's none of my business anyway. I just . . ."

"It's okay," she says, shaking her head.

"I just recognize that box." I laugh, and she smiles a little. "I must have bought about twenty of them, trying to
convince myself each one was wrong, but, lo and behold,
they weren't." I laugh again, then wonder if that was the
wrong thing to say.

"We're trying," Jo says simply. "Maybe next month."

"But Jo, what about Jelly Jar? I mean, even if we could
save it now, how could you have another baby?"

"Wasn't that the whole point?" She shrugs. "To be able
to do both?" I watch her, her carefully composed face

lined with care. "I have no idea how it would work, or if it would at all, but the idea was to make it work somehow."

"I guess so," I say quietly. "I mean, yes. It was."

Jo watches me. Her cheeks are pink.

"It started that way, but now it's so much more."

She smiles, and I begin to suspect that everything is going to be okay.

We've never had wine while we cooked before, but, then, I'm not really sure we've all cooked together before. Not all four of us in the Jelly Jar kitchen at the same time, anyway. It's a little cramped, but with the wine and music, we're all having a good time. Some of us are having a hard time focusing on our task at hand because they're too busy dancing, truth be told. But it's right that we're in a festive mood. We're celebrating tonight.

In honor of our decision to give this whole thing another try, we're catering a party for ourselves this evening. Just us cooking our favorite dishes and enjoying them together. Jo and Ellie won't be getting paid anything for the next few months, we won't be using Lauren's help anymore, and Cate and I have both agreed to figure out how to reduce costs drastically without damaging quality. But we all wanted to make the sacrifices. Tiff and I have been through lean years before. We'll make it through this too.

"Cate, are you done with those potatoes yet?" Ellie says from in front of the stove, where she's melting butter in a large pan for her famous, so she says, mashed potatoes. I say anything made with heavy cream and butter has got to be good, and I can't wait to try them out. Cate already has her Coke chili simmering on the stove, so she's playing sous chef for the rest of us now, a task she has willingly embraced.

"Just about." Cate laughs, then tosses a chunk of peeled potato over Ellie's head and into the pot of hot water on the stove. Ellie jumps back from the splash, then swats at Cate with a dish towel.

"Hey, now," Jo says from the sink, where she's carefully washing lettuce to make a salad. "Be careful. The last thing we need right now is for one of you to be . . ."

"Injured by a flying potato?" Ellie laughs.

"Affected by a medical emergency," Jo says, trying not to laugh.

"Oh, lighten up, Jo," I yell, beating the eggs in my bowl to the rhythm of "9 to 5." I took the liberty of putting together a play list for the festivities.

"I have lightened up," Jo shrieks, gesturing down at her outfit. I have to admit, it took a huge dose of self-control and a kick from Cate to not burst out laughing when Jo walked through the door in jeans tonight. There are just some people who don't look right in jeans, and Jo is one of them. But she's trying, and that's something, I guess.

I take a sip of wine, add the last eggs to the mixture in the mixing bowl, and turn the machine on, then samba my way over to the sink to wash the egg mucus off my fingers. Jo scoots out of my way, but as I turn on the water, something catches my eye.

"Ooh-la-la," I say, picking the shiny platinum ring off the tray on the windowsill. "Whose is this?" I turn the ring over, blinking at the sparkly diamond in a modern setting. I turn to look at Cate, who rolls her eyes and shakes her head.

"Mine," Ellie calls. "It's mine." She stirs the pot on the stove and smiles.

"What'd you do to deserve this?" I laugh, holding the ring at different angles to make the diamond sparkle in the light. Ellie looks nervously at Jo, who smiles at her and nods. Something weird happened between those two, I know that, but Cate and I haven't been able to figure out what.

"I finally told Mike the truth," Ellie says. She smiles at Jo and starts to walk toward me. "I told him I lost his family heirloom ring, and that I always hated it anyway." She takes the ring out of my hand. "And he confessed he'd never liked it much either." She laughs. "We picked this one out together to symbolize that we're really starting over. It will be a long road back, but we've found a good counselor," she says, placing it on her finger and staring at it in admiration. "This ring means what the first one should have."

"He didn't care that you lost his grandmother's engagement ring?" Cate stops peeling carrots for the salad and stares at Ellie, her eyes wide.

Ellie shakes her head. "That ring had bad juju." She laughs and goes back to the stove, where she dances while she stirs the potatoes.

I glance into the other room, where Tiff is keeping the younger children entertained with counting games. They seem to be doing okay, so I turn back to my cake batter. At first we wanted this just to be a night for the four of us, but it was Cate who pointed out that the kids are a part of this too.

"Cate's going to be getting an engagement ring of her own soon." I point at Cate, hoping to get a reaction.

"Daisy. We went out to dinner. We're not eloping anytime soon." Cate rolls her eyes at me again.

"Two dates down and a third next week signals getting serious in my book." I toss a handful of Nestlé chocolate chips and a handful of minimarshmallows into the batter.

The girls seemed skeptical when I told them I was making a S'mores Cake, but we did agree to make our favorite foods, so there you are. They couldn't take that back. "At least it means that you're getting over that creep David."

"Getting there," Cate says, nodding. She takes a sip of her wine. "He called me two days ago. I haven't called him back. That's progress, right?"

"It sure is, honey," Ellie says, stirring the pot. "I'm proud of you."

Cate smiles. "I guess he'll always be the one I never quite get over."

"But you will move on," Jo says quietly.

"She *has* moved on!" I shriek. "Have you seen James's biceps? That man is ripped!"

Cate rolls her eyes at me and turns back to her carrots. We all stand in companionable silence, working on our special dishes, when Jo suddenly speaks.

"I wanted to say thank you to you guys," she says. I turn around to see her weeping over the salad bowl. I look helplessly at Cate, who looks from me to Ellie, uncertain how to respond. This is our fearless leader. She doesn't cry. I didn't know the woman had tear ducts. And how did she start so suddenly? She was fine just a minute ago. "Thank you for sticking with this. For sticking with me."

"Jo, none of us wanted to let this dream die either," Ellie says, walking over to her.

"But you've all made such huge sacrifices," she says, "and for what? To give a failing business another chance? We may fail again, you know." Jo doesn't even wipe away the tears that are running down her cheek. "Thank you for being willing to try." She swipes at her nose with the end of her sleeve. I can see Cate and Ellie are feeling as help- less as I am about how to respond. Jo's just acting crazy.

But then inspiration hits.

"Dolly Parton once said, 'If you want the rainbow, you gotta put up with the rain.' That sounds about right to me."

"That Dolly is a smart woman," Cate says quietly.

"Duh." I roll my eyes. "What do you think I've been trying to tell you?"

"You guys," Ellie says, laughing. "Jelly Jar really is something special. We can make a world of difference for mothers everywhere if we make this idea work."

"That's right," Jo says, tears leaking out of her eyes again. "We can do this. We have to do this. For our families." She looks at Ellie and smiles. "With our families."

"With God's help, we can do anything," Ellie says quietly, nodding.

"Amen." It's weird, because I didn't know Ellie was religious. But somehow it makes sense, now that I think about it. "How about a toast?"

Jo grabs her wineglass, her face still wet and red, and Cate and Ellie follow suit. They look at me expectantly, and I lift my glass.

"To Jelly Jar!" I clink my glass against Ellie's.

"And to friends," Jo adds, looking around the room, her eyes bleary.

"To our children," Ellie says. We all look at Cate, who shakes her head.

"To the tragic old spinsters." She sighs, then clinks her glass against mine. I smile because I know she's joking, but Ellie and Jo both look a bit taken aback. Cate and I burst out laughing.

We all take a sip of our wine, then Jo sets her glass down on the counter and begins to chuckle. "We really might do it."

And though Jo appears a little bit hysterical, we all laugh along. Maybe we're all a little bit hysterical. We've been through the ringer, but we're still here. Financially, things are still rocky, but as a company, we're stronger than ever. "Storms make trees take deeper roots," Dolly says.

For my part, I'm beginning to see that God has given

us each unique talents and blended us into a kind of family. Sure, they may dress a little funny, but somehow in the past few months these women have become everything to me. I look around at them, at Jo, Ellie, and Cate, and I thank God for placing me here with these women.

I think about what Jesus said, that we're all members of the same body. Wait, maybe it was Paul. Or possibly Dr. Phil. Well, anyway, the point is that we're all members of the same body. Somehow, that kind of makes sense to me.

"Of course we're going to do it." I raise my glass for another toast. "To us." As we clink our glasses, I look at their smiling faces and sigh. Maybe we will change the world. But even if we don't, these women have changed me, and maybe that's enough.

~~~~~~

The Jelly Jar Rules

1. Family comes first, and kids are always welcome at work.
2. This is a democracy. We say what we feel. That's what women do.
3. Kids at work are a blessing—never forget it!
4. We don't fire people. Men fire people. Women work through their problems.
5. The customer ain't always right, especially when 'she's just plain wrong.
6. No one talks before coffee.
7. There is no such thing as a "work-appropriate" outfit. God gave us hips, butts, and bags under our eyes. Whatever you need to do to work it, go for it.
8. There's no "I" in quit.
9. Without the support of our families, we are nothing.
10. If you want the rainbow, you gotta put up with the rain.

~~~~~~